DUCKS IN A ROW

MICHELLE GARREN FLYE

·

This book is dedicated with love to my husband Chris, who has always kept his promises to me, no matter how hard they might be. I love you.

1

*C*ady Summers used to love seeing her husband Neil dress for work. He'd come out of the shower wrapped in a towel, his lean, muscular body gleaming with water. When he pulled his neatly creased trousers over his hips and slipped on his shirt, she'd button it for him while he kissed her with a lust that left them both breathless. Sometimes, when there was time, he'd even forgo breakfast and have her instead, right there on the bathroom sink, and afterward she'd fashion his tie in a perfect Windsor. Once upon a time, she couldn't get enough of seeing him dressed in the perfect white shirts, ties and khakis.

Now he was usually gone to work before she woke, and all she could think about was the dry cleaners. Did she drop off his shirts? Did she pick up the last batch? How much did it cost per month? Maybe she should learn to press them herself. And why would he leave on a Sunday morning before she even got up, anyway?

She gathered the dirty clothes he left on the floor, trying not to think that it was only a three-foot trip from the floor to the laundry chute. She bit her tongue to keep from complaining, even to herself. It was only a tiny chore, not too much to ask of her. Neil had other things on his mind. His family law practice took up much of his time. She appreciated the irony that the law practice that kept her and her thirteen-year-old daughter Kelsea living so comfortably in their lovely home very often took away the one thing she would prefer to keep by her side: her husband.

After she made the bed, washed the breakfast dishes and put the clothes into the washer she went out on the deck for a cup of coffee. The house was too quiet without Kelsea, who had spent the night with a friend from school. Cady didn't expect her daughter home until late afternoon.

Even in January the weather in Eastern North Carolina was often temperate, and Cady could sit on her balcony in a light jacket and watch the waters of Haywood Creek, so much less hurried than the Trent River it branched from, meander past. Cady sipped her coffee and breathed.

"Hey, you on the balcony, don't you answer your door?" The harsh female voice cut across Cady's solitude and she blinked down at the woman in her back yard.

"Cam?" She stood and peered over the railing. "What the hell?" She hadn't seen her twin sister in nearly five years, and she could hardly believe she was standing right there in her yard, dressed in jeans, a t-shirt and a threadbare denim jacket with some bizarre emblem on the back.

"Let me into your tower and I'll tell you, Rapunzel."

Camryn Taylor stuck her hands in her pockets and grinned at her sister.

Her sister's mocking tone grated on Cady's nerves, and she made a private bet with herself about how long it would take for them to start arguing but decided maybe even that would be more interesting than drinking coffee alone. She jerked her head at the front door. "Go around front, and I'll let you in there."

Cam waited on the front steps, a gleaming black motorcycle parked next to Cady's minivan. Cady gave it a look of distaste before turning back to her bemused-looking twin. "So what are you doing here?"

Cam smiled a little tightly and shrugged. "Well, your castle is gorgeous, I have to admit, and I sort of need a place to stay for a while."

Cady could tell that it was difficult for Cam to ask. She had the air of somebody who wanted to get a disagreeable task over with. She tried to figure out what could have happened over the course of the past few months to make life hard enough to send her twin sister knocking on her door. The last she'd heard, Cam had been in a steady relationship with a man she actually seemed to like. Her two daughters were in their fathers' custody and Cam rarely saw them, but she'd never been the maternal type anyway and hardly seemed to care.

So why this sudden flight? As Cady studied Cam's face, irritation gave way to anxiety. What once would have been nearly a mirror image of her own face had changed, warped a little with time. Cam was thinner than Cady, her face more drawn, though still beautiful. The pallor of her complexion suggested recent illness.

"Are you okay?" Cady couldn't help asking.

"I'm good." Cam shrugged.

Cady sighed and stepped back from the door. "Come in, have a cup of coffee. You can tell me about it."

In the kitchen, she poured the coffee, refilling her own cup. Cam refused sugar and creamer, and Cady laughed. "You and dad. He couldn't drink anything but the blackest coffee."

"He always said you shouldn't screw with Juan Valdez's beans." Cam smiled, saluting with her cup. "Here's to you, Dad."

Both women drank deeply and Cam stared into her mug for several long seconds, swirling the liquid around. "How's Mom?"

Cady wondered how much that simple question had cost her sister. Cam and their mother had fought bitterly through most of Cam's life, finally ending with Cam leaving home when she was pregnant with her first child. She'd never returned to the little house in the mountains, even when her father passed away five years before, although she had attended the funeral. Mother and daughter had studiously ignored each other, sandwiching Cady between them as a buffer zone.

"She's okay. She's practically taken over the assisted living facility she moved into after Dad died. You know Mom."

"Not really." Cam shrugged. "I never did. I knew Dad pretty well, but Mom was a mystery to me. Her and her junior league buddies. I think that's why I hate the suburbs so much."

"Well, you must really be getting the creeps here, then."

4

Cady gestured at her house. "Although there's not much for Trent Woods to be a suburb of, unless you count New Bern."

"This isn't a suburb. It's a small town. At least, that's what I keep telling myself."

Cady placed a cinnamon roll and a banana on a plate in front of Cam. "Eat. You need some calories from the look of you."

Cam stared at the plate of food for a moment, and finally, as if she'd gained strength from the mere sight of it, she raised her head. "I need a place to stay."

"You mentioned you were in between places." Cady tried not to sound hesitant. Maybe it would be a chance to reconnect with her sister, maybe it would just be painful. She had an idea what Neil's opinion would be. He and Cam had not parted on the best of terms the last time she'd visited. "What happened?"

"Same old thing. I screwed up. I just got to a point in my relationship with Stan where I knew I couldn't go on any longer." Cam shrugged, taking a bite of the cinnamon roll.

"Cam," Cady paused and shook her head. "Relationships are work, you know. It's really hard to stay with one person, but it's very rewarding when you do."

"Really?" Cam shot back and gestured in a grandiose manner at their surroundings. "I mean, yeah, I would guess so. You've got a big house and your husband has a steady job. Is that what you mean? Or is it that he's great in bed? At least I assume he is since you've been married umpteen million years."

"It's not all about that." Cady ignored her sister's second question. Where was her reward? Her husband was gone all the time and had been for years, married more to his job than to her. Her daughter had grown up into a young woman, seemingly overnight. She didn't need her mother as much anymore and Cady felt the loneliness of that intensely, especially without a husband around to share it with her.

"Then what's it about?" When Cady didn't reply, Cam's eyes narrowed. "Is there trouble in paradise? I'm sorry, Sis, I didn't realize you and Neil were having problems."

"We're not…exactly." Cady turned to put her coffee cup in the sink. She paused, looking out unseeing through the trees to the slow moving waters of the creek. "I mean, we don't fight or anything. But then, how could we when he's never here?"

"He's never here?" Cam's voice floated to her from behind. "What exactly do you mean?"

"Just that. He comes home for a few hours and he's either too exhausted to do more than fall asleep on the couch or he has to go back to work. Or he's off on a business trip gathering depositions or something." She sighed, turning back to her sister. "I *know* he loves me, but sometimes I feel like a widow."

"Well, you're hardly the first to feel that way." Cam chewed for a minute. "But if you and Neil are already having problems, I shouldn't add to it. I'll find someplace else to go."

"Don't be ridiculous." Cady fought a sudden sense of rising panic at the thought of not seeing her sister again for another five years. "Where are you going to go?"

"Seriously?" Cam shook her head. "You and I are so different, we've never gotten along. Having me here in the middle of things isn't likely to solve your marital difficulties, either."

Cady fell silent, thinking. She knew Cam was right. Neil wouldn't be happy, and she would never be able to get along with her sister for an extended amount of time. But the panic won out. Cam stood right in front of her, in the flesh for the first time in years. If she walked out the door now, it would be like it never happened, like she'd never come home.

"I don't want you to go." She straightened her shoulders. "We'll figure it out, but don't leave."

"Cady—" Cam sighed and put her hand on her sister's. "Okay. I won't go yet. We'll see what Neil says."

As she sliced cucumbers for the salad, lost in thought, Cady's cell phone rang, startling her from her reverie. She smiled when she saw Will Hubbard's number on the caller ID. Shifting the knife from one hand to the other, she tucked the phone between her chin and shoulder.

"Hey."

"Hi there." Will sounded relaxed, although she knew he had to be busy getting ready for the dinner rush. Even on a Sunday evening, his restaurant, Hubbard's Bar & Grille, was a favorite dinner destination.

Cady frowned at the phone as she continued to slice vegetables. "Shouldn't you be working?"

"Certainly. And I would be but I just realized someone didn't call me with a final headcount for the Historical Society benefit dinner. You know, the one next week that I'm supposed to cater?"

"Oh!" Cady dropped the knife and wiped her hands on a

dishtowel before rummaging through her briefcase. "I'm so sorry, Will. It's been one of those days." She pulled a file folder from the case and began to flip the pages. "Just a sec, I've got it right here."

"No problem." He really did sound as if it wasn't. "What kind of day has it been?"

She smiled at the sincere concern in his voice and pictured him sitting at his desk in the office at Hubbard's. She'd been there innumerable times to have coffee and plan for a benefit. Will's family had run Hubbard's for nearly two decades and under Will's management it had expanded amazingly. In addition to the restaurant and catering business, Hubbard's now included a neighboring banquet hall, which could be rented out for functions ranging from wedding receptions to dance parties to fundraising dinners.

Which was what he was calling about now. Cady scanned the paper in front of her that outlined her latest fundraising venture. Neil called her a "professional volunteer", and she had to admit the title fit. Cady had planned her first event for the historical society three years before and since then she'd been on the top of everybody's list of favorite volunteer event coordinators. It probably helped that she didn't like to say no to a good cause.

"Hey, you didn't answer my question." Will sounded like he was pretending to be peeved.

"Sorry." She found the line item for RSVPs on her spreadsheet. "Sixty-eight have replied yes, but I still have fifteen invitations outstanding. I can't imagine more than half of those will respond yes. Assuming they are all couples or bring a date, let's say plan for about fourteen more and I'll get back with you by the middle of next week with the most definite number I can."

"That's terrific." He paused for a moment and she pictured him writing it down. "But you still haven't answered my *other* question. What's made your day so busy you forgot to call me?"

"Oh." She glanced over her shoulder to make sure Cam wasn't anywhere around although she knew her sister was upstairs either taking a nap or a shower. Nevertheless, she lowered her voice. "My sister showed up this morning. Literally on my doorstep."

"Your twin?" Will let out a low whistle. "That must have been a shock."

"You have no idea." Cady grinned. "And she was riding a hog."

"A hog?" Will sounded amused. "A Harley?"

"Harley, Honda, whatever." Cady snorted. "It's big, black and parked out front right now. I can't wait for the neighbors to see it."

"She's still there?"

"She needed a place to stay." Cady felt a little uncomfortable. Should she be telling Will this before she'd even had a chance to talk to Neil? She could have called her husband at any time during the day to give him a heads up, but she'd decided it would be easier to break it to him in person. Of course, the sight of the "hog" parked in his front drive might be a bit of a shock, to say the least.

"What about Neil?" Will might have been reading her mind. "Does he know he's got a new roommate?"

"Not exactly, but it's not really my fault." She knew she

sounded defensive. "It's Sunday and I haven't seen him since last night."

"Is he working on a case?"

"When is he not?" Cady sighed. "He's probably been buried in the firm's law library looking up some obscure bit of legislation." She paused, feeling guilty. "I guess I should've called him, huh?"

Will's silence answered her question, but when he answered he sounded noncommittal. "None of my business. Just look out for yourself, okay?"

"Of course. I've always been a big believer in number one coming first."

He snorted and she thought again how much she loved talking to him. He had a way of making her feel better about herself. "I look forward to hearing how he takes the news," he said. "Give me a call when things settle down."

As she hung up, she heard the front door open. "Mom?"

Cady smiled, setting her cell phone aside and hurrying to the kitchen door to greet her daughter with a hug. "Hey baby! Did you have a good time? How was it?"

Kelsea Summers shook her walnut colored hair off her shoulders and hugged her mother, but then she stepped back and gave her a puzzled look. "You do know there's a huge Harley sitting in the driveway, don't you?"

"Oh." Cady grinned at a sudden thought. "Did Marie see it?" The thought of her daughter's best friend's mother seeing a Harley in her front drive amused her.

"Um, yeah. She asked if we were having work done on the house."

"Did you tell her it was probably your mother's?"

Kelsea whirled to look at Cam, who stood on the back stairs. She turned to her mother, then back to Cam. "What? I mean, Aunt Cam?"

Cam grinned. "Hey kiddo. You're a little taller than the last time I saw you."

Kelsea laughed. "I was *eight* the last time you saw me." She skipped over and threw her arms around her aunt's neck. "It's so great to see you." She stepped back and looked at her mother. "Please tell me the motorcycle is Aunt Cam's."

"Well, we were discussing trading it for room and board." Cady turned back to the stove with a wink.

"Does that mean—?" Kelsea clasped her hands and turned beseechingly to Cam. "Are you staying with us? For a while, I mean?"

Cam smiled. "I guess. But I refuse to give your mother lessons on how to ride a hog."

"And I was so looking forward to it." Cady arched an eyebrow at her sister as Kelsea threw her arms around her aunt yet again.

"Oh, I can't wait. This is so great. You'll be here for the cheer contest and my recital, too. Oh, you just have to stay for that! It's only a couple of months away. And then—"

"Let's not get ahead of ourselves, honey." Cady felt a little alarmed. "I, um, couldn't get in touch with your father earlier."

Cam helped herself to a slice of cucumber from the cutting board. "Probably best to take it one step at a time."

"Probably so."

Cady turned at the sound of her husband's voice. Neil stood just inside the door of the kitchen surveying the scene in front of him with a slight frown that only showed on his fore-head. He looked tired and rumpled, and she realized her assumption that he had been researching a case had probably been correct. She felt a surge of guilt and set aside the knife to give her husband a kiss. He embraced her absently.

"I was just telling them I hadn't been able to get in touch with you to let you know Cam was visiting." Cady looked appealingly at her husband.

"Really?" Neil patted his front pocket. "Yep. Got my cell phone right there. Didn't ring all day."

"You must've been on it or something. Maybe out of range." Even such a tiny lie tasted sour, but Cady couldn't admit she hadn't wanted to call him about Cam.

Cam seemed to sense the tension between the two and cleared her throat. "Maybe I should wait outside."

"No! Come upstairs with me." Kelsea grabbed Cam's hand and pulled her up the stairs. "I have a million things to show you." Her voice chattered away as Cam followed her up the stairs.

Cady waited until she heard Kelsea's door open and shut. Then she turned to Neil. "Okay, you're right. I didn't call. I didn't want to get into this."

Neil took a beer from the fridge and uncapped it. "Get into what?" He shrugged. "Your sister is visiting."

Cady picked up the knife and turned her attention to the lettuce. She began cutting it into thin strips. "Yeah. I'm, um, not sure how long."

"Great." Neil nodded. "Last time she visited was five years ago. She alienated your mother and nearly drove you insane with worry. It's always great to see her."

"Neil--"

He held up his hand to stop her. He looked tired but resigned. "It's fine, Cady. She's your sister."

Cady nodded. "My *twin* sister. And I get the feeling she needs help."

He rolled his eyes and then sighed, giving her a rueful smile. He took another drink of his beer, set it down and slid his arms around her from behind, giving her a squeeze. "Okay, mother hen. I know better than to try to pull you away from a cause." He kissed her neck. "And I'm sorry. Just a little tired."

She resisted the temptation to lean into his caress. "Speaking of which, where the hell *were* you all day? You left this morning before I even got up, then you're gone all day?"

He took a deep breath and turned away, leaving her feeling bereft and knowing she had only herself to blame. If she missed his touch so much, why did she resist him when he was around? "It's just a case. I got caught up in it. I'm sorry I was gone so long."

"On a Sunday." She nudged him and handed him his beer.

He smiled a little, accepting the bottle. "Yeah, on a Sunday." He slipped his free arm around her waist, kissing her gently. "Maybe I can make it up to you later?"

"Maybe." She smiled and turned back to the oven. "In the meantime, let's get dinner ready. I know you can't wait to catch up with Cam, and I want to hear about our daughter's weekend."

"Right." He opened the silverware drawer and began setting the table. As he passed her on his way to the cupboard for plates, Cady gave him a thoughtful look. She took things like this for granted. How many husbands set the table without being asked? And it was just one thing, just a tiny thing, in comparison to everything else he did.

So what if she had to deal without him some? His work was important to him, and she needed to understand that.

He finished setting the table and she turned back to the spaghetti sauce, stirring it with a long-handled spoon. As Neil passed, he paused beside her and when she glanced at him, he kissed her. "I love you."

"I love you, too." She felt it, too, in that moment, and she swore to herself she'd be better.

KELSEA KEPT them all amused through dinner with a vivacious account of her night. She and Sabrina, her best friend, had been to a movie Kelsea had been dying to see, and it had lived up to her expectations. As she listened, Cody remembered a time when she and Neil would have taken advantage of having a night to themselves. That didn't happen anymore. She squelched the feeling of resentment the realization brought with it, stealing a look at Neil. He listened to Kelsea with an absent smile, asking questions and laughing at the appropriate times, but Cady wondered if he really heard her. Realizing her own mind had wandered, she turned her attention back to her daughter. In a pause, she impulsively reached across the table to take her daughter's hand. "We need to see a movie together. Maybe next week."

"Sure." Kelsea grinned at her mother. "That'd be fun, Mom." She stood, gathering her plate and silverware. "I should get my homework done, though."

"You should." Neil smiled at his daughter. "Back to school tomorrow, young lady."

"Yeah, yeah." Kelsea kissed him and Cady, then startled them all by going around the table to kiss Cam on the cheek as well. "I'm glad you're here, Aunt Cam."

Cam shot Cady and Neil a quick glance, then smiled at her niece. "Thanks. Yeah. Me too."

The three adults listened in silence as Kelsea dropped her dishes in the sink and skipped up to her room. Neil picked up his nearly empty wine glass, swirling the contents with a thoughtful expression while Cady tried to figure out if she should remain in her seat or get up to clear the table.

"Are you all settled in, Cam?" Neil's tone was civil though not overly friendly. Cady decided it was the best she could hope for.

"Sure." Cam nodded. To Cady, her sister looked uncertain. "Thanks for letting me stay."

"Well, any sister of my wife's." Neil downed the last of the wine and set the glass aside.

Cam sighed, looking resigned. "Listen, I won't be here long enough to piss you off this time, Neil."

"Really?" Neil raised his eyebrows. "Is that a challenge?"

"God, you think you're so perfect, huh? Well, listen—"

"Stop it." Cady stood, fearing her sister was about to say something about their earlier conversation about her less-than-perfect marriage. "We're all tired. Let's get the kitchen cleaned up and go to bed."

Neil rose without another word and left the room. Cady watched him go with a mix of emotions. Relief that he had decided to back away from the fight, irritation that he'd started it in the first place, and disappointment that he'd just leave without a word. Once upon a time he wouldn't have left the room without a glance at her, but now she might as well be a piece of furniture. He didn't have to acknowledge her to be sure she'd be there when he came back.

With a sigh and a frown, she turned back to the table but Cam had already started clearing it. She nodded down the hall. "You need to go talk to your husband."

Cady could hear him in the bedroom upstairs, probably getting ready for bed. She considered insisting on helping Cam with the dishes, but decided her sister was right. For better or worse, she needed to have it out with her husband now.

CAM WATCHED her sister leave knowing she had a fight on her hands and it was her fault. She glanced around at the dirty dishes still on the table and knew she should begin loading them into the dishwasher, but she had something to do first, and she needed her strength to do it. Cam glanced at the clock on her cell phone. Six o'clock. Stan would be done with work, probably at the bar having a drink with some of the boys. She bit her lip and decided it was time. She needed to let him know she wasn't home and wouldn't be coming back.

He answered on the second ring, laughter in his voice and the sound of a jukebox in the background. "Hey, baby, where are you? It's payday and we're celebrating. Come on down."

"I'm not there." She wondered what it was about him that made her so tongue-tied, even now. Nearly a year after they'd met and begun dating, the sound of his voice could melt her knees, short out her brain and make it almost impossible to speak a complete sentence.

He laughed. "I *know* you're not here, babe. I'm trying to fix that. C'mon down, I want you."

I want you. The words echoed in her heart. "No, you don't get it, Stan. I'm not there and I'm not coming back. I'm here now and I don't want to see you again." She closed her eyes with the effort of saying the last words. How could she sound so heartless and indecipherable at the same time?

After a moment of listening to the jukebox play, in which she pictured him sitting at a table with a beer in front of him, his chair tilted back and his long legs splayed in front of him, he finally spoke. "Hold on a sec."

She heard voices and a door slamming and then silence. She knew he was standing in the middle of the dirt and gravel parking lot of the little dive bar he loved in Brunswick, Georgia. She knew he was holding his cell phone against his ear, searching for a way to reply to her. "Cam, what's going on?"

"I can't do this anymore. I can't keep pretending I can be your little wife."

"Did I ask you to be my wife?"

"You know what I mean. I'm sick of the whole thing. I had to get away."

"Where are you?"

"I'm at my sister's in North Carolina."

After a moment's silence, he burst out laughing. "You don't want to be my wife, but you run away to suburban hell? Are you serious? I've heard you talk about your sister and her husband and how uptight they are. Cam, are you feeling all right?"

"Cut it out."

"No, seriously, check and see if you have a fever. I'm really worried about you, babe."

"Cut…it…out! I'm serious. I'm not going to *stay* here permanently. Just 'til I figure out what to do next."

"I'll fucking *tell* you what to do next. Come home. Come home now. I don't want to live without you, and I'm pretty sure you don't mean any of these things you're saying. Come home and tell me what's really wrong."

If only she could. But it would ruin everything and she'd just end up back here without him, anyway. At least this way she could do it on her own terms.

"Cam?" His voice was stern. "Come home."

"I'm sorry." She closed her eyes again. She hadn't meant to say that. She hadn't meant to apologize, as if she had anything to really be sorry for, even if she did. "I can't."

She hung up and thought about him standing alone in the parking lot. He'd cuss, he might throw the phone and break it, and then he'd go inside and get drunk. Stinking drunk. Maybe he'd sleep with that little barmaid that'd been flirting with him for a while. Cam tried not to care.

2

$\mathcal{C}$ady closed the bedroom door behind her and turned to face Neil, who was still fully dressed and looked like he'd been waiting for her. He spread his hands, reading her mind. "I'm sorry."

She raised her eyebrows, still angry. "Really? Because it looked to me like you did that on purpose."

He shrugged. "I'd like to say she started it, but it wouldn't be true. She rubs me the wrong way."

"She's my twin sister. Do I rub you the wrong way?"

Neil tossed his jacket onto the bed. "Let's not be ridiculous, Cady."

"Ridiculous? Maybe. But then, too, you've got to look at it from my point of view, Neil." She strode over to the dresser and tossed her watch and her earrings into the jewelry box he'd given her as an anniversary present five years before. For a moment, she paused, looking at the velvet-covered nooks and crannies designed to hold precious things. Then she slammed the lid and whirled to glare at her husband. "Maybe I do rub you the wrong way. Maybe that's why you're gone all the time. Maybe you look at me and see all the ways I've failed you over the years."

"Failed me?" He looked stricken, and she knew her words were close enough to the truth to hurt him.

"Failed you. Failed myself. I couldn't ever give you the son you wanted. I've never had a real job, not since we got married, anyway. Hell, I'm not even much of a housekeeper. If we didn't have a maid once a week we'd be living in squalor." She waved her hand in a despairing flap and leaned on the dresser, surprised at the way her own anger had betrayed her.

"Is that really what you believe I think of you?" He couldn't hide the stunned look on his face. Abruptly he reached for her and pulled her against him. At first she resisted, but then she let herself rest against him. She'd always loved the way he felt when he held her, his chest and arms so strong and gentle. He stroked her hair and she drew away to look at him. She wanted him to say she was everything to him and she couldn't be more wrong and he loved her with all his heart. Instead, he tilted her chin up with one hand and kissed her.

Startled as she was by the kiss, it evoked an immediate response from her. He hadn't kissed her like this in months, and she couldn't deny, even to herself, how much she wanted him. Even when he hadn't been too exhausted to make love to her over the past few weeks, he'd done it an abstracted way, as if more through habit than desire. Not so now. He wanted her and the knowledge excited her as much as if it were the first time they'd made love instead of the umpteenth time in a fifteen-year-old marriage.

He moved his hand from her chin to the nape of her neck, slowing the pace and steering them toward the bed. She reached for his tie, aching to feel his skin against her fingers. She managed to loosen it and he tugged it off, tossing it aside as she sank onto the bed. He followed, kneeling in front of her and reaching for the buttons on his shirt. She surprised them both by reaching down after he'd undone the top three and pulling his shirt tail-first over his head. He laughed and tossed the inside-out bundle into a pile in the corner, then lowered himself onto her as she struggled with his belt buckle. As soon as she had loosened it, he kicked the pants off and set about getting rid of her sweater and jeans before covering her body with his again.

The feel of his skin against hers intoxicated her to such an extent she barely heard the buzz of his cell phone on the bedside table. She almost didn't notice when he reached out for the phone and when she did she thought maybe he intended to silence it. Surely he wouldn't answer it, not with the only thing between them the thin barriers of their underwear.

But he did. Even as she kissed his neck and reached for the waistband of his boxers, even with his hand at the small of her bare back still applying pressure as if to pull her closer and his knee against her damp crotch, he answered it.

"This is Neil."

She froze at the sound of his cool professional voice. "Shit." She wanted to hit him. How could he do this just when things felt right between them again? Angry, she shoved him off of her and stood, crossing to the bathroom without glancing over her shoulder. She could hear his voice outside, evidently undisturbed by her abrupt departure. Maybe he'd even welcomed it. Much easier to continue his business call if she weren't distracting him. She stared at her reflection in the large mirror over her sink. She had some gray hair, and things shook more now than they had twenty years ago, but overall she was in good shape for a woman nearer to forty than thirty. And he'd wanted her. How could he just turn that off so quickly? She couldn't. Her breasts and groin still yearned for his touch, for the completion of what they'd begun. And worse, her heart ached. She didn't like to admit it, but more than her pride had been hurt by his actions.

She hadn't noticed he'd stopped talking until he knocked softly on the door. "Sweetheart?"

"What?"

"Can I come in?"

"No." She turned on the shower and stripped off her panties and bra. "I'm taking a shower."

"I'll wash your back." He sounded amused and she hated him with a passionate surge that startled her.

"Go away." She didn't want to admit to him how much he'd hurt her. "You had your chance. I'll see what the vibrating shower head can do for me now." And she stepped in, closing the door with a sharp snap and letting the water beat over her head and mix with the tears that coursed over her face.

She'd regained an icy self-control by the time she had dressed. She pulled on a t-shirt and sweats so he wouldn't get the idea he might still have a chance, but she paused to put on a little clear lip gloss so her lips looked fuller and more kiss-able in an attempt to let him know what he had missed.

He sat on the bed, his shoulders hunched in such a tired way her first reaction was one of concern, but when he lifted his head she realized he'd gotten dressed again. And not in the rumpled shirt she'd pulled off him. That still lay in the corner. He wore another dress shirt and tie and a neatly pressed pair of khakis. Cady thought about the dry cleaners and her heart hardened in her chest.

"Why did you leave?" He asked the question as if her actions didn't make any sense at all.

"Why did you answer the damn phone?" She glared at him.

He sighed. "Cady, we've been over this before. You know I don't have a job with normal hours. I have to make some sacrifices."

"Right." She nodded and bit back what she really wanted to say. If he had to make sacrifices, how come she felt like the one who was deprived? "Is that where you're going now? Back to work?"

"I have to." He looked uncomfortable. "I should have already left."

"So go." She picked up a magazine and settled onto the bed. "I'm fine. The shower was earth-shattering." She stole a look at him and saw a tiny smile curve his lips. Why was she letting him off the hook?

He leaned over and kissed her tenderly. "I wish you hadn't left." He pushed a lock of her hair back from her face. "I love you."

She sighed. "I love you too." She kissed him briefly.

"Now, go on. Save the world or whatever. I'll be here when you get back."

He left and she flipped through the magazine blindly for a minute before tossing it aside and closing her eyes. "Shit." He meant it, of course. He would have finished what they started, and she wouldn't be left alone with blood pulsing in inopportune spots. He would even have made certain she was satisfied. But all this would have been done with the knowledge that he would be leaving, that something else had already taken his attention from her. And he didn't even understand how that could hurt her.

A light tap on the door made her sit up straighter. Was it Cam or Kelsea? She really didn't want to see anyone right then, but she called out, "Come in."

Cam poked her head into the room. "All clear? I saw his car leave."

Cady sighed. "Yeah, he's gone."

"Well, you look refreshed." Cam bounced over to the bed and flopped down on it. "Man, I miss makeup sex."

"Me too." Cady fought the urge to kick her sister.

"What? You mean you didn't?" Her sister raised herself on her elbows, looking concerned. "I thought you guys made up. It got quiet up here. You didn't throw him out did you?"

"No, I didn't throw him out." Cady felt the tears resurge into her throat. "Go away, Cam. I'm tired."

Cam seemed not to hear. She flipped over on her back and stared at the ceiling. "Well, that's good. That you didn't throw him out, I mean. I think you'd miss him."

"Fuck." Cady got up and went over to the dresser, pulling a tissue from the box and blowing her nose. "Goddamnit,

Cam, would you please just leave me alone? I'm tired and I don't even know if my husband loves me anymore and I just want to feel sorry for myself and cry and go to sleep. I don't need you for any of that!" She dissolved into tears and sank back onto the bed, her hands over her face. She felt Cam get off the bed and heard the door shut and for a moment she thought her sister had actually left her. Then Cam put her arm around her shoulders and pulled her into an embrace.

Cam had always been the stronger of the two of them. When they were kids and Cam fell and skinned her knee, she'd just get up and go on. It was Cady who would wail until her mother came running, usually to scold Cam for some imagined endangerment of her sister. And yet, through it all, Cam had remained protective and loving, until they grew up and their lives diverged.

Cady leaned on her sister's arm, sniffling. "I'm sorry, I'm such a wuss."

"What's going on with you two? I thought you had the perfect marriage. You did the last time I was here." Cam's voice sounded acerbic.

Cady sat up, resenting her sister's tone. "The last time you were here was five years ago."

"Yeah, I remember." Cam frowned. "And Neil hated me then."

Cady dabbed her eyes, thinking that Neil's feelings about Cam probably stemmed from his job. How many mothers had he seen fight for their children when Cam had just given hers up? She decided not to get into that aspect of her sister's life, however. "To be fair, you did smoke pot in the guest bath."

"It wasn't pot. I was just smoking. You guys were so

uptight about it I figured if I smoked in the bathroom you'd never know. But anyway, he hated me." Cam stood and walked over to the bureau, peering at herself in the mirror. "So what's Mr. Perfect done to piss you off?"

"He answered the phone."

"Are you kidding me?" Cam stared at her in the reflection. "Seriously? All this because he answered the phone?"

"He answered it when we were—" Cady stopped. She wasn't sure if she really wanted to get into her sex life with Cam.

But realization had already dawned on Cam's face and she swung around. "Oh! You mean you were…" She snickered, trying to hide her smile behind her hand. "Sorry. Just got a really funny picture."

"Jeez, Cam, thanks for the sympathy. Nothing quite compares with sisterly love." Cady sighed. How could she explain to her sister, the woman with the worst track record ever as far as men were concerned, that she felt alone even when her husband was with her? How could she tell her that Neil was a wonderful father, a perfect husband, a great provider…but he was gone so often and she felt alone and needy and while she hated herself for it, she couldn't seem to stop. Her sister wouldn't understand any of that. Cam had never given her heart and soul to anyone else, even her kids.

Cam sat on the bed again, still grinning a little, but she sounded repentant. "No, I'm sorry, Cady. Really. I'm sure it hurt your feelings, and nobody likes to be left in the middle of makeup sex."

"He didn't leave. I did." Cady sniffed and lay back on the

pillows, punching them with a bit more force than strictly necessary for plumping.

Cam stared. "*You* left? What do you mean?"

"I figured if answering the phone was so damn important I'd take my shower." The words sounded petty, but Cady remembered the hurt when he'd answered the phone as if he had nothing better going on at the moment.

"And when you got out of the shower he was gone?"

Why did you leave?… I have to make some sacrifices… I wish you hadn't left.

"No. He was sitting right here waiting for me, but he was all dressed and *ready* to go, so I told him to go, all right? I know he's got a demanding job and he doesn't need me making it any harder for him, but damn it, did he *have* to answer the goddamn phone right then?" She hit the bed for emphasis, then put her arms over face and sobbed. "God, I'm such a fucking selfish person, but it's like he's never here anymore, you know? And I don't know. Maybe it's my problem, not his. Maybe I'm going through a midlife crisis."

"You're thirty-seven." Cady felt her sister's weight shift as she also lay back on the bed. "That's hardly middle age."

"It could be!" Cady shrugged and dropped her arms to her sides, feeling empty and tired after her temper tantrum. "Seventy's pretty old. I could die then."

"Don't be ridiculous." Cam's voice sounded sharp.

Both women fell silent. Cady thought about all the ways she'd failed Neil over the years, beginning with her inability to have more children. Had that been when he'd become so devoted to work? Maybe he'd sublimated his paternity into his job. She heaved a sigh. "I wish—"

"What?" Cam turned her head on the pillow. When Cady remained silent, she said, "You tell me yours, I'll tell you mine."

Cady turned her head to look at her sister. For a moment she remembered when they'd been kids sleeping in twin beds and telling each other their secrets and dreams. She smiled a little. "Yeah, well, it's not a big secret. I wish we'd had another baby."

Cam stared at her for a second. Then she jerked to a sitting position, facing a little away from her sister. "Why? Do you think it would've made a big difference? In your marriage or your life?"

Cady looked at the ceiling. "I don't know. I mean, we have Kelsea, and Neil loves her of course, but she's getting older and she doesn't need us nearly as much. Maybe it would be easier if we had another one or two coming along after her. And even if it didn't make a difference to Neil and his work, at least I'd feel like there was a reason for me being here."

Cam nodded, sitting very still so only her head moved a little. "You're a good mom." Her voice sounded strange.

"Thanks." Cady sat up, her concern shifting from herself to her sister. "Are you okay? I know you've had your own problems where kids and men are concerned. Is everything all right?"

"I wouldn't say all right, exactly." Cam turned her head to look at her twin. "I'm pregnant."

"Again?" Cady regretted the word as soon as she said it. "God, I'm sorry. I didn't mean it that way." She put a hand on her sister's shoulder and frowned, noticing again how thin Cam was.

Cam smiled mirthlessly, her hand on her only slightly rounded stomach. "It's okay. That was my first reaction, too."

Cady bit her lip. "What are you going to do?" She knew the answer. Cam, in spite of all her other faults as a mother, would never have an abortion.

"I don't really know." Her sister sighed, her head falling forward so her hair hung around her face in a protective curtain.

"Shit." Cady sat frozen for a moment. She thought she knew what Neil's reaction would be to the news, but whether or not she deserved her fate, Cam was her sister. Cady stroked Cam's hair. "What about the father?"

Cam groaned. "What about him? He's out of the picture, just like all the other men I've been with."

Cady took a deep breath. "Have you thought about adoption?"

Adoption. The word hung in the air between the two sisters like a magic talisman. It made sense to Cady. She wanted a baby. Cam didn't. Who knew what would happen to this child if she didn't take it? Cam's other two children lived with their fathers, both of whom made decent livings, had married and had stable lives. Could that possibly happen a third time in Cam's crazy life?

"No." Cam's answer fell like a knife, slicing through Cady's momentary hope. Cam looked her sister in the eye. "I know I've never been much of a mother, and I can see why you'd suggest it. You guys have so much to give a child. But it's like this is my last chance at the mother thing. And Stan... well, he's no father, but he'd never let me give up this baby. I know it." She fell silent for a moment, then added, "If you want me to leave, I will."

Cady sighed. "Of course not. I'm your sister, and you need help." Her shoulders slumped. "You're going to stay here as long as you need to--after the baby's born even. Even if I can only be his aunt and your sister."

Cam sighed with relief and flopped back onto the bed. "Great. Wonderful. Well, unless somebody offers me something better, I reckon you've got yourself a deal. But how will you square this with Neil?"

Cady felt her lips thin with her determination. "My better half will just have to resign himself. It's not like he's here that much, anyway." She squeezed Cam's hand and smiled when her sister squeezed back.

3

*S*houts and running feet outside her door awakened Cam the next morning. "Shit." She rolled over and checked the alarm clock. Nine o'clock. She sat up and groaned. Okay, maybe nine o'clock wasn't all that early, but still. She heard more squeals and yelps from outside her door, and, deciding she needed to make sure the family wasn't being murdered, stood and pulled on a pair of jeans. Not much chance of any more sleep anyway. She pulled a brush through her hair, washed her face and opened her door.

Kelsea stood in the hall with a teenage boy. They jumped and turned when the door opened, looking guilty. "Hey Aunt Cam." Kelsea waved brightly.

"Hey Kelsea." Cam wondered briefly if her sister knew Kelsea had developed an interest in teenage boys. The interest was probably still pretty innocent, though, especially since the boy still had more acne than facial hair. She smothered a yawn as she noticed more yells and thumps from downstairs. "What's up?"

"Mom's coffee group. School's out for a teacher workday, so it's kind of a free-for-all. Sorry if we woke you."

"If?" Cam raised her eyebrows and turned toward the stairs. "At least there'll be coffee."

At the bottom of the stairs, a little blonde-haired baby with chubby cheeks grinned up at her before starting the climb. Cam paused and frowned. "Are you supposed to go up there?" The baby continued upward and she shrugged. "Guess so." She pushed through the swinging door and paused, confronted by a phalanx of curious and unfamiliar faces. She jerked her thumb over her shoulder. "Hey, you guys know the house has been invaded?"

"Sorry." Cady grinned from the other side of the kitchen counter. "Want some coffee?"

"Only if it's hot and black. Oh, and there's a munchkin on the stairs."

One of the women glanced down and gasped. "Oh no. Eric!" She jumped for the swinging door and they heard her scolding the baby in the hallway.

"Tracy's always losing track of her kids." A plump redhead smiled from the bar and held out her hand. "My name's Abby and you must be Cam. We've heard a lot about you this morning."

Cam accepted the cup of coffee as the doorbell rang, precipitating a crescendo of yells for "MOM, THERE'S SOMEBODY AT THE DOOR!" These were followed by Kelsea calling, "I'll get it."

"Wow, they're noisy little fuckers, aren't they?" Cam

sipped her coffee and turned back to find the other women staring at her. Cady widened her eyes impressively, and Cam realized she'd said something wrong. "Well, they are." She shrugged her shoulders defensively.

"I guess we're just not used to hearing the f-word tossed around indiscriminately." A woman with perfect, shoulder-length black hair smiled through very white teeth.

"Shit, did I say 'fuckers'?" Cam covered her mouth. "I meant buggers. At least I didn't say motherfuckers, right?"

Cady began to giggle and Abby snorted with laughter, but the other women turned back to their original conversations with a cliquish rustle. Cam felt a rush of irritation that was prevented from becoming anything more by Kelsea bouncing into the room. "Hey, there's some guy at the front door asking for Aunt Cam."

Cam's hand jerked in shock and she splashed a little black coffee onto the counter. "You're kidding me."

"I'm not. He's really good looking, too." Kelsea grinned, her tone teasing. "Is he your boyfriend?"

Cam stared at her for a second, then stood slowly, exchanging a quick look with Cady. "I don't have a boyfriend, sweetie."

She marched resolutely to the door. Stanley stood on the doorstep, just as she'd known he would be. He looked amazingly good and familiar against the suburban backdrop. She had a wild desire to rush into his arms and beg him to take her away from all this. She grinned at the thought and he looked confused.

"Hey, Stan." She motioned over her shoulder. "I'd invite you in, but I'm afraid we're at capacity now."

"Hey." He glanced past her and she turned to see Cady lingering.

Cady approached, looking at her sister. "Everything okay?" She raised her eyebrows.

Cam wondered what her sister thought of Stan. Well over six feet, his sheer size could be frightening, and considering the long line of junkies, jerks and all around assholes she'd dated in the past, Cady might well be a little judgmental of Cam's latest boyfriend.

And the father of her baby.

"Everything's fine." Cam turned to Stan. "Cady, this is Stan. Stan, my sister."

Stan held out his peculiarly large hand, engulfing Cady's tiny, ladylike appendage. "Great to meet you."

Cady smiled and it seemed genuine. Cam wondered if her sister had already seen past Stan's intimidating façade to his true gentle nature. For most people all it took was a few words or a single touch.

Cam remembered his touch well.

"What are you doing here, Stan?" She focused her attention on him. "Did you follow me?"

"What the hell did you expect me to do, Cam?" He frowned at her. "I wake up yesterday and you're gone. Then you call me with all that cockamamie crap about staying here for a while and how you don't love me and don't want to see me. You sounded half crazed."

Cam folded her arms across her chest to keep from reaching for him. "Be serious, please. What about your job?"

He shrugged as if it didn't matter, but she knew it did. "Well, I've probably been fired by now. I didn't actually have any sick days. But who cares? I'll deal with it. I just want to know why you left. What did I do?"

Cam glanced at Cady, who still hesitated by the open door. "I think we're going to go around to the dock."

Cady blinked as if she were just waking up. "Oh, sure. Just close the gate so none of the kids follow you. Can I get you a cup of coffee, Stan?"

"Sure." He glanced at Cam and appeared to reconsider. "I mean, maybe when we're done."

Cam led him to the backyard. Several kids swarmed around the old play set, but to Cam's relief, they ignored the adults walking past. She felt numb, unable to process what was happening. Why was Stanley here? How had he found her? And was he really worried about her?

Stan held the gate for her and closed it behind them. Their footsteps sounded hollow and loud on the dry wood of the dock. The tall grass and the trees on the far bank were a soft golden color reflected in the still waters of the creek. The sun shone brightly in a perfectly blue sky, but when the wind picked up, Cam shivered, wishing she'd brought a jacket. She turned to face Stan. "So what are you doing here?"

"What are *you* doing here? I thought everything was fine, then you snuck out on me. Aren't you happy?"

"I'm never happy, Stan. You ought to know that." Cam turned away again, folding her arms over her chest. "I'm visiting my sister."

"For how long?" He sounded implacable.

"Until. I don't know. What does it matter?"

"It matters because I love you. I want to know you're coming back."

Cam tried to harden her heart. She had no real desire to listen to him because then she might want to take him up on his offer. She couldn't tell him about the baby. Stan was different from the other men she'd dated in more ways than one, but to Cam the most important one was that he had ambitions. He had a plan for his life. He'd already taken several night classes at a community college, and his plan to start his own construction and remodeling business was taking shape. Cam could close her eyes there on the dock in her sister's backyard and remember the nights she'd lain in his arms in the warmth of his bed listening to him outline his plans.

She had no intention of disrupting those plans with a baby. Cam turned, opening her mouth to tell him to go home, but he caught her around the waist, bending his head to kiss her, his lips gently demanding and familiar. Without even meaning to, she leaned into him, her arms winding around his neck. For that moment as their lips met and parted and met again, she thought about a future with him and their baby. A mix of emotions, led by fear, electrified her, and she took her arms from his neck, pushing him almost violently away.

"Stop! God, Stanley, can't you take a hint? I don't want you. I don't want any of this. I've never wanted to settle down and none of that has changed."

He stood, imperturbable, with the sunlight sparkling off the water behind him. When she finished speaking, he stuck his hands in his pockets and shrugged. "I'll tell you what I know, Cam." As usual, his voice had the timber of a well-educated man caught in the body of a construction worker. "I'm a man of simple tastes. I want the woman I love in the home we've made together. And I love you."

She bit back the obvious reply that wanted to escape her lips: *I love you, too.* She felt extremely tired and scared and too old to be doing any of this. She sighed. "Go home, Stanley. I can't deal with this."

"Can't deal with *what*?" He caught her arm as she started to turn away. "Tell me what you can't deal with! Damn it all, Cam, I only want to help you."

"*You!*" She glared at him. "You. That's it. You're enough, aren't you? If you love me, go *away*, for God's sake." She jerked her arm free and stomped across the dock, trying not to imagine it disintegrating behind her, taking him away with it forever.

CADY COULDN'T WAIT to get her guests out of the house. Cam had not reappeared in the kitchen and she'd seen Stanley's truck drive away so she assumed Cam had either gone with him or snuck upstairs. If she'd gone with Stanley, most likely Cady wouldn't see her for another five years. Maybe that was best, but the thought brought a surge of emptiness with it.

She hurried up the stairs after the last of her coffee group rounded up their brood and left. Kelsea had retired to her room to study for a math test, and Cady couldn't contain her anxiety any longer. She knocked quietly on the door.

"Come in." Cam sounded tired. Relieved to hear her voice, Cady pushed the door open and found her sister lying on the bed.

"Hey, are you okay?" She crossed the room to Cam's side. "You look horrible."

Cam sat up. "Just queasy. That happens, right?"

"Yeah. I guess. I mean, I was never really sick with Kelsea. Well, not like that, anyway." She felt Cam's forehead. "You probably just need something to eat. You never had breakfast other than coffee. Want me to bring you something?"

Cam shook her head. "I'll come down. I guess we need to talk, huh?"

"After you have breakfast." Cady waved as she headed down the stairs. "I'll make you an omelet, you take a shower."

Cady had always liked taking care of someone and Cam was the perfect victim. As she cracked eggs and diced vegetables she thought how nice it was to have someone else in the house, but she wondered if she should be so happy that Cam hadn't resolved her problems with Stan, who Cady knew instinctively was a good man. If Cam was going to keep the baby, she'd do better with the support of the father. Cady quieted the doubts, however, turning on the burner just as Cam pushed through the swinging door.

"Hey. You look better." She passed her sister a clean coffee cup.

"Thanks. I feel better." Cam yawned.

"Yeah, sorry we woke you this morning." Cady flipped the omelet.

"S'okay. I didn't need to be asleep still. I guess my body's telling me I'm too old for this pregnancy stuff."

Cady opened her mouth to suggest they get her an appointment with an obstetrician, but realized she really should establish what had happened that morning. "So." She hesitated. "What happened with Stanley? Is he the baby's father?"

"He is, and I told him to go home." Cam pointed at the pan. "I think that's burning."

Cady flipped the omelet onto a plate and set it in front of her sister. "He doesn't know, then?"

Her sister forked a tentative bite of egg. "I have no intention of telling him."

Cady frowned thoughtfully. "How would he feel about a baby?"

"I know what you're thinking." Cam glared at her omelet. "Didn't I screw things up enough for my girls? Jeanne doesn't even want to acknowledge me as a relative and Selena tells everybody her stepmother is her *mother*. And I'm *glad* she does. I'm glad neither one of them wants anything to do with me. I was never supposed to be a mother. Thank God I picked good fathers for them, at least." She drew in a deep breath. "Maybe you're right. Maybe I should give you my baby. I'm just going to fuck it up, anyway."

Cady felt a jab of conscience. "I'm sorry. I didn't mean it like that. You know I just want to help."

Cam looked up sharply, then shrugged. "Yeah, I know."

"But listen." Cady leaned on the counter. "Neil is very protective of the rights of both parents and he's seen a lot of shit go wrong when one parent isn't up front with another."

"So we don't tell him." Cam raised her eyes to her sister in silent appeal. "Trust me, Cady, Stan doesn't need this. It'll just disrupt his life and he has plans. I can't do that to him."

Cady hesitated. She knew she should be totally honest and upfront with her husband, but her sister seemed so certain she shouldn't tell Stan. What could it possibly help? If Stan had other plans, he might not be happy about a baby interfering.

And if he was willing to be responsible and give up his plans, what kind of life would the baby lead? Surely not the one she and Neil could help provide Cam and her child. She silenced the part of her that whispered that if she told Neil and he forced Cam to tell Stan, both her sister and the baby would disappear from her life.

"Besides, it's a moot point, anyway." Cam took the last bite of omelet.

"Why?"

"Because he's gone. I told him to go home." Cam pushed back her plate and stood to take it to the sink.

"And you think he'll just go?" Cady studied her sister, thinking about the very tall, very good-looking man who'd stood just outside the door looking at Cam with such longing.

Cam turned. "I have no reason to think he won't."

"ARE you sure you're ready to tell Neil you've asked me to stay until the baby's born?" Cam looked a little nervous.

Lady sat across from her at the bar, trying not to feel anxious herself. Neil had called earlier to tell her he'd be home in time for dinner. He didn't ask if Cam would be there too, but Cady sensed it took a great deal of effort for him to resist.

"Of course I'm ready." She looked at her hands, toying with her wedding band. "What's to be ready for?"

"I'm not his favorite person. And when he finds out I'm pregnant, I doubt he'll be any more fond of me." Cam looked at her sister speculatively. "Come to think of it, why are you so supportive? Here I am having a baby, not telling the father, looking for a handout. Why would you be so stuck on having me around?"

Before she could answer, Cady's cell phone rang. Seeing Will's name, she reached for it, but at that moment the front door opened and she dropped her hand. "He'll leave a message."

"Who?" Cam peered at the cell phone as Cady slid it into her pocket.

"Nobody." Cady stood as Neil entered the kitchen. "Hi, sweetheart, how was work?" She kissed him.

"Hi." He glanced at Cam and nodded. "Fine. Where's Kelsea? Still at practice?"

Cady nodded and pulled two beers from the fridge. "I thought we'd order pizza when she gets in, but in the meantime maybe we can talk."

"Talk?" Neil uncapped Cady's beer and handed it to her. As he tossed the cap from his own beer into the garbage can, he narrowed his eyes at Cam. "None for you?"

Cam held up her soda and stood. "I'm good. Besides, I've, uh, got a thing to do."

As she left, Neil raised his eyebrows and sat, turning his attention to his wife. "Okay. Hit me."

Cady had a wild feeling that she was a witness on the stand. If she were, could she take an oath? She had no intention of telling her husband that Cam's baby's father still wanted to be in her picture. She didn't want to jeopardize his willingness to let Cam stay with them throughout her pregnancy and beyond.

Summoning her wits she convinced herself she wasn't

lying by omission and faced her husband. "Cam needs a place to stay."

"I know." He nodded. "We've touched on that before."

She bit her lip, knowing the moment of half-truth had come. "She's pregnant."

He paused with his beer halfway to his mouth. "Really?"

Cady nodded. "And she doesn't know what to do or where to turn." She stepped closer to Neil. "Please, Neil, she's my sister. I need to help her now."

He frowned, setting the bottle down as if he were concentrating hard on the motion. Then he asked the question she'd known he would. "What about the father?"

Cady had already figured out how to handle this. Feeling like a prizefighter dodging a blow, she ducked the question neatly. "Cam doesn't want him to be part of it. And she doesn't think he wants to be." She held her breath, thinking about the handsome, friendly giant who'd stood patiently outside her door. If Neil ever met Stanley, he'd spot the lie, even if it was technically true.

"I thought this one was different. Didn't you tell me they'd been together for a while?"

Cady shook her head. "I don't know. Maybe he wasn't what she thought." That *was* a lie. "Cam just said he shouldn't be part of the baby's life and she didn't want him in hers anymore either."

Neil sighed, looking disconcerted. "Honey, have you really thought this through? What about Kelsea? How is this going to affect her?"

"What do you mean? Kelsea will be thrilled."

"Are you sure about that, Cadence?"

Neil's uncharacteristic sharp tone made Cady stop short. Then she shook off any doubt and glared at him. "She adores Cam. You saw her last night. She's thrilled to have her here."

"For a visit, yes. Who of us isn't thrilled to have Cam here for a visit?" Neil gave her a tired smile to soften his sarcasm. "But she's a teenager. She's going through a lot of changes. Does she really need something else added on? And she needs you! She's had your undivided attention for thirteen years. Now, at a time when she needs you more than ever, you're going to ask her to give that up so you can take care of another baby?"

"That's not what I'm doing!" Cady shot to her feet, anger gathering like a storm. "And who are you to tell me what my daughter needs from me?"

"I'm her father!" Neil didn't back away. "And you've been too preoccupied recently to notice much about your daughter's life, so maybe you need me to point out what you're missing."

The hypocrisy of his words made her laugh, even though she knew it was cruel. "*I've* been too preoccupied? *Me?* You're the one who's never here."

"That's ridiculous." Neil shook his head. "I'm here every night for dinner. I'm here every weekend."

"Even when you're here, you're not here!" Cady slapped her hand on the counter. "You're always waiting for the phone to ring, whether we're sitting at the table with our daughter or making love in our bed. And you say I'm preoccupied? Everything I do, I do for this family."

Neil's expression changed, flickering a little. She knew she'd hurt him, but he just nodded, and she could tell from his unrelenting tone that he hadn't changed his mind. "I know. Maybe that's the problem."

"What?" Startled, she hesitated.

He took a breath. "I don't want to hurt you, Cady, but sometimes you are so centered on yourself and your own activities and concerns you can't see what's going on around you. And I understand your need to help your sister, maybe better than you do. Maybe you need to find some other focus. Maybe that will help you find yourself."

"Find myself." Cady backed away from him. "I know who *I* am. I just can't really figure out who I'm married to, sometimes. How can you say I'm selfish?"

"I didn't call you selfish--"

"Self-centered is the same thing!"

Their gazes locked and they glared at each other, neither one wanting to back down. Somewhere in the back of her head, Cady heard a door slam, but it didn't really register until Kelsea came in, fresh from cheerleading practice. "Hey guys! What's for dinner?" She stopped and Cady knew she'd sensed the tension between her parents. "What's going on?"

Cady dropped her eyes, turning to give her daughter a hug. "Nothing. How was practice?"

"It was great! Coach Taylor says we've finally got the routine down. We're going to use it Friday at the game."

Neil kissed his daughter's head, smiled and went upstairs without another word. Kelsea watched him go with a puzzled expression. "Mom, is Dad okay?"

"He's fine." Cady pulled a pan out of the cupboard. "Tell me more about this routine."

"Okay, what are we having for dinner?"

Cady no longer felt like ordering pizza. She inspected the contents of the refrigerator for something simple and fast. "Taco salad, I think."

Kelsea's face lit up. "That's Aunt Cam's favorite! Can I go tell her?"

"Sure." Cady watched her daughter leave, then set the pan on the counter and slumped, feeling tired and beaten. She and Neil had fought often enough through the years of their marriage, but this argument had an uglier ring to it. Throughout the past fifteen years, they had never argued about anything she hadn't always felt they could work out.

This time, she wasn't sure about that. At all.

AFTER A MORE SUBDUED dinner than was normal, Cam and Kelsea retreated to the den to play Wii Bowling, leaving Cady and Neil alone. Cady noted that Kelsea gave them a worried look but Cam took her arm and led her from the room.

She stole a look at Neil and blinked when she found him gazing directly at her. She sat straighter, but she couldn't think of anything to say.

"We didn't settle anything earlier." He set his drink aside and placed both hands on the table. "In fact, we got sidetracked."

She nodded, wondering if he was going to say Cam could stay and if it would be enough.

"I'm sorry I attacked you." He looked down at his hands and heaved a breath as if he were taking on a heavy load. "You didn't deserve that. I'm working through some issues of my own and I came down on you too hard."

"Neil…" She hesitated. He'd caught her off guard by apologizing, and she didn't want to spoil it by forging ahead. "Thank you. For the apology, and I'm sorry, too. But the baby. And Cam. I still want to do this. I think it could be good for all of us."

He sighed. "I'm willing to do anything we can to help your sister for your sake, Cady. Hell, move her in here and take her to every one of her doctor's appointments. I'm not certain that wasn't what she had in mind, anyway. But in the end, remember. She has to take responsibility for this baby, not you. And I won't let her take advantage of your desire for another child."

Cady opened her mouth to protest, but he shook his head again, looking weary. "I will do what I can. You will do what you have to. But please remember what I said about finding yourself, Cadence. You are a wonderful woman, and you give so much of yourself. I think you need to save some of that for you." He stood slowly. "I also want you to know I heard what you said earlier. About me."

She felt a blush of shame creep up her cheeks. "I didn't--"

"You did." He smiled humorlessly. "It's part of what I'm working on. I know what you said had some truth in it. I'm just not sure how to go about fixing it at this point." He rose and hesitated, looking down at her with a very sad expression on his face. "I don't really think you're the only one who's lost yourself. I just have to figure out what's left of me to find."

The words chilled her and she reached for his hand, but he was already out of her reach.

"He really said that?" Cam frowned. She sat across from Cady at Hubbard's Bar & Grille. The sisters had finally gotten time to discuss Neil's reaction to Cady's request that Cam move in. "Maybe this isn't a good idea, Cady. I should get out of here. You guys don't need me complicating your lives right now."

"Don't be ridiculous!" Cady spoke sharply and lowered her voice when Cam looked startled. "He said you could stay. He even said he understood. It's fine."

Cam hesitated. She knew she should insist on leaving, or maybe just get up in the middle of the night and go, but she honestly didn't know where she would end up. She couldn't go back to Stan, and where else was there? She'd already run to the only person she thought would still be there for her. The only person who would probably be there for her no matter what.

But Cady's life, which Cam had always thought of as perfect, had showed some signs of wear she hadn't expected. Cady had always been so happy before, but now she was moody and disgruntled. And Neil wasn't much better. And if he'd told Cady he felt lost, Cam knew he must be feeling stress from one quarter of his life or another. Even Kelsea, though she seemed pretty normal for a teenage girl, was going through changes in her life and body that Cam wasn't even certain Cady had noticed.

A pregnant sister and a new baby were not what Cady needed now.

She opened her mouth to say so, but was interrupted.

"Hello, beautiful lady." The voice, dark and sexy from over her shoulder, made Cam's breath catch in her throat. Turning to see the speaker didn't help any, either. A well-built, tanned man with handsome features and curly black hair stepped past her to hug Cady. "Why didn't you tell your server to let me know you were out here? You know I never pass up a chance to look at you."

Cady laughed, and Cam realized it was the first true laughter she'd heard from her sister since she arrived. "Cut it out, Will. My sister will get the wrong idea about you."

"Sister?" The godlike young man swung around. "More perfection and all in my restaurant!"

Cam raised her eyebrows and accepted the hand he offered. He smiled as if he realized she wasn't easily charmed. "You must be Cam."

"I must be." Cam nodded. "Nice to meet you."

Will returned his attention to Cady, his brow furrowed. "You never called me back last night. I left you a message."

The concern in his eyes was as unmistakable as the hesitance in Cady's manner. "I wasn't feeling well, but as you can see, I'm fine now. Did you need something?"

"Nothing important. I figured out the answer to my question from what you'd already told me." Will smiled, and Cam noticed Cady lifted her chin a little, as if his smile gave her a little extra strength. Or maybe she was reading too much into it. Maybe it was just friendship. A strong friendship, from the looks of it.

Will and Cady began to discuss a benefit dinner they were evidently putting together, seeming to forget Cam was even there. Feeling a little nauseous in the warm restaurant,

Cam excused herself. In the restroom, she splashed water on her face and waited until her stomach settled before returning to the table. To her surprise, Will was still there, seated now at a chair he'd pulled up next to Cady's. He leaned on the table, his eyes never moving from Cady. For her part, Cady seemed to be thoroughly enjoying the attention of the younger man. Her smile was genuine and when he put his hand on her arm, she didn't tense or try to draw away. Cam felt anxious as she watched the two. With Cady and Neil already having problems, they didn't need something else to act as a distraction.

With a sigh of resignation, Cam reminded herself that she could hardly give her sister marital advice. She bit her lip and crossed the room.

"Are you okay?" Cady looked anxiously at Cam.

Cam nodded. "Sure. I'm fine." She sipped her water, fighting the nausea that threatened to come back at any moment. Was it the pregnancy or her anxiety about her sister? She couldn't be sure. She heard Will asking if he could do anything to help, but she ignored him, unwilling to deal with him when her energy felt so low. She turned her head to ask Cady if they could leave and everything went black.

CADY LEAPT from her seat as her sister slumped in hers. "Cam!"

Will had already reacted, putting an arm around Cam's too-skinny shoulders and supporting her to keep her from falling to the floor. He made a swift motion to a waiter who disappeared into the kitchen while Will felt for Cam's pulse. Cady dropped to her knees next to her sister's chair.

"Is she diabetic?" Will glanced at Cady, a concerned expression on his handsome face. "Allergic to anything?"

"No, nothing like that." Cady hesitated, anxiety finally getting the better of her. "She's pregnant."

Will raised his eyebrows but made no comment as he counted heartbeats. After a moment, he relaxed. "I think she's okay, just fainted. Does she have a doctor you should call?"

"Not yet." Cady covered her face, her mind stalled on the baby. "Oh God, she's got to be okay. She just has to be."

The waiter arrived with a damp towel and Cady watched as Will gently applied it to her sister's forehead. Cam muttered something and opened her eyes. "What happened?" She struggled to sit up and Will helped her.

"You fainted." He gave her a charming smile. "Good thing you hadn't eaten anything yet or you'd give my restaurant a bad rep."

"Yeah, we wouldn't want that." Cam put both hands on her head and sat still for a moment. She glanced around at the anxious faces staring at her. "Okay, I'm fine. Everybody go on about your business."

Will helped her to her feet, his eyes still anxious. "Are you sure I don't need to call an ambulance?"

"That wouldn't be very good for business, would it?" Cam's voice dripped sarcasm.

"Well, on that note, I'll check on your orders." He held Cam's chair for her, then gave Cady's hand a reassuring squeeze.

Cady smiled at him, feeling warm all over like she always

did when she'd been with Will. It was just his personality, his way of making everyone feel special. She liked that about him. Still basking in the afterglow of their conversation, she turned her attention to her sister and recoiled at Cam's glare. "What?"

"What the fuck was that?" Cam leaned across the table, tapping it for emphasis. "Did you forget you're married for a second?" She shrugged. "Doesn't seem like something you should be able to forget, but you know, I've never really experienced marital bliss myself."

"I didn't forget anything." Cady glared at her sister. "Although maybe you haven't noticed, there hasn't been a whole lot of 'bliss' in my marital life recently."

Cam frowned. "I thought that was my fault."

"Not all of it." Cady played with her water glass, making little rivulets of condensation pool and run off onto the coaster. "It's not even just that he's always working and I hardly feel like he's around anymore. Neil's not like he used to be. God, I used to feel so loved. All he had to do was look at me and I knew how much he loved me and wanted me." She paused, remembering other ways Neil had made her feel wanted, but the memories brought no joy. She shook her head, biting her tongue to hold back tears. "Now, he barely looks at me. And the other night he had the chance to make it better. When he kissed me, it was like it used to be. He wasn't making love to me with his mind on something else. He was holding me, loving *me*. And then the phone rang." She sighed and looked back at her water glass.

She felt Cam's hand on hers and looked up. Cam squeezed her hand. "I don't know what's going on with Neil, but I'm sure he loves you. Maybe he's just preoccupied by work."

"For the last four or five years? You'd think he could work through whatever problems he was having, wouldn't you?" Cady shrugged. "Sometimes I even wonder if there's another woman."

"You're not serious." Cam shook her head. "No way. Don't go there. Once you lose that trust, you might as well give up on your relationship. Speaking of which," she glanced around, "how exactly does friend Will fit into things?"

"We've worked on a couple of charitable projects together." Cady tried not to sound defensive. "I do a lot of those and Will's always ready to help. I'm pretty good at raising money, as it turns out."

"An invaluable talent." Cam retorted. "Might have come in handy for me every so often. That doesn't explain the way he looked at you."

"We're just friends." Cady frowned at her water glass.

Cam leaned closer to her sister. "Or the way you looked at him. Are you in love with him?"

"Don't be ridiculous." Cady shook her head, although the idea made her catch her breath. She'd often allowed herself to admire Will. His perfect manners and generous spirit combined with what was undeniably an incredible body and handsome features made him a very attractive man. And she'd often enjoyed the easy rapport she felt with him while working on a project.

But it wasn't possible that she had fallen in love with him. Married women didn't do that.

4

*N*eil got home early that evening. Cady was still fixing dinner, and he came into the kitchen to toss his keys and phone into his basket. "Where's Cam?" He opened the refrigerator, located a bottle of wine and poured two glasses.

"Down by the dock." Cady pointed out the window. "She's helping Kelsea with a science experiment."

Neil raised his eyebrows. "Is that a good idea? I didn't realize your sister was a science expert."

Cady frowned. Was he trying to pick a fight with her? "She knows as much about science as you and me. Besides, the assignment is to observe a habitat for a certain amount of time and make scientific observations about it. I think she can handle it."

"Don't get snippy." He handed her a glass of wine and went to the window. After a moment, he turned with a smile. "You should see this."

She shrugged and followed his lead, peering out the window into the gathering dusk. Cam and Kelsea lay on their stomachs across the dock looking into the creek. Cam dabbled a twig in the water while Kelsea watched the darkening waters with great interest. A notebook lay on the dock next to her.

"They've gotten really close in a pretty short time." Neil put his arms around her and leaned his chin on her shoulder. Cady relaxed into his embrace.

"Yeah. They're peas in a pod, those two. I think it's good for Kelsea to have her aunt around."

"Really?" He turned her around in his arms so she had the sink behind her and his chest in front of her. "Don't take this the wrong way, but I've never thought of your sister as exactly a good example for a young girl."

She sighed, plucking a bit of fluff from his tie, loosening it as she did, enjoying the lingering smell of his aftershave. "Cam's had a hard life. And yes, most of it's her own fault, she had the same chances as me and all that, but she looks at things a different way. I can't even explain it. She's more realistic, and that's great but it's also a drawback. She doesn't believe in her dreams so she doesn't think she can do a lot of stuff I'm sure she can."

"Hmm." He pushed her hair back over her shoulders and bent to kiss her, his hands on the small of her back pressing her hips forward into his. Even as she enjoyed the caress, she wondered in a tiny part of her mind where all the affection was coming from. Could this be the same husband she'd had such a hard time connecting with over the past few years?

The doorbell rang and he pulled back with a little curse. "Damn. You feel so good."

She clung to him a moment longer. "So do you." Reluctantly, she released him and gave him a gentle shove toward the door. "You find out who's at the door and I'll finish dinner before it's totally ruined."

"I'd order you pizza if you burned dinner, you know."

"Well, get the door. Maybe it's a lost pizza delivery guy." She smiled as she turned back to the dinner. Nothing was ruined, and she dismissed her earlier doubts, thinking she and Neil had finally rounded that corner she'd been aspiring to for so long.

She heard Neil greet someone and an answering male voice. Probably a delivery. The back door opened and Cam entered with Kelsea, who darted over to her mother and threw her arms around her waist. "I'm so cold!" she exclaimed, teeth chattering.

Cady put her arm around her daughter's shoulders and gave her a hug. She felt light-hearted for the first time in a long while. "Is it cold out there? I hadn't noticed." She shot Cam a grin and a wink.

"Who's in the hall?" Kelsea tilted her head, curious.

"Your dad. He's home early. And someone rang the bell. Why don't you go see what's keeping your father?"

Kelsea darted into the hall and Cam sidled over, plucking a carrot from the cutting board. "I think I know that look, don't I? What's Neil doing home early?"

"I don't know, but I like it." Cady gave her sister a significant look. She glanced at the hall when she heard footsteps. "Well, whoever was at the door, we may have one more for dinner." She summoned a welcoming smile that froze on her face as the door opened and Stan entered, followed by Neil, who wore a puzzled frown, and Kelsea, who looked nothing short of thrilled.

Stan nodded pleasantly to Cady. "Good to see you again, Mrs. Summers." He turned his attention to Cam. "Hi."

"Hi." She frowned. "I thought you were going home."

"We need to talk." He glanced at Cady as if for permission.

"Why don't you two use the den?" Neil nodded in that general direction although he didn't turn. "Kelsea, you still have a report to write up, don't you?" He gave his daughter a gentle push toward the stairs and Cady realized he wanted her alone.

As Cam and Stanley left the kitchen, Cady plucked the lid off a pot of beans and stirred it, trying to pretend Stanley's arrival was nothing to be concerned about. She knew it was, though, and she bit her lip as Neil cleared his throat. She glanced at him. "What?"

"You didn't mention you'd met Cam's boyfriend."

"It was only briefly. Just a few seconds really. He stopped by and left. Cam said he went home. I figured things weren't going to work out between them." She wasn't really saying anything that wasn't strictly the truth, either, she told herself.

"Well, I don't think I'd count on that now." Neil poured himself another glass of wine, his brow furrowed in a worried way. "He's got a job and is planning to move up here."

Cady dropped the spoon she was stirring the beans with into the pot and cursed. "Damn it." She looked up from the beans to Neil. "Did he say why?"

"He says he loves her and wants to be with her and if she's

going to be here, so is he." Neil's voice was firm. "Is he the baby's father?"

In an effort to avoid looking at him, Cady began to fish the spoon out of the beans. "She said so."

"So you did know. You knew the father of her baby came looking for her less than twenty-four hours after she left? Cady, surely that indicated to you that he cares a bit more about her than she let on?" He caught her arm and when she turned a reluctant and irritable glare to him, he shook his head, looked like he might say something more, then shut his mouth and turned away, dropping his hand from her arm. He walked over to the back door and stood looking out at the Spanish moss dripping from the nearly bare tree branches.

Cady fished the spoon from the beans, tears burning in the backs of her eyes, and wondered when her day had gone so wrong. She'd been so sure everything was all right now, Neil home from work early, attentive, not distracted for a change. And the promise of a new baby to give her a purpose. She swallowed hard and turned from the stove to toss the spoon into the sink.

CAM LED Stanley into the den, her heart quaking in her chest, just as it had been since she entered the kitchen to find him there. She'd sent him away once without a qualm but now that he had returned she wondered if she could do it again. Resolving to do whatever she could, she swung around to face him.

He spoke first. "I got a job."

She froze, unspoken remonstrance stuck to her tongue. Finally, she shook her head, unable to find any other way to indicate she didn't understand. He laughed, sitting on the arm of the sofa next to her and taking her hands. "Construction. I'm staying."

"You can't."

He smiled, so damn sure of himself she wanted to hit him or kiss him or do something, anything to make him stop grinning like a fool at her. "I did. If this is where you are, this is where I am, baby."

"Stop it!" She shook her head, trying not to let his words fill her heart with hope. "You can't stay here. What about school?"

"What about it? There's a pretty good community college. I've already checked into transferring my credit. Might put me a class or two behind, but I don't care." He tugged on her hands until she stepped closer, her thighs resting on the arm of the sofa between his knees. He leaned forward, closing the rest of the distance, nuzzling her neck and shoulder as she drew in a deep breath, smelling his skin. He rested his head on her shoulder for a moment. "I love you."

"Don't!" She tried to pull away, but he held her fast. "You don't understand. I have to start over."

He nodded. "I get that. I don't know why, but I understand. But you have to get this, baby. You and I have a life together, and I don't let go of the people I love that easy." He gave her hands another tiny tug but this time she resisted. He sighed and released her, standing as she took two quick steps away. "It doesn't change anything, Cam. I'm not going anywhere and you don't have anywhere left to go."

As he reached for the door, she recovered her voice. "What do you mean? Why don't I have anywhere left to go?"

He raised his eyebrows, smiling a little. "Because now that I'm here, everybody who loves you, everybody you can count on, anyway, is here in this one town."

She closed her eyes as he walked out, cursing him because she knew he was right.

AFTER STAN LEFT, Cady heard her sister go upstairs. With a sigh, she started to put dinner on three plates, knowing things couldn't have gone well with Stan and Cam wouldn't want to be bothered with eating right then. Neil had retreated to the den, and Kelsea came in. "Gotta run, Mom. Sabrina just called. We're going to pick up dinner on the way to practice."

"Practice?" Cady frowned. "You don't have practice tonight."

"It's a makeup for last Thursday when Mrs. Landower was sick. I told you about it."

Cady opened her mouth to protest, then shrugged. She knew she just didn't want to be alone with Neil and her guilt and his disappointment. "Sorry, Sweetie, I guess I forgot." She kissed Kelsea. "Ask your dad for some money for dinner."

"Thanks, Mom." Kelsea gave her a hug and ran out.

As she put the two remaining plates on the table, Neil came back into the kitchen. "Kelsea's gone. Sabrina's mom says not to worry about pickup, she's planning to stay and help with practice anyway."

"Great." Cady refilled his wine glass and they sat at the

table together. For a moment, they ate the green beans, shrimp and rice in silence, but it didn't have much flavor and she finally set her fork aside, folded her hands in her lap and looked at him. "I know you're angry."

"Angry?" He raised his eyebrows. "Why would I be angry? Because you lied to me?"

"I never lied." Even as she protested she knew she had. She'd known as soon as she saw Stanley that he wasn't the type of man to let his child go, and she'd known he was the baby's father. And no matter what Cam said, it was obvious she was in love with him. Maybe this time Cam would have a real chance of being a mother and having a family.

"You lied." Neil set his fork down and looked her directly in the eyes. "You knew Stan had followed her here and he still loved her."

"I was only going by what Cam told me." Cady held her hands out in a pleading manner.

"She can't deny him his rights, Cady. You saw Stanley. He loves her. He wants her back. Do you honestly think he's going to just let her go, especially when he finds out about the baby?" Neil shook his head, a frown creasing his brow. "You've got to be kidding."

Cady groaned, covering her face with her hands. "I hate being married to a lawyer. Especially a family lawyer. All I know is what Cam's told me, and she's been pretty firm about keeping him out of her life and the baby's."

"Would you listen to yourself, Cady? A decent man deserves his rights as a father. And Stanley's a decent man." He stood and took his plate to the sink.

"How do you know? Maybe he isn't. Maybe he's a total

asshole. You talked to him for what? Fifteen minutes?" She knew she was grasping at straws now.

"Long enough. Besides, has Cam ever said anything against him? I haven't heard anything. And from the look on her face tonight, she'd be happy to have him back in her life."

Cady shook her head in stalwart denial. "I don't care! Cam says she wants to stay here with us to have her baby. She says she doesn't want to be with him."

"For the love of God, Cady, please be sensible. This baby could have a loving home with two parents—its real parents. What you need to do is help Cam realize that with his help she could raise a child and be a good mother if she'll just give it a try."

"I know you're right, damnit, I just don't want to admit it." Cady stared at her plate, then gave him a weak smile. "Maybe I was just looking for something else to take care of. You and Kelsea are gone so much, it gets kind of lonely."

She felt him sit next to her, the warmth of his body next to hers not as comforting as it usually was. She listened to words she didn't want to hear. "Have you thought about going back to work? You need something more than just us."

He took her hands and she looked down at his fingers. One fingertip ran back and forth over the wedding band on her left ring finger. "Maybe." When she spoke, she felt an ending of something, but a possibility of the beginning of something more. Maybe it wasn't such a bad idea.

At the sound of the light tap on her door, Cam considered

feigning sleep but decided she ought to at least talk to her sister. Cady had probably taken hell from Neil, and Cam had pretty much left her to face it alone. She sniffed and rubbed her eyes with her sleeve. "Come in."

Cady entered with a tray, moving with a grace and assurance in the darkened room that could only be achieved from years of practice. Cam realized her sister had lived in this house for more than ten years. Most of Kelsea's life. Most of her married life. Cam wondered what it would be like to have roots that went that deep.

Cady set the tray on the bureau and reached for a lamp. "Okay if I turn this on?"

Cam shrugged and Cady, evidently sensing the movement, flipped the switch. The dim light flared, blinding at first, then softening to a gentle glow that mellowed the harsh corners of the room. Cam hoped the concealing light would hide her own reddened eyes. She gestured at the tray. "Thanks, but I'm not hungry."

"I didn't bring it for you." Cady smiled when Cam gave her a sharp look. "I brought it for your baby." She removed the plastic cover from the steaming plate and set it aside, turning to place the tray on her sister's lap. "It's not my best effort, but it's edible. Although Neil and I didn't do it much justice." She stood for a second, then motioned to her sister. "Scoot."

Cam moved over, careful not to upset the tray. In spite of Cady's deprecations, the food smelled good and she realized she was hungrier than she'd thought. Scooping a forkful of rice and shrimp she raised it to her mouth and hesitated, looking at her sister. "I'm not interested in talking."

Cady shrugged. "I figured. And I'm not interested in going

back out there to be with my husband, so you're stuck with me."

"Great." Cam turned her attention back to the food and ate in silence for several minutes. After the edge of her hunger dulled, she glanced at her sister, who sat silently with her head leaning against the headboard of the bed and her eyes closed. "Was it really bad?"

"Could've been worse, actually, but we said some things we needed to say, so I guess I should thank you." Cady opened her eyes and sat up.

"Thank me?" Cam shook her head. "I doubt it."

"Whatever." Cady pulled out her phone and began flipping through her emails. She paused on one, a little smile playing around the corners of her mouth.

Curious, Cam glanced over her shoulder and noticed a familiar name. She started to mention it but found herself asking something else entirely. "How bad are things with you and Neil, anyway?"

Her sister glanced at her curiously. "Excuse me?"

"Well, you say you don't want to be with him and you're sitting in here reading emails from another man—I figured I'd ask."

"Email, singular, and stop spying." Cady frowned and put her phone into her back pocket.

Cam rolled her eyes and set her tray aside. "What's it about?"

"None of your business." Cady's eyes darted away, as if searching for a sidetrack for their conversation.

"Don't change the subject."

"I didn't!"

"You were going to. You do realize you're playing with fire, don't you?" Cam frowned severely at her sister.

"I'm not playing with anything."

"Good to know because it could be dangerous." Cam relaxed on the pillows, ignoring her sister's glare.

After a moment, Cady lay back next to her, twisting her wedding band in a self-conscious way. "Besides, it wouldn't matter even if I wanted to have an affair with Will. He's too good a person. He'd never ever mess around with a married woman."

Cam turned her head to gaze at her sister. "Even you?"

"Even me." Cady nodded, looking determinedly at the ceiling, but Cam noticed a blush of red creeping up her cheekbones.

5

*L*ike it or not, Cady realized her husband had a point about her getting a job. Especially when Stanley kept showing up, talking Cam into joining him for lunch and dinner. Cady could tell it would only be a matter of time before he wore down her sister's already flagging resistance. Finally, on an unseasonably warm day in February, Cady accompanied her sister downtown for her first OB appointment, but Cam waved her away at the office door.

"I'm a big girl." Cam looked at the red wood door that opened onto a narrow stairway. "It's not like I've never done this before. Besides, don't you have a job to find?"

"Okay." Cady watched her sister trudge up the stairs and sighed. As she turned back to the street, she felt almost as reluctant as Cam had looked. How long had it been since she'd gone job hunting? Twenty years? She wasn't even sure how to go about it.

Her eye fell on the newspaper stand outside the coffee

shop and she made a decision. A latte would be good, and she could browse the help wanted ads. With a plan of action in hand, she got her newspaper, her latte and a seat in the window of the nearly empty shop.

"Good morning, beautiful." Will stood beside her table.

Cady felt the normal boost in her spirits at the sight of him and smiled in response. It felt so natural to want to be near him. "Hey." She pushed the chair next to her out with her foot. "Have a seat."

"You sure?" He looked around at the sparse patrons. "I don't want to interrupt. I could probably find a seat here somewhere."

"I'm sure. I could use the company." She pushed the chair out a little further and he sat.

"So what's up?" He tapped the newspaper. "You looking for a job?"

"Yeah." She leaned back, feeling weary. "I guess I'm bored. Neil thinks so, anyway." She bit her lip, knowing her tone revealed more about her relationship with Neil than she'd intended. "Sorry, Will, I didn't mean to sound like that. Neil's probably right."

He shrugged. "Don't worry about me. I'm not the gossiping kind. You can tell me anything." He put his hand on hers for a moment, not quite holding it, but letting her feel the warmth of his skin on hers. He smiled gently when she looked at him. "You really can. I live to help you."

She laughed because his words had to be ridiculous or she'd have been in a very uncomfortable situation. "Everything's fine. Seriously. We've just been fighting a lot and Neil thinks I need to get out of the house. And he's probably right. Maybe I'm making things up to fight with him about because Kelsea's getting older and is able to do so much more on her own and I don't have to be at every cheerleading practice or volunteering at her school or whatever." She sighed, honestly feeling sorry for herself.

"You do a lot of charity work. The benefit dinner the other night went well. You should be proud."

She glanced up and nodded. "Yes, and that's always rewarding, especially when I get to work with you." Her smile was unfeigned and his hand, which she'd almost forgotten about, tightened on hers.

"Watch it, lady, or I'll start getting ideas." Despite his light tone, his eyes had darkened a little and he cleared his throat as he sat back, his palm sliding to the table. "What kind of job are you looking for?"

"Bookkeeping." She forced her suddenly palpitating heart to calm down. "I'm hoping for part-time."

"Really? I might be able to help you." He tilted his head and observed her and she felt certain she'd imagined the brief vibe she'd gotten from him.

"Really?" Her eyebrows shot up. "You know somebody who needs a part-time bookkeeper?"

"Sure. Me. I just have to fire mine first."

She blinked. "I'm sorry?"

He laughed. "I was going to do it anyway, but if I've got you all lined up and ready to take over, it's all the more reason to go ahead with it."

"Why are you firing your bookkeeper?" Cady tried to remember who kept the books for Hubbard's Grill. She vaguely remembered a pretty young girl who'd seemed very capable.

"She's been wanting to go back to school, but she won't leave until I have someone to replace her. I've sort of dragged my feet about the whole thing. She's damn good." He grinned at her. "What do you think? Want to give it a try? We know we work well together."

Even as she realized what an excellent opportunity it was and knew she'd love working with Will, Cady couldn't deny her own doubts. She didn't need Cam there to tell her she was attracted to this man. And right now she was particularly vulnerable to that attraction. Not that Will would ever take advantage of her. She didn't worry about that. But if her marriage continued to be strained, she knew she would be tempted to lean on Will for support.

"Hey?" He nudged her foot with his. "You okay? I didn't mean to catch you off guard. If you don't want the job, I understand. No hard feelings, I swear."

"It's not that." She hesitated, wondering how to address her feelings to him. She opted for as close to honesty as she dared. "You're just such a good friend, and I'm not sure what's going on in my life right now. I don't want to take advantage of your friendship."

He folded his hands on the table and leaned toward her, his attention completely on her. "By taking the job or by bending my ear about your problems?"

"Bending your ear?" She shook her head. "Yeah, that's pretty apt. Although you'll be lucky if you have any ear left when I'm done."

He laughed and beckoned to her. When she leaned

forward, unable to resist the invitation to be closer to him, he said in a soft voice, "I've been told I have extremely large ears. Maybe you can put them to good use."

She couldn't help glancing at his ears, perfectly shaped and sized and lying back against his head in exactly the right way to complement his features. But then everything about him was perfect, including the way he made her feel. Could she really pass up the opportunity to feel this way on a daily basis? She'd worked with Will regularly before. How was this any different?

You're playing with fire...

"Hello?" He smiled. "You still there?"

"Huh? Oh yeah. I'm here." She hesitated just a moment longer, then nodded. "And yeah. I think you're right. We'd make a good team."

"Excellent." He looked so satisfied, she couldn't help but smile. Maybe everything would be okay. Maybe she could pay Will back for some of his past kindness to her. Just because she looked forward to working with him and seeing him everyday didn't make it wrong.

After all, her own husband had said she should get a job.

CADY MADE meatloaf and mashed potatoes for dinner, one of Neil's favorites, but he didn't mention it. His phone lay conspicuously on the table next to his plate, as if he were afraid of missing a call, and she noticed he glanced at it several times during the meal.

Cam and Kelsea chatted about cheerleading practice,

keeping the tone of the meal light in spite of Cady's dagger-like looks at the phone and Neil's abstracted behavior. Finally, in a lag in the conversation, Cady decided to tell them her news.

"I got a job."

Kelsea stopped chewing. "What? I didn't know you wanted a job, Mom."

Neil spooned more mashed potatoes on his plate. "That's great, sweetheart."

Cam looked suspicious. "That was awfully quick. You just started looking this morning. What kind of job can you find that fast?"

"Exactly what I was looking for, actually. Part-time bookkeeper."

"Isn't that serendipitous? Who offered you this dream job?"

Cady braced herself for her sister's look of disapproval. "Will. He's been looking for a new bookkeeper."

"What's wrong with his old one?" Cam smiled innocently, although her green eyes continued to look skeptical.

"She's going back to school." Smartass. Cady bit off the epithet with difficulty. "I ran into Will at the coffee shop and he offered me the job when he found out what I was looking for." She raised her eyebrows at her sister, giving her a warning look through her amicable expression.

"Sounds perfect." Neil smiled at her and she basked in the warmth of his approval even as she hated herself for taking the tidbit her husband tossed her. "I'm glad you found what you were looking for."

"Definitely." Cam drew out the word in such a sarcastic

way, Cady felt a blush rise unbidden on her face. "That's great, Sis."

"Thanks." Cady ducked her head and for once was actually happy when Neil's phone rang.

"Damn." He glanced at it. "I was afraid of that. Sorry, guys, I have to take this." He stood, taking the phone into the hall to answer it.

Cady watched him thoughtfully, remembering her earlier musings that he was having an affair. Could that be true? Surely she would know. It was a small town and she was well-known and liked. Somebody would have told her. Still…

"So you really want to go back to work, Mom?"

Cady turned back to Kelsea, shaking off the ugly thoughts. Cam was right. She shouldn't doubt Neil's faithfulness without due cause. "Yeah. I guess." She smiled reassuringly at her daughter. "I mean, you're getting so grown up you don't need me anymore. You're not even home until after five most days."

Kelsea toyed with her food. "What about your charity work? Isn't that enough?" Her eyes widened. "We don't need the money do we?"

"No, honey, we're fine, although another paycheck is never a bad thing. And I'll keep doing charity work, but maybe it's time to let somebody else have the spotlight for a while. It'll be nice to have something that's mine for a change. You know, work for me and not for anybody else. Do you understand?"

"Yeah, I guess." Kelsea shrugged and grinned mischievously. "You need something to keep you out of trouble."

Cam choked and Cady glared at her sister. Cam shrugged innocently. "Her words, not mine. *Definitely* not mine." She stood and took her plate into the kitchen.

Kelsea rolled her eyes. "You two are so weird." She followed Cam into the kitchen, taking her mother's plate as well as her own.

Cady remained where she was until Neil came back. She looked up, realizing she hadn't even thought about him while he was on the phone. "Hey, everything all right?"

"Fine." He shook his head but smiled, as if he didn't really think everything was okay but didn't want to say so. He sat at the table, picking up his fork and beginning to eat automatically. "So what about this job of yours?"

Cady sipped her wine. "What about it? The pay is good, no benefits since it's part-time, but that's fine for us. And Will will be a good boss." She eyed him over the rim of her glass, daring him to notice a change in the way she spoke about Will. She'd certainly been aware of a change in the way she thought of him since Cam's revelations. And she still felt the warmth of his hand on hers when she concentrated hard enough. Could Neil pick up on these new vibrations or was he too distracted? Or did he even care?

"Yeah. You guys have always worked well together, so that's good." Neil nodded. His phone buzzed angrily in his pocket. "Damn it." He set his fork aside. "I'm going to have to go back to the office, sweetheart. I'm really sorry." He stood, kissed her on the top of her head and pulled his phone from his pocket as he left the room. She listened to him in the hall gathering his keys and talking on the phone. A moment later the front door slammed and she heard his car backing out of the driveway.

Cady concentrated again on remembering the feel of Will's hand on hers and the way he'd given her his entire attention. Thus armed, she fended off the onset of loneliness brought on by her husband's departure until Kelsea and Cam came back in.

"Did Dad have to leave?" Kelsea looked disappointed.

Cady set her wineglass down. "It was an emergency at work. He said to tell you goodnight and he loves you." The lie came easily to her lips and she was rewarded by Kelsea's smile.

"Well, I have some homework to do, anyway." She kissed her mother in exactly the same spot Neil had. "I'll be upstairs if you need me."

"Don't worry about the dishes," Cam said, her eyes on Cady. "Your mom and I will do it."

"Thanks, Aunt Cam." Kelsea waved and bounded up the stairs.

Cady picked up her glass again and looked directly at her sister. "You are *not* going to make me feel guilty."

"What on earth do you have to feel guilty about?" Cam blinked at her. "Oh, you mean that little matter of taking a job with a guy you want to sleep with?"

"*You* are the only one who's ever said I want to sleep with Will. *I* have known him for years, worked with him on countless occasions and never even considered the possibility of sleeping with him." Until recently. Cady knew her memories of Will's touch were just the beginning. She had already allowed herself to begin imagining what his hands would feel like on other, much more intimate, parts of her body, and later, when she got into bed alone, she planned to allow herself a full-blown fantasy.

Cam's hand on her arm made her jump. "Shit." Her already pounding heart skipped a beat.

"God, you're jumpy. See what I mean? I don't even *have* to make you feel guilty. You already do." Cam looked anxiously down at her sister. "I just don't want you to do anything you'll regret."

"Me either." Cady looked at her husband's empty chair and wondered if he ever regretted leaving. And maybe sometimes you only regretted what you *didn't* do. She stood and picked up Neil's half-empty plate. "Let's get this mess cleaned up."

6

$\mathcal{W}$ill had asked her to come to the restaurant the next morning to meet Brianne, the young woman who had kept the books for him for the past three years. She turned out to be a very pretty, dark-haired girl of about twenty-five. She showed Cady the computer and taught her how and what to enter into the spreadsheets. She gave her the combination to the small safe where the money was kept until the nightly deposits were made.

"Will usually does those so you won't have to stay late very often." Brianne hesitated. "I'm really glad you've taken the job, Mrs. Summers. Will trusts *everybody*, and he really shouldn't. I'm, you know, just happy he's found somebody who won't hurt him."

Cady nodded. She knew all about Will's trusting nature. Usually it paid off just because everybody liked him. However, she remembered working on a silent auction for charity with him. Will hired a young man without references to help move some of the larger items from storage to the convention center. Several small, valuable items disappeared during the course of the move, along with the young man Will had hired. Cady still remembered the puzzled expression on Will's face. He'd insisted on paying for the items himself, and she remembered thinking that he was so intensely honest he just couldn't imagine dishonesty in anyone else.

And of course Will could trust her. So why this feeling of disquiet at the thought? She shook it off and looked at a picture on Brianne's desk. "Is that your daughter?" She smiled. "She's adorable. How old?"

"She's five and not very happy with me." Brianne shrugged. "We'll be moving back to Raleigh so I can have my mom's help while I'm back in school."

"She doesn't want to move." Cady nodded. "It's hard for kids. I had to change schools when I was a little older than her and I *hated* it. I swore I'd never do it to my kids."

"It's not so much her school." Brianne sat behind the desk and began pulling things out of the drawers and putting them in a box next to her chair. "It's more Will than anything, I think. She adores him. She told me the other day she was going to marry him when she grew up."

"Really?" Cady smiled. "What did you say?"

"What could I say? I told her she couldn't do any better, and if he was still available by that time she had my blessing." For a moment, Brianne looked a little introspective, then she shrugged. "But she'll get over it. She loves her grandparents and I've worked too hard to give up the opportunity to go back to school now that I've got the money saved up. A degree will definitely make being a single mom a lot easier." She grinned. "And at least I know I'm leaving this place in good hands."

And Will. Cady wondered briefly how much it meant to the pretty young girl that Will be left in good hands. She suspected it meant a lot. And she couldn't really blame her.

SHE ARRIVED EARLY on Monday to get settled into her desk and make sure she was ready for the day. Brianne had left a long note with the day's routine spelled out, along with a computer manual. Cady could hear Will in the kitchen talking to some of the staff, so she sat at the desk studying the manual until she heard footsteps outside the office and glanced up.

Will passed by the office and did a double take, coming back to grin at her. "Good morning! I didn't hear you come in."

"I snuck in. I didn't want to disturb you."

"You're never a disturbance." He leaned on the doorframe. "Are you finding everything all right?"

"Brianne left some great notes." Cady gestured to the list. "I think I'll be all right, even if it has been a while. I haven't done this sort of thing since before Kelsea was born, but with Brianne's instructions I should be okay. She really cared about this restaurant a lot, huh?"

His smile faltered a little. "Yeah, she was great. And we'll miss her."

"And her daughter?" She studied his face.

"Yeah, that was tough. Polly wasn't happy about leaving, that's sure. But she'll be okay. She's really adaptable and sweet-natured. Kind of like her mom." His face betrayed the warmth of his feelings for the two and Cady felt an unexpected stab of jealousy. She fought it off with difficulty.

"Well, maybe they'll come back when Brianne's done with school." She kept her tone light as she opened the desk drawer and dropped Brianne's list and the computer manual inside. "You should probably put me to work, though."

"Right." He straightened. "I don't want you to get the idea that this is easy stuff. C'mon, I'll introduce you to the rest of the staff, although you probably know most of them." He took her hand as she came to him and walked her back to the kitchen, introducing her to the other chefs and the waitstaff and the hostess. By the time they returned to her office, Cady felt at home in the restaurant.

"So that's it." Will paused by the door to her office. "It's just you and me back here, and I'm in the kitchen or the dining room most of the time. Oh, before I forget…" He fished around in his pocket and pulled out a ring of keys. He selected one and handed it to her. "To the restaurant. You might be the first one here, although I'm in pretty early most days. The hours are flexible like I told you. If you can make the deposit from lunch before you leave, that'd be great."

"Sure. That won't be any problem. I can come back in the evening if you want. To make the deposit from dinner." She wondered why she was pushing for that. Brianne had said Will always made those deposits.

A gentle smile curved his lips. "Yeah, I really want you wandering around the streets after dark with a bag of money." He shook his head. "I always make those deposits. Brianne made the same offer. Maybe one of these days I'll hire a big, ugly dude to keep the books and then he can make the evening deposit for me."

She smiled, looking at the key in her hand. It felt heavy and important, almost intimate in a strange way. She closed her fingers over it and realized she'd been silent for several seconds while he looked at her. She stepped back into the office. "Well, gotta get to work. I hear the boss is a real slave-driver."

"Right." He backed into the hallway. "Just don't let him forget how lucky he is to have you."

She waved and sat at her desk, reaching for a stack of receipts from the morning's purchases.

CADY WAS amazed how quickly she fell back into the work routine. Up early, get Kelsea off to school and then leave for the restaurant. Usually Will and Suzie, another chef, were already there, but sometimes Cady was the first one in the restaurant. She learned to love the empty, sparkling clean dining room, the deserted kitchen and the quiet bar. Unlike her own home, she never felt lonely there.

After spending some time tallying receipts and figuring accounts, Will's arrival with coffee was a welcome interruption. He'd lounge on the tiny sofa in her little office, sipping his hot drink while she tried to make hers last as long as possible, as if that could keep him from leaving.

That hour alone with Will quickly became her favorite of the day.

"How's Cam?" he asked one day about two weeks after Cady started working at the restaurant.

Cady sighed and sat back in her desk chair, wishing she could join him on the couch. She searched for a word to describe her sister's unpredictable mood swings. "Grumpy."

He smiled into his coffee. "Hormones?"

"I don't know. Probably a lot of it. But she's refusing to talk to Stanley and I think she resents the fact that he won't just pick up and leave like she told him to do." Cady didn't add that Cam had also made no secret of the fact that she was afraid her sister was on the verge of doing something foolish.

"Has she told him about the baby yet?"

"No. I guess she'll have to soon, though." Will raised his eyebrows and she shrugged. "What?"

"Nothing." He shook his head. "Nothing at all. None of my business, but why do I get the feeling you'd rather she didn't?"

Cady opened her mouth to protest but decided abruptly she didn't mind Will's comment as much as Neil's accusations. "I guess I don't." She thought about her sister and wondered why she was so opposed to her starting a life with a man who obviously loved her. Could she be jealous? Cady had always been the one with a loving family. Maybe she didn't want to see Cam with what she no longer felt she had. The realization filled her with shame and she stood, thinking blindly that she could somehow escape it. As she stood, her coffee spilled across the desk and she gasped as she watched it soak into the receipts and start to drip off the side of her desk. "Shit!"

She felt rather than saw Will at her side, one hand on her waist to guide her out of harm's way and a roll of paper towels in the other that he used to sop up the mess. He smiled at her as he tossed a stained wad of paper into the trashcan. "No harm done."

His gentle rescue had so startled her that for a moment all she could do was gape at him. Realizing how foolish she must look, she turned away, biting her lip to keep it from trembling. "Thanks."

He stood so close to her in the small office, half of her wanted to move away and the other half wanted to slide closer to him, feel his arm around her waist again, in a more intimate way this time. After a moment, he cleared his throat, however, and stepped back around the desk to a safe distance. Only then did she realize she'd nearly stopped breathing.

"You didn't answer my question."

She stole a look at him and smiled a little. "I'd sort of hoped you'd forgotten. But yes, I guess you're right. It's been nice having Cam around for a while and I'm not really ready to give her up."

"That's understandable." He refilled her cup, adding cream and sweetener without asking.

"Is it?" She raised her eyebrows as he handed her the cup and then sat behind her desk as he resumed his spot on the couch. "Neil doesn't think so."

He gave her a sharp look, then shrugged. "I would think it was understandable. You're a nurturing person. When Cam got here she needed you, and that felt good."

His understanding reply struck her dumb for a second. Then she sucked in a breath and nodded. "Yeah. I guess that about sums it up."

For several seconds they were silent, just looking at each

other. Cady bit her lip and turned away, shuffling papers on her desk and mopping up a little coffee Will had missed. She cleared her throat. "What's for lunch today?"

He paused, pretending to think. "How about carrot and onion potato latkes with pancetta and feta?"

"Yum, that sounds awesome. Is that the special?"

Will shrugged. "I guess so. I just thought of it." He winked at her as he started out the door. "You must be my muse."

Only after he'd disappeared down the hall did Cady realize his comment had made her grin like a teenage girl with a crush. She quickly wiped the foolish smile from her face, but then she remembered his wink and couldn't help the warm flush of pleasure that engulfed her.

CADY LEFT the restaurant feeling happier than she had in days. She arrived home shortly after four o'clock to find Cam alone, reading the newspaper's classified section.

"Looks like heavy reading," she commented with a little smile.

"Not really." Cam pushed the paper away and looked up at her sister. "I need a new car. I sold the Harley this morning."

Cady noticed a resigned tone to her sister's voice and decided it was probably a real sign of acceptance of her pregnancy. She decided not to make a lot of it. "Well, that's good. Can't imagine a babyseat on the back of that thing."

"Ha ha." Cam narrowed her eyes at her sister. "You seem chipper. I guess work agrees with you."

Cady swallowed a sigh. "I guess so." She opened the

refrigerator and began poking through its contents wondering what she should plan to make for dinner. Not that she was hungry. Will had brought her a complimentary plate of the potato latkes for lunch. She smiled, irritation with her sister evaporating as she remembered the luscious, salt-buttery flavor of the dish.

"Maybe a salad would be good tonight," she thought out loud without even realizing she'd spoken.

"Just put some meat in it, please." Cam pulled the newspaper back to her and began scrutinizing the ads.

"Will do." Cady looked over her sister's shoulder. "Help Wanted? Are you looking for work?"

"Congratulations, Sherlock. Of course I'm looking for work. You didn't think I was just going to hang out here waiting for you to come home every day, did you?"

Their eyes met and Cady shrugged. "That's what I've been doing for the past fifteen years." She smiled, feeling sympathetic. "You sure you're up to it, though? You've been so tired. And honey, you're no spring chicken. Maybe being pregnant is all your body can handle."

Cam snorted, her expression disdainful. "I've never done nothing for so long in my life before." She spread her hands. "I can't just sit around reading gossip magazines all day."

"You haven't been." Cady straightened from the refrigerator with a head of romaine lettuce. "You think I hadn't noticed the clean bathrooms and kitchen, the vacuumed floors and dusted furniture?"

Her sister didn't reply, but Cady noticed a tiny smile curve her lips and knew she'd heard. She tossed the lettuce onto the glass cutting board on the edge of the countertop and bent to put her arm around her sister's shoulders. "Thank you."

To her surprise, Cam put her arms around her and they ended up holding each other for a moment, even though the angle was awkward. Cady felt tears well up in her eyes, and blinked them back, determined not to give in to the tenderness. She remembered when she was twelve and sitting in the apple tree in the corner of their yard reading. She heard her mother calling her and remembered she was supposed to sweep the floors. She'd swung down from the tree immediately and run to the door, only to find Cam there, holding a broom and being berated because she'd told her mother she'd switched chores with Cady and forgotten.

After a moment the women drew apart and Cady swiped her eyes dry with the back of her hand, turning to the sink. After she'd gulped back the tears and washed the lettuce, she cleared her throat. "So, have you talked to Stanley recently?"

"About what?" Cam rustled the newspaper as she folded it.

"His new job, where he's living, didn't you say he planned to take some classes at the community college?" Cady bit her lip, knowing what she had to ask but reluctant to broach the subject.

"He called earlier."

Cady turned, arching her eyebrow at her sister, her hands full of wet lettuce. "And?"

"He wants to see me." Cam groaned and put her face in her arms. "Don't say it! I know. I have to see him. I have to tell him about the baby."

Cady plopped the soggy leaves on a paper towel to dry and sat next to her sister. She remembered how protective she'd felt about Cam and the baby before she'd started working. She wasn't sure when her feelings had changed, but she now felt sure telling Stan would be the best choice for Cam.

She sighed. "Is there a reason not to?"

Cam lifted her head enough to pillow it on her crossed arms. "Nothing except he's going to be really angry." She laughed. "Silly, isn't it? I don't want to see him because I'm afraid he'll guess just from the look of me and I love him so much I can't stand the thought of him being angry with me."

"A catch-22, I guess." Cady returned to her lettuce, shaking out the remaining water and shredding it into a bowl.

"You guess?"

Cady shrugged. "I can't *know*, can I? I don't know Stan well enough, but I did see how he looked at you. The man is in love with you, Cam. He might be angry at first, but then he'll forgive you. And you don't have to tell him tonight, either. But you should meet him. You've kept him away long enough, and you're miserable without him."

Her sister sat up, letting her arms fall into her lap, her spine straightening. For several minutes while Cady sliced tomatoes, onions and zucchini into the salad, she remained in one position, her head slightly cocked, her hands folded. Then she stood. "You're probably right."

"Pardon?" Cady's mind had been elsewhere, dwelling on Will's face when he delivered her lunch and waited for her to taste it. His jaunty wink and grin had almost erased Cady's memory of her conversation with her sister.

Cam nodded as if she hadn't heard. "I'll call him back. I guess I have a date. I'll just have to wear some loose clothing." With a grin, she hurried up the stairs as Cady blinked after her, then shrugged and returned to her salad.

As she put the finishing touches on the salad, the phone rang. Recognizing Kelsea's cell phone number, she picked it up. "Hi, honey."

"Hey Mom, just wanted to let you know I'm not going to be home until after eight tonight. A bunch of us are going to MacDonald's for dinner."

"Any parents?" Cady looked at her salad. If she was right, Cam wouldn't be there for dinner, and Neil had already called to warn her he was running late.

"Sabrina's mom is taking us all in her van."

"Does she need any help? Should I come?"

"I don't think so. It's just five of us. And I've got my allowance to pay for dinner. Sabrina's mom will bring us home after."

Cady hesitated, her eyes still on the salad. She reached for the plastic wrap. "Okay, well, I need to go back by the restaurant for a couple of hours, anyway. I'm leaving a salad for your dad. If you want some, there should be plenty."

"Thanks, Mom, I love you."

"I love you, too." She hung up the phone, thinking again about Will. He'd be at the restaurant, and she really couldn't think of any reason *not* to go back. The evening receipts could be totaled, and with Cam, Kelsea and Neil all out, the house would be lonely. She sighed and stuck the salad into the refrigerator, grabbing a piece of paper to write a note.

SHE SPOTTED Will behind the bar when she went in but he was busy enough so he never glanced her way. With a wave at Melanie, the hostess on duty, Cady ducked down the short hallway leading to her office. Within a few minutes she'd buried herself in acquisition forms and receipts and had totally lost track of time when a shadow crossed her door, paused and backed up.

"Hey." Will had one hand on the doorsill as if he'd used it to pull himself back to her door. "What are you doing here?"

Cady shrugged, gesturing at the account book she'd just finished totaling. "Nobody's at home so I thought I'd come get a little work done. I figured I could help with the receipts tonight. You're short-handed, aren't you?"

He gave her a thoughtful look. "No more so than usual. You sure nobody's missing you? I never intended to take you away from your family."

"They're fine. Really. Neil's working late and Kelsea is out with her friends." Cady glanced at her watch and gave a soft exclamation. "Well, at least she *was*. I didn't realize how late it was getting to be."

He smiled. "Happens to me all the time. Back when I first started managing the place for my dad, I'd close, clean up, take care of the books and suddenly realize it was almost dawn. Even now I'll come in on my day off and mess around in the kitchen. This place gets into your blood."

"It's almost not like work sometimes."

"Yeah."

A silence fell between them, and finally Cady sighed and stood. "I should probably get home, though. I'm sure Neil and Kelsea are wondering where I am."

"Probably so." He smiled and saluted. "Thanks for coming in tonight."

As he started to turn away, Cady spoke without even knowing she would until the words forced themselves between her lips, "I could stay, you know, to help you with the deposit tonight."

"What about your family?" He gave her a narrow look.

"They're fine without me." She tried to keep the bitter hurt out of her words but knew she'd failed by his raised eyebrows.

"I doubt that." He took a step toward her, and she could see the concern in his eyes. "Are you okay?"

"I'm fine." She shook her head, trying to laugh at herself. "Really. I just…" The heaviness in her heart wanted to be turned loose, and she could see from Will's expression that he would help her. She bit her lip. "I'm sorry. I should go."

She grabbed her bag and tried to push past him, but he caught her arm. "Cady."

His touch seemed to pulsate warmth into her veins, spreading through her body. She placed her hand over his and looked up at him, summoning enough strength to smile, though she felt tears in the back of her throat. "I'm fine, really."

"I'm here if you need me."

She caught her breath at the offer she could so easily read into his words and nodded, dropping her gaze and forcing herself to walk out into the corridor, leaving him behind.

7

*C*ady had just gotten home Friday afternoon and was sorting the mail she'd brought in with her when she heard the front door close and turned to find her husband. He entered the kitchen, kissed her lightly and opened the refrigerator door. "Hey."

"Hey." She couldn't keep the surprise out of her voice, although she wasn't sure if she should be pleased or not. She and Neil hadn't sorted out their conflict yet, and Cady was conscious of a continued resentment about his attitude toward her sister. Still, she knew it would take very little for him to convince her to let go of her anger. If he had come home early to make his other absences up to her, she'd forgive and forget it all.

He glanced at his watch. "Kelsea still at school?"

"Yeah." She tried hard to squelch the hope that flared in her breast. "She's got practice until four."

He nodded, his expression absent. "I won't have to leave until after that."

"Leave?" The word tasted bitter.

He refocused on her. "Yeah. Sorry. I was going to tell you. I have to go to Utah."

She half raised a hand as if to ward off his words, then dropped it in resignation. "Why on earth would you go to Utah?"

"It's this case. It's a child custody case with the mother here in North Carolina and the father in Utah. They have family members and friends in both places, and some of them might be willing to give testimony for her. I have to collect affidavits from the ones I can."

"When do you leave?" She found it difficult to speak. Disappointment lodged in her throat like an ice cube.

"My plane leaves at eleven. I'll have to get to the airport by nine." He took her hands in his. "I'm sorry."

She squeezed his hands and gave him a little smile before turning away. "What for? It's work. Do you know how long you'll be gone?"

He heaved a sigh. "Unfortunately, at least the weekend. Probably Monday. I should be back by Wednesday at the latest."

She nodded, opening the refrigerator and pretending to search its contents. "It'll probably be pretty quiet around here. Kelsea's got that cheerleading convention she's been talking about for weeks."

"I forgot about that." He put a hand on her shoulder. "You'll be okay, though? What about Cam?"

His concern irritated her. "Cam's got her own stuff going

on. She's trying to work up the courage to tell Stan about the baby. Doesn't matter, though. I'm working this weekend, anyway."

"That's good." A look of obvious relief spread over his face and she bit back a sudden rush of anger. He didn't seem to notice as he pulled her into his arms. "I'm really proud of you, you know. This job has been great for you."

You have no idea. She made herself relax against him for a moment, but for the first time, it wasn't her husband she thought about as he held her. "Anything that keeps me out of trouble, right?"

He kissed the top of her head. "Yeah, right. I better go pack."

SATURDAY WAS ALWAYS busy at the restaurant. Cady wasn't actually scheduled to go in, so she lingered in her house waiting for Cam to get up. When her sister hadn't made an appearance by ten-thirty, however, Cady left her a note and went to work.

She'd intended to slip circumspectly through the pre-lunch preparations and into her office, but she spotted Will at the bar wiping glasses and shaking his head at Suzie, who looked upset about something. Suzie spotted her and waved and Will turned, his brow furrowing at the sight of her. "Hey, what are you doing here?"

"Thank heavens you are!" Suzie turned with a relieved air to Will. "She can fill in at the hostess desk and you can be in the kitchen. Won't that work?"

Will frowned. He handed Suzie the towel and walked around the bar, taking Cady's arm and leaning down to whisper in her ear, "Did you forget you're only part-time?"

She glanced at him as she let him guide her down the hall to her office, wondering if he was upset, but saw only concern in his expression. Gaining courage from that, she replied with as much truth as she could muster, "I still haven't gotten the books the way I want them, so I thought I'd come in for a couple of hours. Why, what's up?"

As she placed her purse on her desk and turned, Will sighed and sank onto the couch. "Suzie's upset. Collette called in sick again, so I was going to put Sandra at the hostess desk and take over the bar. But that puts Suzie short-handed in the kitchen."

"No problem." Cady tried to contain her delight at the prospect of being truly useful. "I can do the hostess desk."

He shook his head. "That's not exactly in your job description, is it?"

"Who cares?" She grinned. "Just have one of the waitresses show me what to do."

"Sandra can show you. She's done it often enough. She prefers bartending, though."

"Well, don't ask me to tend bar. I can pour beer and wine, but that's about it."

"We'll work on that." He grinned, obviously relieved, stood and kissed her cheek. "Thanks a lot, Cady. This is a huge help. I can't afford to lose Suzie. She's too good a cook, and she's the only other person besides me who knows everything about this restaurant. Plus, she's really a good sport. This has just happened once too often, even for her."

Fighting the urge to put her hand on her cheek where he'd kissed her, Cady nonetheless felt herself leaning slightly toward him. Flustered, she turned and tucked her purse into a drawer of her desk. "Well, we can't have that." She glanced at her watch and turned back. "Let's get me trained before the early birds get here."

By the time the first of the day's hungry customers came through the door, Cady had learned how to read the map of the restaurant's tables and Sandra had clued her in on how many tables each individual waiter or waitress could reasonably handle.

"How's it going?" Will paused by the hostess stand on one of his customary greeting forays around the dining room.

"Good." Cady studied the dining room map in front of her and hoped she'd marked off the correct table. She looked up and gave him a reassuring smile. "I think I've pretty much got it."

He smiled back. "Since ninety percent of the job is just being pleasant and charming, I'd say you have all the experience needed." He winked at her, and as she blushed, he disappeared back into the kitchen.

By the time three o'clock and the end of the lunch rush rolled around, Cady felt as if she'd worked a twelve-hour shift. Will emerged from the kitchen, wiping his hands on a dishtowel he threw over his shoulder. He paused to speak to Sandra, who was tidying up the bar, then came over to the hostess stand. "You look dead on your feet."

Cady smiled a little, leaning on the stand. "I feel like a herd of really hungry elephants trampled me and I had to keep smiling the whole time."

He laughed, coming around to put an arm around her shoulders. "I'll never ask you to do that again, I swear. But you saved my ass this afternoon and I am in your debt." He gave her shoulders a squeeze just as the front door opened.

A handsome young man in a police officer's uniform stood there, a curious expression on his face. He took a cautious step into the restaurant. "Hey, Will."

"Hey, Patrick." Will grinned in an easy way, stepping away from Cady, his arm slipping away from her shoulders as casually as if he'd forgotten it was there. "Just getting around to lunch?"

"Actually, Mom sent me by to see if you were going to be home for dinner tonight." Patrick glanced at Cady, then back at Will.

"Sorry." Will turned to Cady. "Cadence, this is my little brother Patrick. He just transferred back home from Raleigh."

Cady forced a smile, thinking the muscles in her face had received more of a workout during the course of the afternoon than her yoga usually gave the rest of her body. The smile felt unnatural, as if she didn't use that particular expression much. "Nice to meet you, Patrick." She glanced at Will. "If you don't need me anymore right now, I thought I'd go back to my office for a bit?"

"Sure." He gave her arm a gentle squeeze. "I'll bring you some lunch in a bit."

Cady sank into the chair behind her desk, kicking off her pumps and breathing a sigh of relief at just being alone for a few minutes. She tried to sort through her confused feelings of the morning, but exhaustion overrode any guilt she might feel for her continued and unchecked attraction to Will. Besides, she told herself, it wasn't like she'd actually done anything about it. She closed her eyes, remembering how he'd kissed her cheek and fantasizing he'd chosen her lips instead of her cheek to kiss.

A light touch on her shoulder pulled her out of her daze with a startled exclamation. She whirled, her cheeks burning with embarrassment, to find Will, amused, balancing a tray with two steaming plates and a pitcher of ice tea.

"Hey, relax. You're too tense." He set the tray on the desk, turning to put both hands on her shoulders. Her muscles tightened at his touch, then she took a deep breath and forced herself to relax. "That's better." He continued to massage her shoulders, finding the knots in her muscles as if he could feel the pain himself.

"God, that feels good." She surrendered herself to the pleasure of his touch, even in a non-intimate, although familiar, way. After a few minutes, however, she forced herself to pull away, smiling at him to indicate her gratitude. "Just what I needed. Thanks."

"No worries. The least I could do. Speaking of which." He took one plate from the tray and placed it in front of her, then took the second one to the couch. "Just a grilled cheese and fries. Hope that's okay?"

"Sounds great. I could eat everything on the menu, I think."

They ate in silence for several minutes. Cady thought how nice it was to have a relationship like this with a man. They could eat in silence without feeling awkward or neglected. She remembered the mute dinners with Neil when Kelsea wasn't around and her heart ached. He would call her later, and what would she say?

She looked up and caught Will's sharp glance. He took a sip of tea, setting aside his plate. "You okay?"

Cady winced. "Yeah, I guess. I mean, I'm sorry. I shouldn't be--" She tried to hide her confusion, aware that everything about her situation was wrong. She shouldn't talk about her marital problems to a friend, especially when she hadn't even talked to her husband about her feelings. It shouldn't feel so natural to talk to Will about personal things.

"Sorry, I shouldn't have asked." He set his glass on her desk and sat forward. "If you do need to talk, though…"

"Thanks." She bit her lip, setting aside the crust of her grilled cheese and wondering in an absent way about her clean plate. When was the last time she'd been so hungry? She looked up at him and smiled. "Really. And the sandwich was great, too."

"Sure." He stood and started to gather the empty dishes.

"Are you leaving?" The startled question was drawn almost involuntarily from her.

"Gotta get back to it. It'll be dinner time before you know it." He smiled at her. "You should go home."

"I will." She gestured at the books in front of her. "Just going to get some of this straightened out first."

He paused at the door. "Look, I understand you've got something personal going on and you don't want to talk about it. I'm just…" He shifted the tray in his arms and the empty plates clinked. "I don't like to see you hurt."

She nodded, unable to voice a reply, but as he turned away, she covered her mouth to keep from calling him back.

CADY WORKED STEADILY for the next several hours, burying herself in facts and figures of the restaurant that was so important to Will. By delving into the inner workings of the business, she felt a tenuous connection to the man she'd come to look at as more than just a friend over the past few weeks. Or had she always seen him this way?

So lost was she in her work that the dinner hour came and went before Cady finally realized how late it was. For several minutes she sat at her desk, feeling fulfilled in a way she'd missed for years. A day's work had left her tired in a way that exhilarated her. At that moment, she heard Will's footstep in the hall.

He paused in the door, his face creased by a frown. "Are you still here? I thought you left hours ago."

Nothing to go home to. She forced a smile. "Just catching up a little. The time went faster than I thought it would."

"Have you eaten?" He looked concerned. "I was about to make myself a shrimp and grits sub out of some of the leftovers. I can make two, and if your family won't be worried about you, I'd love the company."

"Sure. Sounds better than the bologna and cheese I would've made at home." She sighed and stood, stretching her neck to alleviate the crick in it.

A frown creased his forehead. "You've been working too hard. And I don't think it's the boss's fault."

"No, the boss is a sweetheart. But that just makes the people who work for him want to do their jobs really well."

"Bastard." He took her hand. "Let me make you dinner and you can tell me why you're here so late."

She followed him to the kitchen where Suzie and Joe were finishing up. Will pulled an apron on over his t-shirt. "You guys go on home. I'll finish up here after I eat dinner."

Joe grabbed his jacket and left but Suzie hesitated. "You sure? The dishwasher still needs to be unloaded. I don't mind staying."

"I can unload the dishwasher, Suz." Will waved her on. "Isn't your daughter visiting with that grandbaby you're always talking about?" He pulled a loaf of French bread from the "day old" drawer. Cady knew he'd make croutons from the stale bread the next day. She hadn't realized he sometimes made himself dinner from it. It made her a little sad to think of him eating dinner alone in the deserted restaurant. How was it that such a wonderful, giving man didn't have his own family to go home to yet?

She didn't realize Suzie had left until Will pulled a covered bowl of shrimp and grits from the refrigerator. She frowned. "That's not much leftover."

"There's enough for two. I try not to have leftovers. I don't like waste. But I had a taste for shrimp and grits so when I made it tonight I saved a little extra." He sawed off two sections of the bread, split it open with a deft cut and spooned shrimp and grits inside. As he placed them in the warmer he gave her a bemused look. "I suppose it's embezzling in a way. Care to join me in my life of crime?"

"Sure." She grinned. "Where should we eat? Back here?"

"I usually do, but since you're here, let's do it up right. Let's eat in the dining room." He placed the sandwiches and a plate of warm rolls on a tray with a bottle of wine and two glasses. Grabbing a lighter, he hefted the tray to his shoulder with a practiced sweep. "After you."

He guided her to a booth near the back of the restaurant. "You're full of surprises," she said as he set the tray on a neighboring table and lit the candle. She slid into the booth and he smiled at her as he poured the wine and put the plates on the table. "I had no idea you could wait tables."

"You don't really think it's possible to run a successful restaurant without being able to do most every job, do you? I worked as a waiter all four years of college. I think I can do just about everything I ask anybody else to do. It helps me be more sympathetic to the people who work for me, plus if there's a crisis, I can fill in."

"You'd wait tables? Now?" She sipped the Chardonnay. "That's good stuff."

"Thank you." He sat across from her, taking his own glass and admiring the wine before tasting. "My favorite. And yes, I would wait tables now. I have, as a matter of fact. Not much use owning a restaurant, making terrific food, if there's nobody to get it to the customers. I'd even hostess if I thought I wouldn't scare the customers away."

He grinned at her and she found it difficult to look away. She turned her attention to her plate. She felt oddly displaced, sitting in an empty restaurant after midnight with a handsome man, eating one of his favorite meals and drinking his favorite wine…by candlelight.

"You never told me why you're here so late." He buttered a roll and handed it to her. "I know *I'm* a loser, but you've actually got a life. What's up?"

"Having a family doesn't automatically equate to having a life." She tore a piece of buttered roll and chewed it thoughtfully, then, realizing he was waiting for her to continue, she shrugged. "I guess they all have lives and I have theirs. Cam's out all the time with Stan, and Kelsea's off at a cheerleading convention this weekend. She won't be back until tomorrow evening."

"And Neil?"

Cady tore another piece of buttered roll and glared at it. "Neil's out of town on business. He'll be back Wednesday."

He nodded and took a bite from his sandwich. She sighed. "So you see, when my family's off living their lives, I suddenly find myself alone. Thank goodness for this job or I'd've sat at home feeling sorry for myself. Instead, I get to wind up a productive evening with a pleasant dinner."

"Well, here's to pleasant dinners and lovely company, then." He held up his glass and she grinned.

"I'll drink to that." They clinked glasses and ate in companionable silence for a few minutes. The shrimp and grits sandwich was tasty and Cady found she was hungrier than she'd thought.

"That was excellent." She wiped her mouth. "I never would've thought about putting shrimp and grits into a sub. You should add it to the lunch menu."

His eyebrows shot up. "That's not a bad idea."

"Well, it might be a bad idea for those of us who need to watch our carbs, but it'd be a hit, I'm sure."

"The lunch menu could use revamping, that's for sure." He studied her thoughtfully. "You have plans tomorrow night?"

"I--" She hesitated, caught off guard. "No, not really. I

mean, not at this hour. Kelsea will be home by dinner, but she'll be asleep by nine. And Cam will be there tomorrow night, I think."

"If you can get away, maybe you and I could look over the menu together. Figure out a way to update it without getting rid of too many favorites."

She hesitated. Ducking out after her daughter was asleep and while her husband was away felt like cheating. For the first time, she realized Neil hadn't called her all day. She felt in her pocket for her phone and discovered she'd left it in her office. An unexpected feeling of freedom surged through her.

"Sure." She ducked her head to hide the fact that the invitation pleased her more than it should. "Are you sure I'm who you need to go over this with, though? Seriously, I can barely make a decent meatloaf."

"You can make a decent meatloaf?" He raised his eyebrows. "Now that's a secret you need to share with me."

"Sure, it's—" *Neil's favorite.* She hesitated. "It's easy. You just throw in a lot of the same spices you use to make hamburger patties. Breadcrumbs, egg yolk, oregano, garlic, thyme."

"Thyme?" His eyebrows shot up even higher this time. "You're kidding."

She gave him a suspicious look. "You're just humoring me."

He laughed, his eyes crinkling in a very friendly way. "I'm not. Seriously. I never would've thought to add thyme to either hamburger patties or meatloaf. This is why I need you. You may not be professionally trained, but you've got plenty of experience making dinners your family is willing to eat."

She shrugged. "So *that's* why you need me."

"It's not the only reason." The words were stated simply, but when she looked up at him, he didn't quite meet her gaze. After a moment's silence, he looked at his watch. "It's late. You should get home. C'mon, I'll walk you to your car."

"Don't you want me to help you finish the cleanup?" She looked guiltily at the dirty dishes on the table, knowing he wouldn't leave for at least another hour. "I can wash these dishes at least."

"You do enough dishes. Let's pretend I just took you out to a nice dinner and neither of us has to do the dishes." For a moment they looked at each other and Cady wondered how far she could take a game of let's pretend with him. *Let's pretend I'm not married and you're going to kiss me good-bye at the car. Let's pretend you're going to take me home to your house and make love...* The game quickly got out of control in her imagination, but he broke it off by taking her arm. "And now it's time to go home."

He walked her to her car after she'd collected her purse and cell phone from her office. When she opened the door and hesitated a minute before getting in, he kissed her cheek. "Good-night."

"Good-night. Thanks for dinner."

"Thanks for the company." He stepped back as she got in and drove away.

CAM SAT up on the sofa as Cady entered the house quietly. She glanced at the clock. Well after midnight. She didn't really need to ask where her sister had been. She did wonder what she had been doing, though. Will didn't really seem like the cheating type. Of course, Cady wouldn't be attracted to the cheating type, either. Cady had always valued the good guys. And she'd been lucky enough to have them value her.

Cam felt sad when she thought of Neil, who might not even realize how much jeopardy he was placing his marriage in with his too-constant work ethic. Neil was a good guy, even if they'd never gotten along. And she believed he still loved Cady, even if Cady had her doubts.

Cady hadn't spotted her in the darkened room, so when Cam flipped on the lamp, she jumped. "What the hell are you doing sneaking around here?"

"What the hell are you doing sneaking *in* here at this time of night?"

"I was working." Cady tossed her purse onto the couch and sat. "How was your date?"

"It was great. He wants to work things out. He loves me and I love him. And no, I didn't tell him about the baby yet. But don't change the subject."

"I wasn't aware I was changing the subject. I was working. See? End of subject."

Cam narrowed her eyes suspiciously. "Pardon my ignorance. I thought the restaurant closed two hours ago."

"I stayed to help Will with some stuff. He made me dinner."

"Well, a man who cooks is certainly very sexy." Cam shrugged. "A man who does the dishes is even sexier."

Cady shot her a look but said nothing. Cam gaped at her.

"He washed the dishes, too? You're kidding. What exactly *were* you 'helping' him with, anyway?"

"Cut it out, Cam. I'm not fooling around with Will. He's not that type."

"Neither are you. But I get the feeling if you weren't married, neither one of you would waste any time getting down to the fooling around."

Her sister looked startled, probably by being confronted by the truth, but then she sighed. "He's such a great guy, Cam. You may be right. I've probably been half in love with him for as long as I've known him. I guess I just never noticed when things were good between Neil and me."

"How bad are things with you and Neil, really?" Cam frowned at her sister. "I mean, he's not changed that drastically. I know he's not cruel to you."

"Not on purpose. And you don't have to tell me I'm an idiot. I know what a wonderful man my husband is. But he's so tied up in work and when I try to talk to him about it, he just says he's got a demanding job and has to make sacrifices. Well, that's all well and good, but he's sacrificing *me*, and I'm sick of it." She grabbed a pillow and hugged it, looking like a little girl for a minute.

Cam sighed, touching her sister's arm. "Look, I don't know what's going on with you and Will. Maybe I shouldn't know anything. And as for Neil, well, maybe I should hate him for treating you like this. But I just don't want you to ruin your life just because your husband's not paying enough attention to you."

"I'm not trying to ruin anything. I love Neil. I've never denied that, and I know he loves me, too. But I love the way

Will makes me feel. I'm more of a whole person when I'm with him. Can you understand that?" She turned pleadingly to Cam.

Cam shook her head but sighed. "Yeah, I understand it. I've been there. Never with a guy as great as Neil *or* Will, but yeah."

"Thanks." Cady smiled a little. "But you haven't told me about Stanley. How's his job going?"

Her sister shrugged. "I think it's good. He seems like he wants to stay in town. He says he won't leave without me, anyway." She found it difficult to look at her sister. "I guess he loves me a little more than I thought."

"So how come you didn't tell him about the baby?" Cady sounded a little more detached from the subject than she had up to then. Cam studied her thoughtfully. Maybe Neil had been right to encourage her to get a job. Of course, she was pretty sure he hadn't intended his wife to fall in love with her boss.

She cleared the thoughts from her head with a shake. "It didn't seem like the right time."

"Is there a right time, Cam? Seriously? I think you just need to tell him."

Cam groaned. "I know you're right. I do. How come you're so much better at living my life than I am?"

"Same reason you're better at living my life. We're twins, maybe we should switch places, huh?"

"You don't think Neil would notice anything was up in a month or so, anyway?"

"Maybe, although he doesn't take much notice, anyway."

Cady sighed. "Listen, I'll quit giving you advice if you'll quit giving me advice."

"Deal." Cam smiled and thought for a minute. "So are you going to sleep with him?"

Cady's eyes widened in shock. "Cam! What the hell? You just said--"

"I'm not judging. I'm just curious. If Will asked you to sleep with him, would you?"

A tiny smile touched her sister's lips and Cam had no doubt that, plan to or not, Cady had already imagined a dozen ways of making love to Will. She kept her dismay to herself, however. It hadn't happened yet, and might not.

"It's a moot point, Sis." Cady stood, tossing the pillow she'd been hugging back into its spot with a practiced twitch of her wrist. "Will would never ask."

Would you? Cam longed to ask the question, but she bit her tongue and Cady left the room, probably assuming she'd put her sister's doubts to rest.

8

Just as Cady had figured, Kelsea arrived home from her conference exhausted. She was content to have a quiet dinner with her mother and aunt before heading up to her room. As Cady finished cleaning the kitchen, she glanced at her watch. Eight o'clock. The restaurant closed at nine on Sundays. If she left in the next hour, she could help Will get the evening deposit ready and probably be finishing up just as the last of the wait staff left.

"So what are your plans tonight?" She tried to keep her tone casual.

"TV and bed. Stan might stop by later if it's okay." Cam rinsed a wineglass and handed it to Cady, catching her looking at her watch again. She raised her eyebrows. "You got some-place to be?"

"I do, actually." Cady dried a wineglass and put it in the cupboard, turning with resolve. "I told Will I would come by to help him with the deposit tonight. He's been shorthanded this weekend, so whatever I can do is a big help."

"Oh, right." Her sister nodded, and Cam did a double take. "Really?"

"What?"

"That's it? No objections?"

"Why would I object to you going to work?" Cam tried and failed to look innocent and unworried.

"Right." Cady considered her sister for a minute, then decided not to look a gift horse in the mouth. She gave Cam a hug. "I love you."

"I love you, too." Cam smiled but as Cady pulled away, she seized her hands. "Just be careful, okay?"

"Sure." Cady tried to sound reassuring. "Don't worry about me, Cam. I know what I'm doing."

OF COURSE, if she knew what she was doing, why did she have butterflies in her stomach? Cady sat in her office thinking of Will, who she'd spotted earlier behind the bar chatting with some customers. He'd smiled when he saw her, but when she ducked into the back, he hadn't followed her. Cady closed her eyes for a second, aware of a distinct feeling that she was in the wrong place.

Pushing the thought away, she shuffled through the receipts she'd already totaled twice, then put them in the safe along with the bank deposit bag. Just as she turned back to her desk, she heard his step in the hall.

"Hey!" He sounded ebullient, and she shook her head. He

had to have been there since eight o'clock in the morning. Did he never run out of steam?

"Aren't you exhausted?"

His eyebrows shot up and he laughed. "Of course not. I've been thinking about this all day and have I ever got a surprise for you."

He grinned, took her hand and pulled her down the hall into the empty dining room. She hesitated at the swinging doors and he glanced over his shoulder. "It's okay. Everybody's gone."

She let him draw her into the kitchen, realizing as he did that he'd understood she was hesitant to be seen alone in the restaurant with him again. She accepted a glass of wine, thinking that it was paradoxically his own open nature that had revealed his awareness of her desire to be subtle.

"No leftovers tonight." He began assembling ingredients on the counter. "We'll fix dinner in a bit, but in the meantime, I thought we could experiment with appetizers."

"Appetizers?" She raised her eyebrows. The appetizers currently on the menu ran the gamut from calamari to onion rings, but she could think of nothing that matched the motley assembly of ingredients on the counter.

"Sure. I told you I wanted some new stuff on the menu. This is something my aunt makes for her kids. Well, sort of. I've added a couple of my own touches."

She watched him layer a flour tortilla with ham and grated cheese. "Ham and cheese pinwheels? You're kidding."

"Wait. There's another ingredient." He produced a whole pineapple from below the counter and deftly peeled it with a large serrated knife. She couldn't help admiring the way his hands moved, seemingly without conscious thought of what he was doing. He quartered and cored the pineapple, sliced one of the quarters in half and offered one half to her on the blade of the knife.

Feeling absurdly honored, she accepted the slice of fruit while he diced what remained into tiny bits. "Now what?"

"We add it to the pinwheel."

"That won't work." She began to giggle. "You've got to be kidding me."

"You've never had a ham, cheese and pineapple pinwheel before? You're kidding *me*."

"Will, be serious. We're trying to revamp your menu with stuff people will actually eat."

"Trust me, they'll eat this." He sprinkled the pineapple over the ham. "Wait!" He paused in the act of rolling the tortilla.

"What?" She grinned at his deliberately intense face. "What now?"

"We almost forgot the secret ingredient."

"Secret ingredient?" She couldn't help laughing. "I don't care what you put in those things, nobody's going to pay seven bucks for an appetizer plate of them."

"You'd be surprised." He poked through the commercial-sized refrigerator. "You know those sautéed vegetables I'm always getting compliments for?" He turned, a mischievous look on his face. "Want to know the secret ingredient?"

"Sure." She had to admit she was curious. "Those veggies were the only green things we could get Kelsea to eat for a while."

"I've heard that a lot." He grinned. "Lemon pepper."

"You're kidding."

"I'm not." He shook his head vehemently. "Lemon pepper. And the vegetables were sautéed in butter. It's really all it takes. I learned early on it didn't even matter what kind of veggies they were. Whatever was freshest. Carrots, broccoli, snow peas. As long as I included the lemon pepper, everybody loved them."

"So what's the secret ingredient this time?" She tried to see what he'd taken from the refrigerator.

"I'm not sure you're ready for this." He gave her a narrowed glare. "This one is really top secret."

"Cut it out." She tried to grab the jar but he held it behind his back, grinning. "Oh come on, Will! Don't be ridiculous. Show me!"

"On one condition. You have to take an oath."

"An oath?" She raised her eyebrows, then shrugged. "Fine. Tell me what to say."

"I, state your name."

She kept a straight face. "I, state your name."

He frowned playfully at her. "Do solemnly swear to never, ever reveal the secrets of this restaurant."

"Do solemnly swear to never, ever, under any circum-stances, even if I'm placed on a rack and tickled mercilessly, *ever* reveal the secrets of this restaurant."

He cocked one eyebrow at her, pausing for a long moment. Then he grinned. "Sorry, that was just sort of a fun image."

She hit him and he fended her off. "Okay, are you ready? Here goes." He displayed a small jar with a flourish.

"Dijon mustard?" She looked at him doubtfully. "Seriously?"

His face became very somber. "Have you ever tasted Dijon mustard?"

"Of course I have."

He shook his head. "Not on a sandwich. By itself."

She stared at him in astonishment. "Seriously?"

"Why do you keep asking me that? I'm always serious about food."

He did look very solemn as he produced a spoon. "Here, I'll show you." He squeezed a bit of the condiment on the spoon and held it out.

Cady backed away. "Huh-uh. No way. Dijon on bread can burn a path through your sinuses."

He shook his head, waving away her objections. "The key is moderation. If you know your medium, you know how much to use. In this case, it's Dijon with nothing else. So there's barely even a taste of it here." He held the spoon out again, and when she still hesitated, he raised his eyebrows and grinned. "Don't you trust me?"

She looked at him doubtfully, then shrugged. "Can't kill me." She tasted cautiously and was startled by how good the mustard actually was. "Mmm." She closed her eyes, focusing on the flavor. "You're right. It's not really that hot. And there's a sweetness there, too."

"You're tasting the honey. This particular brand adds honey and uses both burgundy and white wine. The original recipe for Dijon mustard called for unripe grape juice." He sounded pleased. "Added—in moderation—to the pinwheels, the Dijon will complement the pineapples."

"Yummy." She opened her eyes and smiled at him. He stood very close to her, but she didn't feel uncomfortable and she didn't back away. "Okay, so add your secret ingredient."

"Secret ingredient?"

Will and Cady swung around, startled, at the new voice. Neil stood in the doorway to the kitchen, head cocked and smiling. "Sorry. Am I committing kitchen espionage?"

Cady regained her equilibrium with difficulty and started across the kitchen to him. "Neil! I didn't expect you home until Wednesday." Her heart pounded absurdly in her chest. She hadn't been doing anything wrong. She put her arms around her husband and kissed him, telling herself she had a clear conscience.

"There wasn't any point in staying longer. I tried calling when my plane got in but your cell went to voicemail. I called the house and Cam said you were here. Lucky for me the front door was still unlocked."

"Oops." Will had finished the pinwheels while Cady greeted her husband. "I should fix that." He placed the pan in the oven and smiled as he left the kitchen. Cady looked after him for just a second, wondering if he wished, as she almost did, that he had remembered to lock the door earlier.

"Anyway," Neil said as she turned back to him, "I wanted to see you, so I came on over. I didn't mean to interrupt. Are you still working? I was hoping to take you home."

"Actually, Will and I are going over the menu…"

"We were planning a literal working dinner." Will tossed his keys on the counter as he returned. "Have you eaten? I have some ideas for new menu items I was going to try out on Cadence. You should join us."

"Cadence?" Neil smiled a little at Will's use of Cady's

full name and glanced at his wife. "I thought I was the only one who called you that. Maybe I will join you. Sounds like fun."

"Great." Will produced another glass and filled it with wine. "It's a good thing you're here, actually. I'm planning grilled meatloaf sandwiches for dinner. You can tell me if I got Cady's recipe down."

"Cady's recipe?" Neil accepted the glass. He smiled at his wife. "You have a recipe? I thought you just threw everything but the kitchen sink in and it turned out great."

Cady felt the color creep up her neck. "I mentioned it to Will last night. Just that, actually. That I threw in everything I could find."

"You said, if I remember correctly, breadcrumbs, egg, oregano, garlic, thyme." Will ticked off the ingredients on his fingers.

"You got a recipe from that?" Cady blinked. "You're obviously more attentive than me."

"It sounded good." Will flipped on the grill. "I could barely wait until this morning to make the meatloaf. Turned out pretty well, but I figured I'd try something different with it tonight."

"You guys did this last night, too?" Neil glanced at his watch. "I guess the hours of restaurateurs are different from lawyers."

Cady noted the dark circles under his eyes. "You don't have to work tomorrow, do you? You look exhausted. Maybe we should head home."

He put an arm around her and pulled her to his side. She felt a little thrill of desire as he kissed her lightly. "I am exhausted." His smile contained a definite invitation. "I might plan to stay in bed all day."

She couldn't help grinning back, but when the timer went off she was abruptly reminded of Will's presence. She turned, feeling awkward, as the man she'd been fantasizing about removed ham, cheese and pineapple pinwheels from the oven.

"Your wife," Will indicated Cady with a spatula, "didn't think these would be good enough to be on the menu."

"I just said I didn't know who would pay seven dollars for them." Cady accepted one on a napkin.

Will leaned on the counter. "Even with the secret ingredient?" He waggled his eyebrows at her and she giggled.

"Nobody wants to pay seven dollars for an appetizer anymore." Neil blew on his pinwheel to cool it. "You should have a selection of this type of thing for three bucks. Something cheap, tasty and easy to fix. People would pay for that and you'd make your profit."

Will nodded thoughtfully. "Not a bad idea. Lots of this sort of thing I could make."

A little thrown off by the friendliness between her husband and her boss, Cady popped the pinwheel into her mouth and was startled by the explosion of sweet spiciness. She closed her eyes in ecstasy. "Mmm."

She opened her eyes to find Neil watching her with amusement and, to her surprise, a thinly disguised desire. His voice sounded a little husky. "Is it that good?"

"It's fantastic!" She turned to Will to tell him the same thing but stopped when she saw his expression almost exactly mirrored Neil's. He gave her a quick smile and turned away to pull the meatloaf from the refrigerator and begin slicing it.

"Wait til you taste the sandwiches." His voice was light enough so she wondered at first if she'd imagined the longing in his eyes, but she remembered it too well and her breath caught in her throat. He wanted her. Maybe he'd never act on it, but now that she knew, a certain amount of the damage had been done. Because she wanted him too.

AFTER A DELICIOUS MEAL and more friendly conversation than Cady ever remembered having with two men, Neil walked her to her car and they left. At home they lingered in the kitchen. Neil thumbed through the stack of mail and Cady rinsed a couple of stray dishes to put in the dishwasher.

After a few moments of silence, he put his arms around her, turning her to him so he could kiss her. "God, it's good to see you."

She snuggled closer, kissed his neck and enjoyed the lingering smell of his aftershave. "You too, although you did sort of startle me just appearing like that."

"Yeah, I got that vibe. Sorry, I didn't mean to sneak up on you. I just really needed to be with you."

How long had she wanted to hear him say something like that? She couldn't remember the last time he'd spoken so plainly of his need for her. "What happened? Why did you come back so early?"

He sighed. "I can't really talk about it. I just went on a wild goose chase, apparently, trying to get an affidavit that might help my client keep her kids. It didn't work out, though."

"I'm sorry, Neil." She knew he hated to fail his clients. "Maybe something else will come up, though."

"Maybe." He set the mail aside and smiled at her. "It really helped to just hold you, though. You have no idea how much I need that some days."

"Really?" She couldn't hide her surprise.

He reached across the counter and took her hands. "Of course. You're the most important thing in my life and sometimes when everything's going wrong, the only thing I can hold onto is you. You didn't know that?"

"No. I mean, yes, but you've never…well, it's been a while since you said anything like that to me." She hesitated, not wanting to hurt him but unable to hold back her feelings.

He drew in a deep breath, squeezing her hands. "I know I've screwed up a lot. Tonight, I'm feeling really discouraged about life and the state of the human experience, and you're the only one who can take that away from me." He turned to her. "I want to hold you tonight." The words were simple, but the underlying emotion wasn't. She responded instinctively, leaning across the counter to kiss him.

She didn't allow herself to think of Will until after she'd made love to her husband, and by then the memory of the desire in his eyes had dulled.

She might have even imagined it.

9

*I*n spite of his earlier claim that he might stay in bed all day, Neil rose earlier than Cady the next morning. He woke her with a kiss to tell her good-bye, and only with difficulty did she resist the urge to put her arms around his neck and pull him back to her. She knew he'd only leave anyway, and she felt certain her heart would break at any more rejection. As the door closed behind him, however, her thoughts changed to wonder when she remembered the expression in Will's eyes the night before.

She'd never given much credence to Cam's assertions that Will was attracted to her. They'd worked together so often over the years, she'd come to take his cheerful compliments and friendly but harmless flirtatiousness for granted. She valued his friendship, and she knew he felt the same way. Only recently had she become aware that her own feelings had the potential to become much more. She wondered how long he had wanted her. The idea that he'd felt that way about her all along excited her in an incongruous way.

"Jeez," she muttered, sitting up. "What the hell's wrong with me?"

Too restless to lie still, she got up and went downstairs. She had waffles and sliced fruit ready when Kelsea came down a few minutes later. "Hey Mom." Kelsea looked at the breakfast Cady had prepared with surprise. "What's this?"

"Breakfast. I thought you could use a little extra something after your tough weekend." Cady kissed her daughter.

"Mom, I can't eat all that." Kelsea frowned at the plate. "I'll get sick for sure. I was just going to grab a banana. My ride'll be here in a minute."

"Well, eat what you can. Try the fruit." Cady sat across the bar from her daughter. "I want to hear about your conference."

Kelsea sat and took a bite of fruit. Just as she swallowed, however, a horn honked in the driveway. "Gotta run, Mom. I'll tell you all about it tonight. Love you."

Cady blinked as her daughter seized a banana and bolted to the door. She sighed and shrugged, pulling the plate over to her side of the bar. As she contemplated the golden waffles and multicolored collection of fruit, her cell phone rang. Glad of the distraction, she pushed the waffles aside and grabbed the phone.

"Cady? It's Brenda Carlisle."

"Brenda, so good to hear from you." Cady smiled at the receiver. Brenda Carlisle, the principal of Kelsea's school, had helped Cady on several fundraisers for the historical society, and Cady had been very active in the school's PTO—until she'd started back to work.

"I haven't seen you around much." Brenda's gentle voice so closely echoed Cady's thoughts she frowned, wondering if she'd said something out loud.

"I haven't had as much time recently. I went back to work." Cady took a sip of her coffee. "At Hubbard's, actually. You remember Will Hubbard?" Saying his name felt wrong, a little more intimate than she'd intended, especially when talking to another person.

"Of course." Brenda's voice contained warmth, but Cady thought she detected something else there as well. "A charming young man."

"But you didn't call to talk about charming young men, did you?" Cady tried to keep the worry out of her tone. "What can I do for you?"

Brenda sighed. "It's Kelsea, actually. I'm a little worried about her."

"Why?" Cady straightened, spilling a little of the coffee over her hand. As she did so, Cam entered, looking rumpled and sleepy. She made a beeline for the coffeemaker. "What's wrong with Kelsea?"

Cam, looking a little more awake, raised her eyebrows, but Cady ignored her as she waited for Brenda's reply.

"Nothing's exactly wrong. I don't mean to alarm you. I just wondered if she'd mentioned a new friend of hers to you."

Cady thought frantically. Had Kelsea said anything about a new friend? Someone who'd moved there recently or joined the cheerleading squad? She couldn't think of anyone. Immediately a horrible feeling that she was a bad parent began to haunt her. Had her preoccupation with her new job—and Will —translated into a lack of attention to her daughter's life?

"I only mention it because he's a little older and, well, a bit more experienced than Kelsea. It's really easy for a young girl to get carried away when one of the upperclassmen pays attention to them, and I thought you might want to keep a close watch on the situation."

"Wait!" Cady shook her head, trying to process the other woman's words. "Seriously? Her new friend is a boy?"

Cam frowned, sitting across from Cady. She picked up the fork and began eating the waffles, still obviously listening in to the conversation.

"His name is Rob Watson. He's sixteen and really very bright, but I wouldn't say he's one of our better students." Brenda sounded hesitant. "He's not exactly the type of boy I would think you would want for Kelsea's first boyfriend."

"Kelsea's not even allowed to date yet." Cady felt numb. Her sweet thirteen-year-old daughter dating a sixteen-year-old boy—she couldn't wrap her mind around it. "Not until she's fifteen. We've discussed it since she's so much younger than her classmates, but it's never been an issue."

"Well, you might want to discuss it again." Brenda's voice contained a hint of asperity tinged with humor. "And while you're at it, whatever your feelings are about motorcycles, you might want to reiterate them, too."

Cady slumped in her seat, too weak to do more than murmur assent. "Yeah, I'll do that. Thank you, Brenda." She hung up and looked at her sister.

"Kelsea's dating?" Cam took a sip of coffee to wash down a mouthful of waffle. "Did you approve that?"

"What do you think?" Cady stared at her phone, thinking about Neil. She wished he were there.

"Well, it might not be so bad. The age difference isn't that big, is it?"

"Three years." Cady slapped the phone down on the counter. "It might as well be twenty. He's sixteen, rides a motorcycle and from the way her principal talked, he's got more than a little experience with girls." She laid her head on her arms. "I just got you off a motorcycle, now my daughter's in danger of riding one! What am I going to do? If I tell her she can't see him, she'll resent it, and it might just make him that much more attractive to her. But what if she gets hurt?"

"Set some boundaries." Cam took another bite of waffle, then chewed quickly and swallowed when Cady's head snapped up. "Really, Cady, your daughter is a reasonable person. Just approach her as the intelligent girl she is and you'll be fine." She picked up the discarded cell phone. "But the first thing you need to do is call your husband."

Cady looked blankly at the phone. She had Neil on speed dial, of course. All she needed to do was press the tiny picture on the screen of his face. She'd used one of her favorite pictures of her husband, taken on their last vacation two years ago. Her gaze drifted over to Will's grinning image on the second line of important contacts. She couldn't help thinking how good it would feel to hear his voice right then.

"I said your husband, not your lover." Cam's voice cut across her thoughts and Cady glared at her sister.

"He's not my lover."

Cam assumed an innocent expression. "Who?"

"Damn it, Cam, I don't need this." Angry that she'd let her sister trick her into an acknowledgment she'd never intended to make, Cady marched out of the kitchen, hitting the speed dial for Neil as she did so.

The swinging door cut off her sister's snorted laughter behind her.

NEIL'S PHONE went straight to voice mail, so Cady left a message and got ready for work, mulling Cam's advice as she did so. If Brenda's tone had indicated anything to her, it had been that there was no time to waste. Cady knew she needed to act now, so she fidgeted as she prepared for work, keeping the phone beside her. When he hadn't called by nine-thirty, she left for the restaurant.

She reached the restaurant before ten and slipped into her office. Now that the moment had come to actually see Will, her nerves failed her, and she realized her fantasies hadn't helped her at all. How could she face the man she'd imagined kissing and even making love to when she suspected he now might be thinking about the same things?

As the morning wore on, however, she realized she didn't have to worry about it. Will passed her office briefly late in the morning, pausing to say good morning. His manner hovered between friendly and formal, the perfect tone for a boss to take, and Cady couldn't help but feel a little sad. She had no doubt their barely hidden, almost acknowledged mutual attraction could destroy the tenuous bonds of their friendship. To distract herself from her guilt about Will, her worry about Kelsea, and her growing irritation with Neil, she concentrated on her work.

Around two o'clock, Will surprised Cady with a sandwich and chips. He set the plate on her desk. "You've been working so hard I thought you might need some sustenance."

She smiled. "Thanks. I guess I have been kind of lost in it." She sat back and stretched, rolling her head from side to side. "Wow, how long *have* I been working?"

"It's after two." Will sat with a plate of his own. "You should've stopped an hour ago for lunch."

"After two?" Cady frowned, glancing at her purse where her phone remained silent. "I need to finish up the deposit, Will. I'm afraid I have to leave by four."

"Not until you've eaten. I can't be getting a bad rep. Nobody'll want to work for me."

She laughed, wondering if he knew he always made her feel better. "Right. Fat chance of that."

"You never know." He took a bite from his sandwich and they ate in companionable silence for a minute, then Will said, "So, what's up? You've seemed pretty tense all morning and if you don't stop glaring at your purse, you're going to give it a complex."

Cady tried not to smile but couldn't help it. "Stop. I'm not."

"You are." Will gave her purse a fixed stare, then grinned and turned to her. "So tell me who hasn't called you that should have by now."

"Who else? My wayward husband. I'm sure he's got a good excuse, though." She added the last out of a little lingering guilt from the night before.

"Of course he does. I'm sure he's been busy today. But what's so urgent?"

She bit her lip, holding back just a moment longer as she tried not to worry that she shouldn't discuss her family problems with Will, in fact that she shouldn't share any more intimacy with him than she already had. But her need to talk to someone about her worry for her daughter overwhelmed her need to avoid sharing details with someone who should be an outsider. Before she could stop herself, she blurted out everything about Brenda Carlisle's call, jumping up and pacing the office as she talked.

He frowned. "You don't know this kid?"

"No." She collapsed on the couch beside him and massaged her temples.

"But the principal thinks he's not a good idea." He seemed to be casting around for a way to help. "I could ask Patrick to check him out. Nothing official since he's a minor, but just ask around."

"Surely Patrick won't have heard about him." The thought filled her with dread.

"Probably not, but I could ask. Wouldn't hurt, would it?" He took her hand without seeming to think about it.

"Thanks." When he raised his eyebrows, she blushed. "No, really. I mean it. You don't have to worry about my family's problems, but you are. Thank you for that."

He smiled and brought her hand to his lips, kissing it as if it were the most natural thing in the world. "I care about you, Cady. I don't like seeing you upset and worried."

She dropped her gaze and at that moment her phone rang. He released her hand without being asked and she grabbed her purse, yanking out the phone and punching the button. "Neil?"

Will mimed leaving, but she waved him back to his seat on the couch.

"What's going on, Cady? Your message was a little garbled." Neil sounded preoccupied.

"Brenda Carlisle called me this morning. She's worried because Kelsea's been seeing a sixteen-year-old boy."

"What do you mean, seeing? Kelsea's not dating. When would she? The only place she ever goes is out with her friends or to cheerleading practice."

"I'm not sure exactly what Brenda meant by 'seeing'. But she was worried. She said he's not the type we would want for Kelsea's first boyfriend."

During the silence, she pictured Neil's forehead creased, a frown on his face. She closed her eyes and waited, hoping he could give her some guidance. When he sighed, however, he sounded more irritated than concerned.

"This is not the time for this."

"Neil?" Cady frowned. Neil had never failed her before. No matter what his work worries were, he always came through for her, especially when she had a concern about Kelsea.

"I'm sorry, Cady, I just—I can't deal with this right now. We'll talk to her tonight and make it clear we know what's going on and will keep an eye on it, but I have to go out of town tomorrow and—"

"Tomorrow?" Cady half-turned away from Will. "You just got back."

"I know it's bad timing. And I'll try to be back as quickly as possible, but I can't guarantee anything before Friday."

"Oh." She felt as if her heart had turned to a block of ice in her chest. It couldn't be beating anymore when all that reached her extremities was a cold breeze that whispered to her she'd been mistaken about her husband all along and especially the night before. He didn't love her anymore, no matter what he said when he tried to get her into bed. She shook off what she knew was nonsense with difficulty. "You're right, we'll talk about it tonight, then." She hung up without saying good-bye and stood for a long second trying to bite back tears that threatened to overcome her in the face of what she couldn't help but see as her husband's desertion.

"Everything okay?" Will spoke from close enough behind her so she knew he'd stood and taken a step toward her.

"Sure." She tried to keep a bitter edge from sharpening her voice. "Yeah, Neil says we'll talk to Kelsea. He's concerned. It's just that he has to go out of town. Totally not really a problem. I mean, it's been going on for a while, anyway. So we'll talk to Kelsea, tell her we're concerned. Tell her we'll be paying attention and that she's not allowed to date anyone, let alone a scumbag, motorcycle-driving, *sixteen-year-old* who'll steal her innocence when she's too young to know how to protect it."

She paused, breathing hard, seized with an irrational desire to throw her phone against the wall. She might have done it if Will hadn't turned her around to face him and pulled her into his arms. She stiffened at first, then relaxed into the temporary sanctuary he offered. How long they stood that way, she couldn't be sure, but eventually she realized if she didn't step away from him, she might never want to, and she pulled back. "Thanks."

"Anytime." He scanned her face. "Are you going to be okay?"

"Sure. Yeah." She drew in a deep breath. "Now, anyway." She gave him a half smile that he returned. "I'm sorry. I shouldn't have— I just get irritated when Neil's job comes first. And that seems to happen more and more often."

"You're worried about your daughter."

She wondered if he steered the conversation back to Kelsea because he was more at ease comforting her than defusing her anger with Neil. It made her like him even more to think so. "Yeah, I should go pick her up from cheerleading practice." She glanced at her watch, then back at Will. "I'm sorry I don't think I'll make it back this evening."

His lips curved a little. "Don't worry about it. You're supposed to be part-time, remember?"

She picked up her purse, stuffing the almost forgotten cell phone back inside. She hesitated, then turned. "I'll plan to be here early tomorrow."

He put his hands in his pockets, looking uncomfortable. "You don't have to do that."

"I want to." Her gaze met his. "Really."

For several seconds he remained silent, as if her offer to come in early was something totally different. Then he nodded. "Okay. I'll see you in the morning."

SHE KEPT her promise to come in early, arriving even before Will did. By the time she heard his step in the hall she'd composed herself, determined not to dump more of her anger and frustration with Neil on Will. Friendships could only stand so much of that, and she knew the person she should discuss marital problems with was her husband.

He paused in the door to her office. "Hey, how'd it go last night?"

"Fine." She smiled. "Kelsea's a sweetheart. She didn't think she was doing anything wrong, and I'm sure she wasn't, not really. She wants us to meet him and we're going to do that as soon as Neil gets back from his trip." She bit her lip, looking down at the desk. She couldn't quite rid herself of the feeling her husband was deserting her by leaving at a crucial moment in their daughter's development. Not to mention that he hadn't even gotten home until eight o'clock last night. By that point, Kelsea had confessed every-thing and Cady had struggled to explain her position about dating.

Will came in and sat across the desk from her. "Neil left this morning?"

She nodded, and he placed a hand on hers. When she raised her gaze to meet his, he looked so concerned she had to smile. "It's fine. It's what he does, you know? He works. He deals with life-changing stuff. Divorce, child custody and even worse. It's pretty poor of me to resent it when he's helping someone through what might be the worst part of their lives."

"You're not being selfish." As he spoke, he lifted her hand and sandwiched it between his. She closed her eyes, suddenly too aware of his touch to trust herself to look at him. His voice betrayed nothing when he spoke again. "Maybe you just need a break."

She forced herself to open her eyes and look directly at

him. "What do you mean?" Her reply sounded more cautious than she'd intended.

He grinned. "Nothing serious. I just have two tickets to the symphony. I was going to offer them to you and Neil, but since he's out of town, I wondered if you'd go with me."

"I love the symphony." She hesitated, looking down again. "I just feel sort of guilty."

"You have no reason to feel guilty." When she looked up at his slightly sharp tone, he shrugged and released her hand as he sat back. "I know things are difficult right now. For both of you. Neil's dedicated to his work, but maybe he doesn't realize how much it costs you to give up his company so often."

She gulped against sudden tears at Will's unexpected empathy. She blinked rapidly and smiled. "Cut it out, you're appealing to my self-pity instincts."

"I'm not trying to." He spoke seriously, his brow creased. "I'm worried about you, though. You seem lonely a lot recently."

"It's that self-pity thing." She straightened and picked up her coffee mug, then put it down, taking a deep breath. "I know Neil works hard because he has to…"

"…but it's tough when you want him around." Will smiled. "Seriously, why don't you come to the symphony with me?"

She hesitated. The thought appealed, but what would Neil think? And how would it look? She couldn't help remembering how easily Cam had spotted the attraction between her and Will. What if somebody else did?

His expression and tone were persuasive. "C'mon, let's do it. It's a win-win proposition. We both get to enjoy the symphony but I don't have to find a date and you don't have to miss out because Neil can't go. I can't think of any reason not to do it, can you?"

Only the one, but she couldn't exactly tell him that. Besides, it was silly. There was nothing going on between her and Will. She loved her husband and he respected that; it didn't matter if she and Neil were going through a rough patch. They'd always recovered before. With a smile, she nodded. "Okay. Let's do it."

10

*C*am's search for a car she could afford had been fruitless so far. And she needed one. Cady was great about taking Cam to doctor's appointments whenever needed, but Cam wanted the freedom to get out of the house when she wanted. And she couldn't keep calling Stan for rides, especially since she hadn't told him about the baby yet and even the looser fitting clothes she'd bought from Goodwill would soon be too tight to conceal her pregnancy.

But the cars she could afford weren't ones she wanted. She'd owned a 1987 hatchback in high school and she had no desire to go back to that. She sighed as she scanned the classifieds. She missed her motorcycle, but she had to admit it would be hard to go back to that at this point. Her growing belly threw her sense of balance off anyway, and it would only get worse over the next couple of months. She laid a hand on her stomach. It was still possible to conceal under a bulky sweater, but the weather was getting warmer. Soon a bulky sweater would look ridiculous.

"I should just tell him already, shouldn't I, Junior?" Her last doctor's appointment had included a detailed ultrasound and the tech had asked her if she wanted to know the baby's sex. She did, but it didn't seem right to find out before Stan did, so she said no.

She turned to the last page of cars for sale ads and paused, her eye caught by one ad. "1971 Chevy Camaro, $15,000 OBO. Must sell." Cam couldn't believe her eyes. She grabbed the phone and dialed the number listed. After setting up an appointment for twelve-thirty, she dialed Stan.

STAN PICKED her up at twelve fifteen. He looked confused. "What is this, anyway? You sold your Harley?"

"I've always wanted a classic Camaro." Cam didn't look at him, knowing she wasn't answering his question.

"Yeah, but your *Harley?* I figured you'd get rid of anything else than that." He shot her a look. "Are the 'burbs affecting you that much?"

"It's not a minivan. It's a '71 Camaro."

He snorted. "Hate to break it to you, babe, the seventies were not great years for the Camaro. Late sixties, maybe, but not seventies."

"Whatever, can you just drive?" She tried not to sound too impatient.

He shrugged and they fell silent. Finally he said, "I miss you."

"I know what you miss." She smirked, but he took her words as encouragement.

He grinned. "I miss that too. But I mostly just miss holding you at night, knowing you're there. You know?"

"I know." She said it without thinking, then shook her head. "I mean, I know what you're talking about."

"Good." He slid one hand over the truck seat to hers, folding his long fingers around hers, caressing. "But I think it's more than that."

"What do you mean?" She tried to keep her mind on what he was saying, but when he touched his lips to her palm, her own desire threatened to overcome her. She fought it down.

"I think you feel it too." He dropped her hand and glanced sideways at her before returning his attention to the road. "I don't know why you're shutting me out or how long you're planning to keep it up, but if you could just stop it, I'd appreciate it."

She took a deep breath and looked out the window, cradling the hand he'd kissed as if it held something precious. Scenery passed unseen and she wished she could move over on the seat, lean her head against his shoulder, and feel his arm around her. But the growing life in her belly remained between them. "I can't." Her words came out in a whisper, and since he didn't acknowledge them she decided he hadn't heard her. Which was probably best.

The Camaro was everything she'd hoped. Not the classic muscle car of the sixties, but still very traditional with the softer curves that had emerged in the seventies. Stan checked out the engine and pronounced it sound, then stood by his truck while she haggled with the owner, finally walking away with the keys and a grin.

Stan shook his head at her as she approached. "I'll never get you figured out, girl."

"Probably not." She jangled the keys. "Follow me back to New Bern and I'll give you a ride."

"Can't." He shook his head. "Gotta get back to work. I've already gone over my lunch hour. I had to text my boss and ask for an extra half hour of comp time."

"Oh. Sorry." She shrugged. "I'll make it up to you."

"Make it up to me now." He slipped one arm around her waist and pulled her close, bending his head to kiss her before she could pull away.

Panicked at the thought that he could probably feel her pregnant belly, even through her jacket and sweater, Cam quickly disengaged herself. "Later. I gotta drive my baby home." Wincing at her own choice of words, she blew him a kiss and left him gazing after her with a puzzled expression on his face.

"You're really going to the symphony with him?" Cam frowned. Something wasn't right. Here she was helping her sister get ready for a date with a man she was obviously halfway in love with while her husband was out of town. But then, could she say anything? Really? She was pregnant with the baby of the man she loved and she was afraid to tell him.

"I am." Cady twisted her hair up into a French knot.

"Don't do that."

"Don't do what?" Cady frowned at her sister in the mirror.

Cam heaved a resigned sigh and pushed her sister into a chair in front of the mirror. "You are constantly twisting your hair up into the same hairstyle. Be adventurous! Haven't you noticed we have beautiful hair?"

As she spoke, she picked up a curling iron and began adding waves and curls to her sister's hair. Cady dropped her hands to her sides and sat obediently. "I thought you didn't approve of me going out with Will?"

"I don't. I think you're inviting trouble and heartbreak for one or both of you. The man is obviously already crazy about you. And don't say he's not." She glared at her sister who had opened her mouth to protest, and Cady shut her mouth slowly. "You know it's true. And you know you're vulnerable and lonely and half in love with him yourself."

Cady sighed and shrugged. "Okay. I won't deny there's an attraction that neither one of us *would ever act on*."

Cam turned her sister around to face her, hands still busy as she pulled her hair up into a loose double bun with several long curls artfully pulled out. She applied the curling iron again, then stood back and gazed with satisfaction. "Okay." She nodded. "I'll accept the word attraction to describe the way you feel for each other. But you have to admit, this is pretty awesome."

She turned Cady around and watched as her eyes lit up at the sight of her reflection. "Oh, Cam. That's gorgeous. You should do this professionally."

"Well, if Will can keep his eyes off you tonight, I'll take back everything I've said about you two." Cam smiled.

"What does that mean, Aunt Cam?" Both women turned,

startled, as Kelsea came into the room. She looked at her mother. "You look gorgeous, Mom. But why would you have to worry about your boss keeping his eyes off you?" Her own eyes widened. "Are you being sexually harassed? You should report it!"

"No, no, honey, nothing like that." Cady shot her sister a murderous look and Cam felt acutely ashamed of herself for her indiscretion. "Your aunt was being silly, that's all. Mr. Hubbard would never sexually harass anyone, and please don't ever say he would. That could really hurt his reputation."

"Well, what did she mean, then?" Kelsea obviously wasn't going to let it go.

Cam decided to redeem herself. "Just that your mom looks hot. Don't you think? And it's a pity your dad isn't here to enjoy it. I'm sure your mom is safe, though."

Kelsea frowned, still trying to piece it all together, but the doorbell rang. "That's probably Sabrina coming to pick me up. Are you coming down to talk to her mom?"

"Sure." Cady picked up her wrap and purse and Cam followed mother and daughter down the stairs. Cady tossed her things onto a chair in the den as Kelsea grabbed her overnight bag and ran to the door. Cam watched as she flung the door open, kissed her mother good-bye and swung out the door past the woman standing there.

Cady laughed and shook her head. "Hi, Marie. I'd ask you in for coffee, but obviously my daughter's in a hurry."

"I'll say!" The other mother laughed. "Don't worry, I'm used to it. Sabrina's the same way." She paused, her eyes scanning Cady curiously. "You look fantastic. Hot date tonight?"

Cady smiled. "Just the symphony. My boss had some extra tickets."

"Well good for you! We all need a break sometimes. I thought Kelsea said Neil was out of town, though?" Cam wondered if her sister noticed the other woman's curious look.

"He is. I'm going with my boss. You guys know Will Hubbard, right?"

"Will? Oh yes." Marie looked a little startled, then shrugged. "Well, great. Have a good time." She grinned mischievously. "Not that you shouldn't. He's a good-looking guy."

Cady's smile froze a little. Cam wondered if she'd even have noticed if she didn't know her sister so well. She recovered quickly, however, nodding. "Thanks. Don't let the girls drive you nuts. I'll be by to pick Kelsea up around ten tomorrow."

"Sure. And if you need to sleep in, go for it." Marie waved her hand dismissively. "If it's a late night, you know."

Cam watched with amusement as Cady barely waited for the other woman to turn away before shutting the door, practically in her face. "Did she strike a nerve or something?"

"She's just a gossip, that's all." Cady glanced at her watch and wandered into the kitchen. "I can only take so much of her."

"I didn't hear any gossip." Cam sat on a barstool and watched her sister pour herself a glass of water. She touched her belly and thought about Stan. She hadn't spoken to him since buying the Camaro. She'd need to talk to him soon, though, or chances were he'd hear about her pregnancy from someone else.

"She wasn't gossiping *now*, but she was mining for it. I could almost see her trying to figure out how close Will and I are. She'll be telling everyone we're having an affair before you know it." Cady rolled her eyes and took a sip from her glass. "Geez, it's hot, isn't it? I thought it was April."

"It is. Don't you guys usually take a trip around this time of year?" Cam decided a change of subject would be in order.

"Camping." Cady sighed. "Yeah, I've been so busy I've barely even thought about it." She looked thoughtfully at a picture of Neil and baby Kelsea in a magnetic frame on the fridge. "I guess Neil hasn't thought about it either." Her voice sounded sad, then she straightened her shoulders and put her glass aside. "I better go. I'm meeting Will in half an hour and parking may be a challenge."

"He's not picking you up?" Cam frowned.

Cady gave her sister a significant look as she paused in the kitchen doorway. "It's not a date, Cam." The door swung shut behind her.

Cam stood for several seconds looking at the closed door, worrying about her sister for a reason she wasn't quite willing to name. If Cady's life fell apart, where did that leave her? Her hand drifted to her belly and her cell phone beeped. She glanced at the screen to find a text from Stan. "OK to come over?"

"Got house to myself. Come on." Cam stared at the reply she'd typed, took a deep breath and hit send. Just like that, she'd made a decision. Whatever might happen to her sister that night, Cam would make a stand for herself and her child. She touched her hand to her abdomen again, aware of a sense of wonder she'd never felt in either of her previous pregnancies. She wondered if it could come from her love for Stan. Could love alone transform an obligation into a miracle? And would Stan see it that way?

It might not have been a date, but the moment Cady saw Will standing on the sidewalk outside the Riverfront Convention Center, she realized how dangerous the territory she traipsed along was. He spoke to a young policeman she recognized vaguely as his brother Patrick, completely unaware that she had paused to admire him.

Will looked incredibly good in a suit and tie, his curly dark hair neatly trimmed and his face clean-shaven. She'd seen him dressed up before but had never been his date on any of those occasions. It made a difference now, especially when he turned from Patrick in mid-sentence and stopped speaking entirely for a second at the sight of her. In the back of Cady's mind, she thought maybe she should at least smile at Patrick, see if he'd noticed Will's sudden silence, but her eyes were caught by Will's, by the way he grasped his brother's arm in farewell and came toward her, a smile working its way from his mouth to his eyes.

"You look fantastic." He gave her a quick hug of greeting and a light kiss on the cheek. Nothing wrong with any of that. He'd done it before. Why did the warmth of his lips on her cheek linger this time?

"Thank Cam for that. She did my hair." She reached up to touch one of the curls in a self-conscious manner and his smile warmed her.

"I'll remember to do that." He took her arm and they started down the walk toward the convention center. Other well-dressed couples walked beside them, near them, all around them, everyone heading to the same place. Will had folded her arm into the crook of his and he didn't walk too fast for her heels, as if he could sense exactly how to make her most comfortable. She felt as if they had all the time in the world to stroll through the unseasonably warm and pleasant evening air to the double glass doors of the large brick building.

All too soon, however, he held the door for her, took her wrap and handed it to the coat-check girl. They turned into the hubbub of people milling about and Will left her side for a moment to work his way through the crowd around the ticket table. He returned in a moment with the tickets, and she replaced her hand in the crook of his arm without a moment's hesitation as he led her into the auditorium.

Members of the symphony were already in their seats on the stage, tuning, practicing, their soft strums and hums and blurts a pleasant background cacophony to the chatter rising from the concertgoers taking their seats. Will led her right to the front where two seats were marked "RESERVED HUBBARD'S". He shrugged when she glanced at him as she sat. He'd just started to take his own seat when his attention was claimed by an acquaintance and he chatted for a few minutes.

When he sat next to her, she leaned closer. "You weren't kidding. It really would have been a shame to waste seats like these."

He gave her a sheepish grin. "It's a weakness of mine. I like good seats at the symphony."

"To get seats like these you must have done a bit more than pay for them." She glanced sideways at him, a little wicked grin on her face. "You've never struck me as a patron of the arts."

"Really? What do I strike you as?" He pulled out his program, flipping idly through the pages.

"Hmm." She looked at the pages over his shoulder, hiding a smile. "Sort of an altruistic redneck."

"Really?" He turned to her again. "So all this time you've only been taking advantage of ignorant altruism, then? Just because I'm nice, you figure you can hit up my restaurant to aid every benefit you find yourself on the board of?" He shook his head. "You know, I hadn't thought about it, but it's a good thing I hired you."

"Why is that?" She tilted her head, grinning, noticing a half page ad for Hubbard's Bar & Grill in the program where he'd stopped flipping. She knew it wasn't on purpose, but she had to appreciate his timing.

"Because now you're working for me, you'll have less time to work on benefits. It'll probably end up saving me money."

She frowned, pretending to be put out. "You could just say no."

"Can't be done." He shook his head, his expression solemn. "I find it impossible to say no to you."

She laughed, even as she blushed. He'd sounded so sincere she couldn't help but wonder if there might not be some truth to his words. Before she could find a suitable reply, the emcee stepped out to thank the sponsors and then the concert began.

It was the spring concert and the familiar songs filled Cady's heart with joy, as they always did. At the same time, however, she felt sad and lonely. Why wasn't it Neil beside her so she could lean on his shoulder? She didn't realize a tear had rolled down her cheek until Will's hand closed over hers. She glanced at him to find his eyes full of concern. He held out a tissue and she smiled weakly, wiping away the tears. She wished she could whisper a thank you, but instead she tightened her fingers on his and hoped he wouldn't pull away.

She concentrated on regaining her composure until intermission. She excused herself quickly and went to the restroom while Will chatted with another friend. As she looked at herself in the mirror, she wondered again how she'd come to this point. Why had she accepted Will's invitation? Once upon a time if Neil hadn't been able to accompany her to the concert, she wouldn't have gone with another man, no matter how good a friend he was. So why give in to the loneliness now?

As she left the bathroom, she admitted to herself she knew the answer. She was tired of being lonely. Yes, she loved Neil, and she didn't want to hurt him, but his continued absences and the many nights she spent alone combined with his distraction when he was with her had begun to add up.

"Cady?" The gentle voice behind her made her wheel around, her face as hot and red as if she'd actually been caught in some debauchery. She searched her mind for a way to answer the obvious question of where Neil was tonight. Why hadn't she considered how to reply to an acquaintance when she ran into them?

It was Mrs. Carlisle, the principal from Kelsea's school. An older woman with a short stocky figure and salt-and-pepper hair, she looked so concerned, Cady searched for a way to reassure her.

"Mrs. Carlisle." She gave the other woman a quick hug. "It's so good to see you. And thank you for calling the other day."

"Of course." Mrs. Carlisle hugged her back. "I know your lovely daughter isn't here tonight. I caught her discussing plans for a slumber party with Sabrina this morning."

Cady laughed. "When you're a teenage girl you live for those slumber parties. I hope they weren't being disruptive."

"Not at all." Mrs. Carlisle smiled. "Reminded me of being a girl. In fact, I think that's why I do what I do." Her face became more serious. "I wondered if you'd had an opportunity to discuss matters with Kelsea?"

"We did." Cady was momentarily glad she'd done so, but her smugness faded at the frown on the other woman's face. "Why?"

"Nothing really." Mrs. Carlisle tried to look unconcerned. "I'm glad to know you're looking into it, though."

Cady would have questioned her more closely, but Will came up with two glasses of wine. "Mrs. Carlisle!" He handed one of the glasses to Cady and gave Mrs. Carlisle a one-armed hug before offering her the other glass. "It's nice to see you outside the restaurant."

"And you." She gave Will a puzzled look, shooting

another one toward Cady even as she smiled and shook her head at the offered glass. "Are you here together?"

"Cady took pity and agreed to come with me so I wouldn't have to go stag." Will sipped from his glass.

"I see." The older woman looked thoughtful, then nodded and smiled as if their being together made perfect sense. "Well, enjoy the rest of your evening then."

Cady watched her leave with a rush of misgiving that must have shown on her face. Will put a hand on her shoulder. "You okay?"

"I'm fine." She took a sip of the wine and abruptly wanted to get out of the throng of people. "Let's step outside."

The air had cooled from earlier, a crisp feeling taking the place of the softer mugginess. Cady took a deep breath and went to stand at the railing beside the river. Will joined her. "Are you sure you're all right? I get the feeling you're not enjoying this evening as much as I'd hoped you would."

She sighed. "Sorry, I know I'm not good company." She made a decision. "I should go home."

He nodded, reaching out to push a tendril of her hair back from her face. "You could. I can walk you to your car. Or we could find a quiet place to sit and you could tell me what's going on in your life."

Her heart lurched in her chest as his hand barely touched her face. "Yes." The word escaped her lips without her even meaning to speak.

"I'll be right back." Without waiting for her to change her mind, he took her wine glass and disappeared inside the building. She remained where she was, trying not to look conspicuous as the lights blinked and the milling crowd began to move inside.

"Cady?" She turned to find John Wright, one of the partners in Neil's law firm, and his wife looking at her curiously.

"Hi, John, Nancy. How are you?" Cady decided it wasn't time to feel guilty.

"We're fine, hon." Nancy gave her a hug. "What are you doing out here all by yourself? The concert's about to start back."

"Sure, walk with us," John said. "I didn't expect to see you tonight with Neil out of town."

"I, um, came with…" She gulped and felt the blush come back.

"She's with me, but I'm afraid she's not feeling well." Will emerged from the mass of people headed into the auditorium and put Cady's wrap around her shoulders.

Cady nodded. "John, Nancy, do you know Will Hubbard?"

"Of Hubbard's Bar & Grill?" John held out his hand. "Nice to meet you. I'd heard Cady had returned to the working force."

Nancy looked at her with concern. "You're not feeling well? Do you need a ride home?"

"I'll be fine." Cady shook her head. "You guys should get back inside. I don't want to make you late."

"Are you certain?" John honestly appeared anxious. "With Neil out of town, we need to make sure you're taken care of." He glanced at Will. "You'll make sure she gets home all right?"

"Of course." Will's voice wasn't simply polite. He sounded honestly surprised John would even question it. Cady fought against yet another blush as she hugged Nancy and said good-bye to John, thankful for the darkness that hid some of her discomfiture.

They stood together for several minutes while the crowd streamed back into the building. When all was quiet again, Will took her arm. "Do you want to go home?"

Now that they were alone, she knew the answer was no. "Can we walk for a bit?"

"Sure." He started walking and she fell into step with him as easily as she had earlier. They wandered aimlessly under the drawbridge that spanned the Trent River and into deserted Union Point Park. The moon was high and bright, lighting their way while leaving the shadows dark and secretive, but she couldn't imagine feeling frightened with him beside her.

When they reached the point of the park where the Trent and Neuse Rivers met, they paused, looking out over the moonlit waters. She wondered if he knew how guilty she felt even being with him like this. It didn't help to know Neil wouldn't even object to her being alone with Will. Neil would never suspect her of being capable of developing feelings for another man.

He interrupted her thoughts. "Why don't you tell me what's happening in your life to keep you so unhappy, Cadence?"

Although he'd used it before, the sound of her full name on his lips still made her catch her breath a little. Even Neil only called her Cadence once in a while, and usually at their most intimate moments. Sensing her sudden tension, he moved away. "What's wrong?"

"Nothing." She found it difficult to look at him. His

simple, innocent use of her name had called to mind the carefully guarded fantasies she used to keep herself company in the long, lonely evenings when Neil wasn't around. Will called her Cadence then, too, or rather whispered it in her ear…

"Cady?" He sounded worried. "Did I say something wrong?"

"No, no, it's nothing, really." She looked at him then, eager to dispel his worry. He wasn't to blame for her faults as a wife. "You just startled me when you said my name—my full name. Not many people use it."

"Oh." He looked thoughtful. "Yeah, I guess you might startle me if you suddenly called me William. Sorry about that. It's a lovely name, though, and it fits with the evening."

"I'm so sorry I made you leave the concert. You could still go back…"

"Don't be ridiculous." He shook his head, took her hand and went to sit on a bench, pulling her down next to him. "You're my friend and you've been sad for a while. I want to know what I can do."

"Oh, you know me. I'm just moody."

"Really?" He raised his eyebrows.

"Really. I mean, what do I have to be sad about? I have a great husband and daughter, wonderful job, no reason to worry or fret..."

He shook his head. "We're friends, remember. I want to help you and I can't if you won't let me."

She sighed. "I feel like such an idiot. There's nothing you can do. Really. It sucks knowing you've got nothing to complain about but still wanting to complain, you know? I mean, I know Neil has an important job, and he's dedicated and, hell, it's the reason I can live the way I do, but it still gets lonely not having him around. And I'm thrilled Kelsea is living the life of a healthy, happy teenage girl, but she's not around anymore, either. And it terrifies me at the same time that it thrills me. And that's it. That's what I have." She held her hands out, palms up and fingers splayed.

He placed his hands on top of hers. "That's not it." She dropped her eyes, wondering if what he thought to offer her was forbidden, but he continued. "You have friends, you have your job, you have beauty and intelligence. Life is full for you, and if your husband isn't there to enjoy it with you—" He broke off, looking away but still holding her hands. Then he gave her a crooked grin. "Well, that's his tough luck, isn't it?"

She dropped her gaze, feeling much as she had when he'd said her name "Cadence" as if he had every right to it. And did he? Had she given him that right? Sitting there on the bench holding his hands, she realized she had.

11

Stan smelled like aftershave and leather, and Cam wanted to bury her face in his neck. She held back, however, turning after he'd kissed her cheek lightly and leading him into the living room where she'd already uncapped a beer for him and a soda water for herself.

He frowned and she knew he'd picked up on her serious manner. "Are you okay?"

"I just have to talk to you." She sat and handed him his beer.

"Great, I have to talk to you, too." He took a sip of the beer and set it aside. "I've been thinking a lot about why you left." He held up a hand to silence her and she bit back a reply. "I think I know why now. You say you don't want what your sister has, but you've settled in here pretty well."

"That's not it." She shook her head. "You don't understand—"

"I know you have a complex relationship with your sister.

That's not the issue." He placed large warm hands over hers, bringing them to his lips and dropping to one knee in front of her. "The issue is I love you and I want you to have what you want. I thought we were happy the way we were, but obviously I was a fool. I should have known I couldn't have a woman like you with no commitment."

She shook her head again, panic starting. "No, wait—"

He laughed. "Can't you just let a guy propose in peace?" She felt something cool slip over her left third finger, and he smiled. "Camryn, I've never been so sure of asking any other question in my life; will you marry me?"

She stared at him, astonished by how off kilter her life was when the question she'd never expected to hear from the man she loved was the one thing she realized she'd always wanted him to say and the last thing she needed from him right then. Tears welled up in her eyes, and she looked down. "Shit. This sucks."

She felt him freeze. "Cam? What's going on?"

Cam sighed and looked up, realizing there was no help for it. "I'm pregnant."

"Pregnant?" His gaze dropped to her abdomen, then he reached for her, his hand on the gentle swell under her shirt. "Dear God." As if the realization had shocked him out of complacency, he rose, stepping backward at the same time, his hand falling to his side. He paced across the room and turned, his gaze fixing on her face. "*That's* why you left? You fucking left me because you found out you were pregnant? Jesus, Cam. How could you do that to me?"

"It's not you." She shot off the couch, taking a step toward him. "I'm so sorry, Stan. The whole thing scared me. I didn't know what to do with it, so I took off."

"You could have started by *telling* me!" He stared at her and she saw how much she'd hurt him. When she took another step toward him, he shook his head. "No. No, I can't listen to this. I can't even look at you."

She stood where he left her, listened to the front door slam behind him and only then did she realize she still wore the ring he'd put on her finger.

WILL WALKED Cady to her car shortly after ten o'clock. They'd lingered in the park until the concert was over, lulled into a sense of security by the darkness. Even now they stood beside her car for several long seconds before she sighed and turned to him. "I should get home."

She wanted to bite back the words as soon as she'd said them. They reeked of reluctance to resume her everyday life. Why hadn't she just said thank you and good night? She felt a surge of guilt followed by a wave of embarrassment.

He didn't seem to notice anything out of the ordinary and when he bent to kiss her good-night on the cheek, she pretended she didn't notice his hand on her waist and that her own fingers were reluctant to release his. And when she got home, she closed the door and leaned against it wondering how she could handle the feelings growing so rapidly inside her breast.

Cam appeared in the kitchen doorway holding a half-full

wineglass. "Hey, sis." Her voice sounded funny and Cady frowned, looking pointedly at the glass.

"What's that?"

"Relax." Cam walked back into the kitchen, the swinging door closing behind her.

A feeling like angry panic rose in Cady's throat like bile. She pushed into the kitchen and grabbed her sister's arm. "Cam! You can't drink when you're pregnant."

"Chill." Cam shook her off and took a sip from the glass. "Grape juice, see. I'm just pretending it's something stronger, and I won't say I didn't think about it, either."

Cady took a deep breath and a step back. "Sorry." She surveyed her sister's face and saw the traces of tears in the red around her eyes. No wonder she'd sounded strange. "Shit. What's wrong?"

"I told him." Cam set the glass on the counter. "He finally asks me to marry him and I have to tell him I lied to him." She laid her head on her arms, her voice muffled by her sleeves. "He didn't take it too well."

The sparkle on her sister's finger caught Cady's eye. "Oh my God. That doesn't look like he didn't take it well."

Cam propped her chin on her right arm and examined her left hand with a bleak expression. "Yeah, right? I mean, he comes over here and says all these sweet things to me and I tell him I'm pregnant. He couldn't even *look* at me, Cady. I think he totally forgot about the ring." She bit her lip and laughed, her voice a little harsh. "I can't seem to take it off, though."

"Try butter." When Cam glared at her, Cady giggled. "Sorry. I know what you mean. You can't take it off because it belongs there. And he didn't take it off you because he knows that too."

Her expression dubious, Cam nonetheless sounded hopeful. "Do you think so?"

"I'm sure of it." Cady gave her a hug.

Cam sighed and set the glass aside. "What about you? You're home early. How was your evening?"

"It was fine." Cady turned to the coffee maker, pulling a mug from the cupboard.

"Cadence!" Cam frowned at her, hands on her hips. "Seriously. Did you or didn't you?"

"Camryn!" Cady frowned back. "Of course not."

Cam shook her head. "Don't say 'of course' like that. There's no 'of course' to it. You can't tell me you haven't already done it in your fantasies, anyway."

Cady felt a hot blush on her cheeks. "Don't be ridiculous, please."

Cam shrugged and took the mug her sister offered her. "Well, just watch yourself. You're treading on dangerous territory and there's a point of no return, you know. Once you've cheated, there's no going back."

"Right." Cady nodded. "I'll be sure to keep that in mind if the situation presents itself." And even as she tried to look at her sister with scorn, she knew she half-hoped that moment would come.

NEIL RETURNED TWO DAYS LATER, tired and withdrawn. Cady had hoped he'd be in the same mood he'd been in after his earlier trip, but she could tell his efforts had not paid off and the disappointment of it had left him silent and filled with an anguish she couldn't touch.

Conversely, she felt irritable instead of loving and attentive as she knew she should be. She couldn't find it in herself to give him what she knew he needed when she felt she wasn't getting the same thing from him. She stabbed a green bean on her plate after Kelsea excused herself from the dinner table to do homework and Cam quietly followed. Why was this case so much more important to him, anyway? How come it mattered more than any other ever had? She wished she could ask, but Neil never discussed work with her. He'd already said more about this case than he usually did.

"What's up with Cam?" His voice sounded abrupt in the still room.

Cady looked up. "She told Stan about the baby. He didn't take it too well." She tried to sound casual. "She hasn't heard from him since."

"Did he go back to Georgia?" His words sounded callous.

"Jesus, Neil." She stared at him.

"I'm just trying to figure out where we stand. Is he gone for good or is he going to do the right thing?"

"What the hell's wrong with you?" She let the anger come, glad of the excuse to be angry with him.

He took a drink of his beer. Neil never had beer with dinner. Sometimes he'd have a glass of wine with her, but beer was usually before dinner, occasionally after when they sat on the deck together. He shook his head, looking at his plate. "She should put that baby up for adoption."

"My God, Neil, what's wrong with you? Cam loves that

baby. And she loves Stan. Her life isn't a cookie cutter perfect one, no, but you could have a little more sympathy for her."

"I can't help it." He shook his head. "I've seen too much happen to kids whose parents don't want them, aren't ready to take care of them. You have to admit your sister doesn't have the best track record where kids are concerned."

Cady held up her hands to stop him. "No. But she's ready for this one. She wants this baby. And Stanley…"

"What about him? Sure he's a good guy, but they're both a little old to start the parenting thing, aren't they? Poor guy's probably scared to death."

"For God's sake, Neil! Stop letting your job color your view of life. I know you see a lot of bad stuff, but…"

"You don't know!" He flung his arms wide. "You don't know anything about it, Cady! You've lived like this" he shook his arms at the ceiling "all your life with a family that loves you. You can't possibly understand what it does to a child to grow up without that."

She froze, her face set in anger. "Maybe not. But I'm starting to get a handle on what it's like to have a husband who can't separate his work frustrations from the rest of his life. And I really don't like it."

She stood, took her plate into the kitchen and dropped it into the sink. Then she grabbed her keys from the counter.

"Where are you going?"

She swung around. "To work. I left some stuff undone so I could come home and make dinner for you. And yes, it could wait until tomorrow, but I don't want to be with you right now."

She saw the hurt on his face, but she left without feeling sorry for him, telling herself he didn't deserve her sympathy.

CADY SLIPPED IN UNNOTICED, or so she thought, but she hadn't been there long when Will came to her door. "Hey, didn't think you'd be in tonight." He didn't add that the last time her husband came home from a trip he'd barely been able to keep his hands off her…so what had happened this time?

Because she didn't want to answer that question, even if she didn't think he'd actually ask it, Cady smiled and shrugged. "Neil was tired and went to bed right after dinner, but for some reason, I'm wired. I couldn't sit still so I thought I'd come in and put my energy to use."

Something in his expression made her think he wasn't buying her story. She looked away for a moment and heard him say, "Great, it's always good to see you. Let me know if you need anything."

She looked back up in time to catch his friendly wave as he disappeared back into the busy restaurant.

HE DIDN'T COME BACK. The hours slipped past and Cady knew everyone had left—staff and diners. She even thought Will might have gone too. Though she'd kept her cell phone beside her the whole time hoping Neil would call to apologize, it hadn't rung all night. Maybe he was angry or maybe he'd just gone to bed. The thought that their argument hadn't meant as much to him as it had to her dispelled the last of her anger with sadness, and she wondered if she'd really finally lost her husband. As she locked up the safe, she glanced at the little couch in her office and wondered if she could sleep on it. For the first time in her married life, she didn't want to go home.

She ventured into the quiet dining room. All was neat and clean, ready for the next day. Will never left it any other way. Cady glanced at her watch, surprised to note it was after midnight. Just as she realized that, the swinging door to the kitchen opened and Will stood there, silhouetted in fluorescent light.

"You still here?" He rubbed his hands together, not pausing to give her a chance to reply. "Excellent. Come here, I need your opinion about something."

He disappeared from the doorway and Cady hesitated. She knew following him would be dangerous for her marriage. And yet. Will was so uncomplicated, nothing like Neil. She loved being with him, and she knew he liked her. She thought of Neil's continued absences and neglect. Without allowing herself any further debate, she pushed through the door to the brightly lit kitchen.

He stirred something in a pot on the huge stove. As she entered, he glanced over his shoulder and nodded to a spot next to him. "Over here."

She shrugged and joined him. "What's up?"

"I've been working on the lasagna sauce. For the Lasagna Cook-off for the Riverkeeper's Foundation." He continued stirring.

She nodded. The Riverkeeper's Foundation had actually called her to ask if she'd consider organizing the Cook-off, but she had refused, knowing Will would want to compete. "That's over a month away, you know."

"Can't start too early." He turned, holding a spoon of red sauce. "Wait a second." He blew on the spoon to cool it, then, his gaze on her face, he offered her a taste of the lava-like liquid.

She hesitated only a second before accepting it, her eyes still locked with his as she let him tip the sauce into her mouth. She licked her lips with unfeigned appreciation. "Mmm. That's fantastic."

"Yeah, um, thanks." He seemed distracted, his gaze still on her mouth, but then he shook his head and refocused. "Sorry. I've been toying with it for a while. Tonight I think I finally hit it."

"I think so." She smiled. "Is there a secret ingredient?"

"Yeah." He gave her a half-smile. "Here, have another taste, see if you can figure it out." He dipped the spoon back in and she fought a purely motherly desire to tell him not to do that, it would spread germs. This time when he brought the sauce to her lips she couldn't deny the glimmer of awareness that hadn't been there before—in his eyes, and she suspected, hers also.

His lips parted a little as she accepted the spoonful of sauce. His expression excited her and she felt her breath shorten. "God." The single word startled them both and he blinked, stepping away from her. "Sorry, just, for a second there…" He shrugged. "Hell, you can't really blame me. I thought about what I'd like to do if you weren't a married woman." He turned away. "I'm sorry, Cady. I really am. I shouldn't be saying these things. I just can't seem to keep my mouth shut anymore."

The silence stretched between them. He stood with his arms braced against the counter, his head bowed. She bit her lip, still hesitating, but her feeling that she'd lost Neil a long time ago persisted and she longed to fill the hole in her spirit that had been empty for so long. She reached out, running her hand experimentally over his forearm. When he turned his head to look at her, she said, "It's nutmeg, isn't it?"

"Yeah." He turned completely, putting one arm around her waist as he pulled her toward him. "It's nutmeg." He bent his head and covered her lips with his and she pushed the guilt away, enjoying the sensation of being the whole focus of a man who wanted her.

As if the mutual desire they'd denied for too long had suddenly built to a breaking point, the kiss turned to unthinking, animalistic passion in moments. He pushed her back against the wall, his hands fumbling with her blouse and she reciprocated, forgetting everything as she undid the buttons of his double-breasted chef coat. He shrugged it off and came back to her immediately, his body warm against hers now, his lips burning hers, the only relief for it to open her mouth to his tongue… As if the contact of their bare skin had brought him to his senses, however, he paused, brushing her hair back from her face and looking at her with wonder. "Are you… God, I can't even ask. I want you so much, but I just…can't."

He stepped away, covering his mouth with one hand and breathing hard. Cady realized how close she'd come to doing something irrevocable and terror squeezed her heart. She searched quickly for her blouse and stopped when he held it out to her. She took it with a trembling hand. Even now, he was a gentleman.

"Will, I—"

He shook his head. "It's not your fault. I should've known better. I've been in love with you long enough to know it's not a good idea to be around you too much."

"You've been in love with me?" His revelation stunned her into forgetting her apologies. She'd known Will liked her, that he was attracted to her. She'd never imagined that he might be in love with her.

He snorted mirthless laughter. He'd pulled on the chef's coat but hadn't done the buttons. "I've been in love with you since the first benefit we put on together. Remember?" He stepped closer to her, his eyes on hers. "You were so beautiful that night. Neil was working so you were alone, and I was officially working since we catered the event, but all I had to do was keep an eye on the food, make sure the waiters made the rounds. We danced, do you remember?"

She did. He'd smiled and said something about how she should enjoy some of the delights of the evening herself and he'd put his arms around her and guided her onto the dance floor. He'd been very gallant and handsome and she'd told herself she needed to be sure to approach him again about catering another benefit. She nodded, dropping her gaze. "I remember."

He put a finger under her chin and tilted it up so she looked at him again. "You're half the reason I kept doing the damn things. Hell, maybe you're the whole reason. Half to keep seeing you on a regular basis and half so maybe I could build up some brownie points or whatever so I won't go to hell for coveting my neighbor's wife."

Her cheeks burned and she found it difficult to look at him. She recognized the value of what he offered and at least half of her wanted to accept it. She also felt guilty for not realizing earlier that he was in love with her. The pain must have shown on her face because he drew away. "Go home."

"Please Will, we should talk about this." She touched his arm as he turned away.

"Talk about it?" He looked down at her hand on his arm. "There's nothing to talk about. It doesn't matter how I feel about you or even really how you feel about me. You're married and I have no intention of destroying your family."

"You're not!" She tightened her grasp and he turned slowly. She lowered her voice, forcing herself to speak calmly. "You're not to blame, Will. Any damage that's been done to my marriage was done by me and Neil."

"Maybe." His voice sounded bitter, and he touched her face gently. "So how do I keep myself from taking advantage of it?"

She hesitated, wanting to tell him she wouldn't let him, but she knew she would.

At her continued silence, he turned away again, dropping his hands to his sides. "Go home, Cadence." His voice shook. "Your family needs you more than I do."

She nodded although he couldn't see her. And she fled because she wanted so badly to stay.

12

*I*n spite of her late return from the restaurant, Cody woke when she heard Neil getting ready for work the next morning. She lay in bed listening to him shower, then rustle quietly around in the bathroom. She considered getting up and making coffee, but the fear that he might spot some spark of guilt in her eye made her roll over and burrow deeper under the covers. Besides, she told herself, Neil never took time for coffee anymore. He was always in too much of a rush.

Lost in thought and remorse, Cady almost didn't realize Neil had paused beside the bed. She felt his warmth behind her, hoped he would kiss her good-bye. She didn't realize he was gone until the moment had lasted too long and she rolled over to find he'd left. Cady sighed and closed her eyes.

Without meaning to, her thoughts turned to Will. She remembered how good he'd felt against her, warm muscle and skin taut against hers. She banished the fear at the thought of what might have happened if he hadn't stopped them. Her heart pounded inside her chest as she imagined his hands removing her bra, her skirt and panties, exploring places only her husband had ever touched before, and her breath quickened.

The alarm startled her from her half-awake dream, and she shut it off, sitting up and forcing herself to face the reality of her life. She was a married woman with a teenage daughter who had never needed her attention more. She had to stop the fantasizing.

For all she knew, Will would probably fire her. He should. For that matter, she should save him the trouble and quit. The thought brought almost immediate relief from her pressing conscience. It was Friday—payday. She could close out the books on the week for him and leave.

Right after she made breakfast for her daughter.

CADY WAS EARLY TO WORK, and she headed straight to Will's office to tell him she would have to leave her job but found it empty. He was probably in the kitchen. She walked quickly across the restaurant, determined to get it over with.

Suzie looked up from dicing vegetables. "Good morning."

"Good morning." Cady looked around, surprised. "You're here early."

"Will called. He said there's a minor emergency at his family's vineyard. He'll be there today. He did leave you a message, though."

Fighting a sinking feeling in her chest at the thought of not seeing him, even to resign from her job, Cady raised her eyebrows and Suzie paused, looking at the ceiling as if trying to remember his exact words. "He said to tell you he's signed the payroll checks for everybody and they're waiting for you in the safe. He said to just fill in the correct amounts for everybody, and he's sorry you'll have to handwrite them instead of printing them through the computer."

"Oh." Cady shrugged as if it didn't matter. "Thanks, Suzie." She walked swiftly back to her office. She hoped Will had left her a note with the checks but when she swung the door of the safe open, she didn't find one. Disappointed, she picked up the checks he'd signed. Each one was addressed to the employee in his handwriting. She touched his signature and sighed. So much for quitting. At least for now. She decided to complete the payroll, close the books and leave him a note. He'd have the weekend to find somebody else. He'd understand. She knew he felt the same way. They couldn't continue working together after last night.

Her heart lighter, Cady turned to her work. She finished the payroll just as Jeanette poked her head in. "Hey, Cady, Clarice just called and wanted to know when they should stop by for the waiters' paychecks."

"Shit." Cady frowned and flipped through the checks Will had left. He'd forgotten the waiters from the previous weekend's wedding. The restaurant had catered the wedding but hired waiters from a temp agency. Will had been adamant about making sure the waiters were paid on time because he'd been so impressed by them and wanted to use the agency again. He'd even told her to remind him. Cady glanced at her calendar and saw the sticky note she'd put there for that purpose. Double shit. He'd forgotten and he wasn't there to remind.

She took a deep breath. "Tell Clarice I'll bring the checks by before five." She glanced at her watch and swallowed panic. "I've got to get in touch with Will. He forgot the waiters."

"Must be something pretty bad going on over at the vineyard." Jeanette paused in the doorway as Cady dug for her cell phone and located Will's number.

Cady looked up curiously. "Why would you say that?"

"Well, I only remember one other time when he wasn't around for payroll. When his dad died. It's just not like him not to be here."

Cady felt guiltily that she probably knew why Will wasn't around for payroll and it reinforced her determination to quit before the day was up. But she couldn't let Will's reputation be marred by something so simple to remedy. She dialed his number. The call went straight to voicemail and she cursed. "Hey, Will, listen, it's Cady and it's eleven o'clock. I need to talk to you as soon as possible about payroll. It's—it's really important." She bit off an apology, not wanting to risk leaving anything personal on his voicemail.

She finished entering the payroll into the computer and frowned at the stack of checks. Abruptly she stood, stuck the checks into the safe and grabbed the checkbook ledger. It would take an hour to get out to the vineyard and an hour to get back. If she was going to have to go and get back before five, she'd better go ahead.

Jeanette readily agreed to distribute the payroll checks and get them for anyone off duty who came in when Cady explained the situation. She also provided directions. "You sure you'll be okay?"

"Sure." Cady tried to convince herself it was true. The thought of facing Will again brought butterflies to her stomach. She tucked the directions into her purse and hoisted the ledger. "I'll be fine. Thanks."

THE HUBBARD FAMILY vineyard was a lovely place of 400 acres. Cady drove through the stone pillars at the entrance and followed the gravel drive through fields of thriving grapevines. She wondered vaguely where she could find Will. The place was enormous. Just as she was thinking this, however, she spotted a side road and glanced down it. Several trucks were parked there, and she saw men working on the grapevines. As good a place as any to try.

She saw him from a distance. He had on jeans and a sleeveless white t-shirt that stuck to him in some really good places. His gloved hands full of yellowed grapevines, he wore a grimmer expression than Cady had ever seen. She forgot her earlier nervousness, hopped out of the car and strode toward him, barely noticing the warmth of the early spring sun on her shoulders. "What's wrong? What happened?"

"Black rot." He showed no surprise at seeing her as he tossed the vines into a rapidly growing pile. "It's been so hot and wet this spring, it's hitting us early. We have to get rid of the infected vines before it spreads."

"Oh no." Cady turned to look across the vineyard. She knew the grapes grown by the Hubbards were used by several local wineries, and the money they brought in helped supplement the restaurant's income. What would this blight do to their crop? She turned back to find him talking to a young Mexican in fluent Spanish. When he finished and started back into the field, she followed him. "I didn't know you spoke Spanish."

"Gotta know a lot of stuff in the restaurant business." He paused and glanced at her. "What are you doing here, anyway?"

"Payroll." She wondered why he sounded so unwelcoming. Yes, their kiss had been a mistake, but she'd assumed they could continue to interact on a professional basis, at least until she quit. "You forgot to sign—"

"I signed everything this morning before I left." He looked suspicious and she tilted her chin, a little irritated by his attitude. As if she'd followed him out to bumfuck to tempt him into evil.

"You forgot the waiters at the wedding we catered last weekend. Remember the ones from the temp service?"

He regarded her for a long moment, then sighed. "Yeah, sorry. You didn't have to come all the way out here for that, though."

"Actually, I did. You specifically told me to make sure they got paid on time, and since I haven't been able to reach you on your cell to find out if you'd be back before five, I had no other choice but to throw my books into the car and come out here after you. Now, if you'll just sign the damn checks, I'll get out of your way."

She turned away, biting her lip and fighting to keep back the tears that seemed to always be so near the surface. She hadn't meant to show her anger, but the "damn" had slipped out unexpectedly. Determined not to reveal any more of her distress, she tossed her head and walked away, refusing to look back until she reached the car. Seeing him following, she reached for the door to take out the ledger. He stopped her with a hand on hers, and she looked up at him.

"Get in." He jerked his head at the car. She hesitated. He opened the driver door and she started to do as instructed but he shook his head and took the keys. "I'll drive."

The road was dirt and gravel and seemed to wind forever through the acres of vineyards. He rolled the windows down and she felt the warm breeze on her face with gratitude. She looked out over the flatness of the plain and wondered again about the advisability of growing grapes in such a place. She'd visited vineyards in California and even in the mountains of North Carolina where the soil was rich and the ground so hilly it was terraced to create the fields. What grape could possibly grow in such arid, sandy earth?

Will pulled the car to a stop and she looked at him in surprise. They were apparently in the middle of the vineyard with nothing but grapevines around them. "Sorry." He didn't sound at all apologetic. "We can't talk at the house. Too many people around."

"Your family?" She remembered Will had a brother and sister. No wonder he'd been so understanding about Cam and the baby. Will understood her yearning for a larger family. "I'm sorry. I shouldn't have come."

He stared out the windshield. "Not your fault. I'm not sure any of this mess is your fault, although I'd really like to have someone to blame it on."

"Will, I—"

He shook his head. "Don't. I knew what I was doing last night. God help me, I've wanted you as long as I've known you, I think. I was always able to tell myself you were taken. You were a married woman, off limits, don't even think about it. Then, last night…" His voice trailed off. "You know I actually convinced myself I wasn't hiring you just so I could see you every day. Within a week I knew I was wrong, though. I was coming into the restaurant earlier so I could spend a few minutes with you before getting ready for the lunch rush. And when you stayed later, so did I. Those minutes we had alone were the best of my day."

"Me, too." Her face grew hot with shame.

"Yeah, I know. Knowing that didn't really help, either." His dry voice made her smile a little, although she felt certain he hadn't intended to be funny. He made an impatient movement and got out of the car. She followed. He stood with bowed head and shoulders, hands on the hood of the car. "How the hell am I supposed to look your husband in the eye again?"

She shook her head. "I don't know. I don't honestly know how *I* will, either. I don't regret what we did, though."

He groaned and ran his hands through his hair, throwing her a despairing look. "Really? You don't regret betraying your husband and daughter? I do."

"That's not what I meant." She closed the door and came over to stand next to him. Hesitantly, she reached up to touch his shoulder. "I would die before I hurt Kelsea—and Neil, too, in spite of our problems."

They stood in silence, the sun warming them, and Cady

wondered if she could actually hear the vines twisting and growing, responding to the rhythm of the earth in the same mysterious way that all plants and animals did.

"I know." Will spread his hands in a gesture of helplessness. "I know that and I should fire you and never see you again, but the thought of not seeing you…" He shook his head. "What are we going to do?"

Cady thought of Neil and her inability to face him that morning. If she continued down the path she'd started, she knew it would only become more difficult. She'd be choosing something different from trying to mend the cracks in her marriage. She looked at her hand, still on Will's shoulder and wished she could lay her head there for a while. "I came here to quit. I had every intention of doing that. And then I saw you, and I remembered how *wanted* you made me feel last night. And I wondered how I could continue living as the wife of a man who really doesn't need me anymore."

"That can't be true." He shook his head, touching her face with gentle fingertips. "I can't believe anybody could have you and not let you know every single day how wonderful you are."

"I don't want to have an affair." She knew the words were truthful even as she spoke them. She saw the belief in his eyes.

So why did her hand spread out on his shoulder, spanning the bare skin, feeling the muscle beneath? Why did she tilt her head, feeling his hand trail over her face to the more delicate skin of her neck, her eyes half-closed in pleasure? She heard his breath coming faster, and felt his lips on hers, knowing she'd made the decision she hadn't thought she could.

He moved his hand behind her neck and pulled her closer,

lips caressing hers in a light kiss. He shifted them so she was between his body and the car, lifting her onto the hood, still kissing her. She gave herself up to the passion in his caresses, remembering the pleasure of the previous night with a sudden hot longing. But she doubted she would be satisfied with where they'd stopped before. This time she would want more.

She hadn't even noticed the rain until he drew away. It fell gently, cooling his sun-warmed skin under her touch. He shook his head as if coming out of a trance. "We've got to stop."

Drops of rain beaded on the skin of his shoulder. She had a sudden longing to taste them, but held back, reaching out to touch them instead, drawing her fingers over the tanned muscle and sinew of his body and watching the raindrops follow. He trembled at her touch and she hesitated, looking up at him. She felt like a child who had found something that fascinated her. Something forbidden. "I'm sorry. I know I shouldn't touch you."

"God." He stared at her. "I want you in so many ways. But if we're not going to hurt your family…"

She shuddered at the thought of Neil finding out, or worse, Kelsea. She closed her eyes, knowing she loved Neil in spite of everything. If everything was what it should be between them, she'd never have come this far with Will, attraction or not. How many years had she known Will, been friends with him, enjoyed being with him? Could she have been in love with him all along but unwilling to acknowledge it until now when her heart was breaking from Neil's seeming disregard for her feelings?

As if understanding her unspoken terror, Will took her

hand and kissed each finger tenderly. The rain fell harder around them, soaking them, blinding them. He held her hand for a moment. When he spoke, his voice sounded broken. "I don't know what this is for you, Cady, but I've been in love with you for so long, I can't imagine not being there for you. I don't promise to remain satisfied with what you can give me, but I'll try for as long as I can."

She nodded, knowing guiltily that she'd take what he could give her, even if she had nothing to give back.

HE TOOK her to the big white farmhouse to dry off. She hesitated outside, uncertain about meeting his family. Surely they could read the guilt on her face? She wouldn't be just the bookkeeper of his restaurant to them. She would be the married slut who was destroying Will's life, preventing him from finding a real relationship...

She hung back and Will looked over his shoulder. "They don't bite. Well, usually."

"Will, thanks, but I don't want to intrude. I should get back..."

"You're not going back soaked to the skin like that. Haven't you noticed how much cooler it is? And you've got plenty of time. It's not even two o'clock yet." He took her hand and pulled her with him. "Besides, it's lunch time."

"Lunch time?" Cady would have redoubled her efforts not to enter the house but by that point they were at the door. Will released her hand as he opened it, placing one hand on her shoulder to guide her in.

Two women sat at the kitchen table drinking coffee. The younger one looked up and gasped. "What the hell happened to you?"

"Will!" The older woman frowned, standing. "Have you been dragging people through the muddy vineyard again?"

"Sorry, Mom." Will took off his muddy boots at the door and Cady followed suit, slipping off her pumps. "Cady needed me to sign some checks and you know I can't resist giving a tour."

"Especially to a captive audience." The younger woman shook her head at him before smiling at Cady. "I'm Will's sister Lisa. C'mon, I'll get you some dry clothes. You can't drive all the way back to New Bern like that."

"I don't want to be any trouble." Cady hesitated on the threshold.

"Don't be ridiculous, honey." Will's mother smiled warmly at her. "It's the least we can do when my son's dragged you all over the muddy yard. Go on and I'll fix you a sandwich while you're changing. Will, before you change, can you check the porch gutter? I think it's clogged again."

"Sure, Mom." He gave his mother a quick kiss on the cheek and smiled encouragingly at Cady before disappearing out the back door into the rain.

Deciding graceful acceptance of their hospitality would be less suspicious than insistence on leaving, Cady followed Lisa upstairs. A white carpet runner softened the hardwood floors and family photos peppered the walls. Cady found it was very easy to imagine Will growing up in this house, tossing a football from the balcony, teasing his sister, celebrating Christmas and Thanksgiving with his family. She felt a pang of guilty envy. She'd always longed for large family celebrations, probably part of why she'd wanted more children.

Lisa interrupted her musings. "It's nice to finally meet you. Will's talked a lot about you. Patrick's even teased him about being in love with a married woman."

"Patrick?" Cady was glad she'd been guarding her emotions so closely or she was sure she would have revealed the dismay Lisa's casual remark produced in her.

"Our brother. You've probably seen him at the restaurant. He's a police officer in New Bern?"

"Of course. Sorry, I'm not thinking straight today."

"Well, I guess not!" Lisa snorted with laughter and continued to chatter like the friendly girl she was. "I can't believe Will making you come all the way out here."

"He just forgot." Cady shrugged as if it didn't matter much.

"Sure, he forgot. I guess he told you he forgot his cell phone too. And it's totally not like him to leave the restaurant for something so minor. That's certainly not what Mom meant for him to do. She called him last night to tell him what was going on and he seemed fine with it, then he shows up this morning to help. None of us know what's going on with that boy half the time." Lisa shook her head and her short blonde hair bounced.

Cady couldn't help smiling. Lisa was either younger than she'd originally thought or just had a young way of acting. Either way, she was adorable. They were both startled by the sound of running feet in the hall behind them. Turning, Cady saw Will barreling toward them. Lisa shrieked as he grabbed her in a bear hug. "You butthead! Now I'm all wet!"

"Serves you right for keeping my best employee waiting for her change of clothes while you listen to your head rattle!" Will grinned and waved before slamming the door to a bedroom down the hall.

Lisa giggled. "Well, he's a butthead, anyway, but when he's right, he's right. Sorry, I do tend to chatter."

Cady gave her a warm smile. "It's okay. I don't mind."

"Well, here's my room. I'll grab you some clothes and you can change in the bathroom down the hall if you don't mind. I guess I'll have to change now, too."

She found Cady a change of clothes and pointed her in the right direction. Cady quickly swapped her wet clothes for the dry ones and drew a comb through her tangled wet hair before starting back down the hall. As she passed Will's bedroom, the door opened and he reached out, catching her by the arm and pulling her inside.

"Shit." She gasped, too startled to formulate anything else to say.

He grinned like a boy. "Sorry, I couldn't resist. Might have something to do with being here in my old room." He bent his head and kissed her, lips tasting hers with a thoughtfulness that belied his claim of boyish lust.

When he drew away with obvious reluctance, she looked around at the typical teenage boy's room. "So you've had a lot of women in here, huh?"

"Actually, I've never had a woman in here before." He looked around, too. "Just girls. And not many of them. Mom was pretty on the ball about that kind of stuff."

At the mention of his mother, Cady stepped away. He grinned. "You scared of my mom? I told you she doesn't bite."

"I wouldn't bet on it." She frowned, remembering her own guilty thoughts about how she was keeping Will from forming a real relationship with a girl. A relationship that would blossom into a family. She had an anguished feeling that Will's mother would be very, very angry if she knew what Cady was doing with her son. "Let's go down and get this over with."

"So charming." Will rolled his eyes and held the door for her. Cady stepped outside, almost directly into Lisa who looked, startled, from one to the other. Will spoke as if they were continuing a conversation from inside the room. "So I guess you'll believe me next time."

"Oh geez, what's he talking about? What bit of sports trivia did he have to prove you wrong about?" Lisa groaned, covering her face and shaking her head.

"She insisted the Tar Heels had only won the national championship five times. I proved to her it was actually *six* times counting their undefeated season in 1924."

"They've only won the national tournament *five* time, Doofus. And nobody cares, anyway."

"Well, you don't, Dookie. We all know where your sympathies lie."

"You'd've gone to Duke if they'd been letting in doofuses, but Carolina was the only one with standards low enough for *you* to get in."

By this point, they'd arrived at the kitchen and Lisa ducked inside as Will pretended to try to tickle her. Cady couldn't help smiling at the good-natured sibling banter as she followed Will into the kitchen.

Will's mother waited for them at the table with two hot

cups of coffee and a large plate of sandwiches in front of her. Cady wondered when she'd had a chance to make so many sandwiches and who could possibly eat all of them. She glanced at her watch and did a double-take. It was nearly two thirty.

Will noticed her look and pulled out a chair for her. "You've got time." His voice was soothing. "Just chill for a minute. My mom's chicken salad is worth it."

Cady gave in and sat. As she ate the delicious chicken salad sandwiches and chatted with Will's mother and sister, the back door opened and Will's younger brother Patrick dressed in his police uniform stepped in. Patrick gave her a startled glance before looking at Will. "Hey."

"Hey, little brother." Will spoke easily and Patrick raised his eyebrows, then shrugged and took off his shoes, pushing them to the side with his toes.

"Hey." He kissed his mother's cheek and gave his sister a one-armed hug, looking at Will with a frown. "Didn't expect to see you here."

"Was the restaurant still standing when you left? Without me and Cady, I wouldn't be surprised if it exploded."

Patrick poured himself a cup of coffee. "No reports of explosions. It's been pretty quiet over there. But why are you here?" His eyes slid over to Cady and she felt the question directed at her and shifted uncomfortably. She wondered how much Patrick knew about her and Will. Maybe he just suspected something. Surely Will hadn't told him. But then again, maybe Will had the same relationship with his brother that she did with Cam. Maybe he didn't have to be told.

Will stood, taking his own and Cady's plates to the sink.

"Just came to check on the blight in the northwest vineyard. Mom's got it under control, though." He glanced at Cady. "We should get back to town."

Cady seized the opportunity, and after she'd thanked his mother and sister for their hospitality, Will walked her to her car, holding an umbrella over her. "Will you be all right?" He sounded anxious. "It's raining pretty hard. I could drive you back…"

"And do without your car?" She shook her head. "No, besides it would look suspicious." Of course, she felt like anything they did together had a taint of suspicion now. Including standing too long in the rain together.

She looked up at him as she reached for the car door. "I'll see you back in New Bern?"

He nodded. "I'll be about an hour behind you."

13

For the first time ever, Cady was thankful Neil was preoccupied at dinner. Her heart felt lighter than it had in a long time. She couldn't stop thinking about Will's lips and hands, and, surprisingly, his big home in the vineyard with a mother and two younger siblings. When she thought of how he'd chased Lisa down the hall or clapped Patrick on the back she couldn't help smiling at her meatloaf, and she was just as glad Neil couldn't take his eyes off his cell phone where it lay beside his plate.

At one point, however, just as something Kelsea said about Sabrina's mother reminded her of Will's mother and how dutifully he'd kissed her and gone out to check the gutter she'd been worried about, Cady looked up to find Cam regarding her with slightly raised eyebrows. She realized her sister had noticed something.

Cam waited only long enough for Neil to retire to the study. Then she shooed Kelsea up the stairs, promising to help

Cady with the dishes. "Unless of course, you're going back to the restaurant tonight?" She turned to Cady and nudged her, lowering her voice. "By the look of you, you're just itching for an excuse. Although maybe that's not the only thing you're itching for."

Cady frowned, disliking her sister's crass view of her relationship with Will. Telling herself it wasn't like she was having an affair, not really, she frowned at Cam. "I guess there's not much need in telling you you don't have any idea what you're talking about." She tossed her head.

"Not really. I know a bitch in heat when I see one." When Cady swung around angrily, Cam spread her hands. "Tell me I'm wrong. Please." Cady dropped her gaze and Cam sighed. "I didn't think you could. I'm sorry, Cady, I just think you're going to regret it."

"We're not having an affair." Cady glanced over her shoulder, keeping her voice low as her sister cleared the table.

"What would you call it?" When Cady didn't answer, Cam set the plates she'd brought into the kitchen aside and faced her. "Did you kiss him?"

"It wasn't like that." Cady bit her lip. "I mean, yes, but—"

"But nothing." Cam shook her head, turning on the water in the sink to rinse the dishes before handing them to Cady to put in the dishwasher. "Kissing's more intimate than sex, if it's done right. Did he do it right?"

Cady couldn't help a little smile at the memory, and that was evidently all her sister needed. She shook her head. "See? You know what I mean then. Cady, you're going to regret this."

"I know." Cady faced her sister and turned off the water

Cam had absently left running. She glanced at the stairs her daughter had gone up a few moments before and the closed study door. She could hear Neil's voice on the other side. Either he'd gotten the call he was waiting for or he'd grown too impatient to wait any longer. She sighed and looked back at Cam. "I already do. Not just for me or my family, either. For Will. He should have a family, somebody he could love."

"So why the hell are you doing this?" Cam grabbed her sister's arms and shook her. "Why are you taking this chance with your life and his?"

"I love him." The words felt right in her mouth, even while she knew how wrong it was to say them.

Cam stared at her, then sank into a seat at the kitchen table. She stared at nothing while Cady finished the dishes and made two cups of coffee. When Cady sat across from her, Cam accepted the coffee automatically.

"Are you okay?" Cady peered at her sister anxiously. Cam looked so pale in the dim light.

"I just can't believe this is happening." Cam shook her head. "You're really in love with him?"

Cady nodded. She took a sip of her coffee. "And you don't have to tell me how wrong it is. We both know. We didn't mean to—it just happened." She reached over and touched the glittering diamond on her sister's hand. "Like that, actually."

Cam pulled her hand back, covering the ring as if it were too precious to be subjected to the current conversation. "That has nothing to do with it. What are you going to do?"

"What do you mean?" Cady raised her eyebrows, leaning back in her chair.

"You know damn well what I mean." Cam made an impatient movement as if to push something out of her way. "Are you going to have sex with him?"

Cady winced. "Geez, Cam. Way to couch those words in gentle expressions."

"It's sex even if you call it making love. It's giving something intimate to someone besides your husband." Cam's expression challenged her sister. "And you didn't answer the question."

"It's not about that." Cady shifted uncomfortably in her chair. She thought of Will's gentle touch and her heart pounded but when she remembered the tenderness he'd shown his family, something inside her shattered, and she felt a longing to be part of that life, even a peripheral and unacknowledged part.

"Cady?" Cam looked anxious. She frowned and put her hand across the table, covering Cady's in a protective way. "What is it about, hon?"

Cady fought for words. She wanted to make Cam understand, even though she knew forgiveness was too much to ask for now. "It's his spirit. He's so gentle and loving. I saw it today with his family. I knew it before but somehow seeing him there, cleaning the gutters for his mother, teasing his sister…I don't know." She blushed and looked away. "I can't walk away from him, Cam. I know I should but it's like I just don't know how."

Cam sighed and squeezed her sister's hand, and Cady squeezed back, hoping that would be enough.

It wasn't enough, though. Cam worried about her sister long after she'd gone to bed. Cady had an inborn need to take care of people, which was part of her desire for a large family. With only one daughter to worry about and a husband who'd grown distant, she'd found someone else with the same altruistic desires to fill the void in her heart.

Cam lay on her back looking at the ceiling. Of course, the breach with their mother didn't help. Cam knew that was her fault. Cady had stood up for her, and her mother had never forgiven either of them, although she'd stayed in contact with Cady at least. Cam groaned, remembering the summer she'd left her family home for the last time.

Susan Taylor always wanted the life her husband Edgar, a C.P.A., gave her. A part-time nurse and full-time mother of beautiful twin daughters, Susan's life was full and happy and everything it was supposed to be. They belonged to the country club, knew the right people, went to the best parties in town and were generally known as a good family. Susan liked her life and she loved her family.

Everything was perfect until the girls hit puberty. Cady remained as quiet and bookish as always but Cam discovered boys and her effect on them at an early age. To make it worse, she persistently ignored her mother's best efforts to calm her down, rebelling at any constraints Susan tried to place on her. When she had sex with her boyfriend in the backseat of his Camaro at the tender age of sixteen, she went home and asked her mother for birth control. When Susan asked her why, Cam told her everything, knowing how much it would hurt her. Susan slapped her, sent her to her room and ignored her request.

The day Cam came home from the free clinic with a handful of brochures outlining different plans of action to deal with teen pregnancy, Susan had refused to talk about anything. Cam still remembered the cold look in her mother's eyes when she'd said the two words that froze her young heart in her chest. "Get out."

And she'd gone. Cady had tried to intervene, begging her mother to relent, but Cam had never hesitated. When Wade, who eventually became her first ex-husband, drove up in his Camaro, Cam threw her bags in the trunk and never looked back.

"UNTIL DAD DIED." Cam spoke the words to the dark ceiling. By that point, she hadn't spoken to her mother in more than fifteen years and the damage was done. Susan had never met her granddaughters, although Edgar and Cady had made the two fruitless excursions to sit by the hospital bed and ooh-and-aah over the two children Cam, lost in a battle with drugs and alcohol, had never made the effort to care about.

Now, three ex-husbands later, Cam knew she was partly to blame for the fact that her mother lived a lonely life in her old hometown with her daughters more or less estranged from her. And Cady, the only person still alive who had never wavered in her love of Cam, stood on the brink of losing everything that could ever really make her happy.

Cam rolled over in bed again, closing her eyes and feeling the weight of guilt settle on her. She'd left home and stayed away from Cady for so many years to avoid that guilt. Without Cady around to remind her, she had escaped the knowledge that she'd killed something in their family.

But it wasn't something in their family that she'd killed. It was the family itself. Even though her mother had told her to get out, Cam suspected Cady and her father could have brought her around. She knew Susan had loved her, maybe still did. Somewhere in Susan a mother's heart still beat, and Cam had never appreciated that until now when she was so aware of the heartbeat of her own child.

She shifted again and kicked off the sheets, sitting up and looking at the clock. It was late. She wondered where Jeanne, her eldest daughter, was. Jeanne had started college two years before. Was she embroiled in exams right now? Did she have a boyfriend? Cam realized she didn't even know what her daughter's major was. She thought about calling Wade. Over the years she'd touched base with him from time to time, but he'd been clear that he didn't want her around when she was off the wagon.

"It's too late." Cam knew it wasn't just the hour she referred to. She paced over to the window and looked out. Selena, her sixteen-year-old daughter, was asleep, she hoped. What did she dream about?

Cam groaned and put her head in her hands. She looked at the cell phone in her hand and she knew there was only one person she could call. She'd dialed Stan's number before she thought she'd given it any real thought. He answered on the second ring. "Hey." She closed her eyes, so thankful to hear his voice the relief was like a cool shower of water on a hot day. "Can we talk?"

He picked her up at the end of the drive half an hour later.

CAM CAME DOWNSTAIRS EARLY the next morning, Saturday. Cady stood by the back window, her cell phone held to her ear and a gentle smile on her lips. Cam winced and cleared her throat, intentionally rattling coffee cups in the cabinet. Cady turned, said something quietly into the phone and hung up. "Good morning."

"Morning." Cam tried to look uninterested.

Cady sighed. "Don't ask and I won't tell."

"Fine." Cam gave her sister a weak smile. "Where's Neil? And Kelsea?"

"Asleep. Maybe not for long if you keep making such a racket." Cady raised her eyebrows and sat on one of the stools next to a half-full cup, motioning for Cam to do the same.

"Good." Cam accepted the invitation, easing herself off her feet with a sigh of relief. She was amazed by how cumbersome her body felt so suddenly. It was as if, at seven months, her baby had decided to take over her body. "How is it that we never remember how much of a pain pregnancy is?"

Cady smiled. "Could have something to do with survival instinct. Subconsciously we know if we remember we'll never do it again and the species will die off."

"Probably." Cam grasped her cup in her hands, enjoying its warmth. Outside the sun looked promising, but she thought it might be deceptive. The past few days had been cooler and after the unseasonable warm temperatures of the previous months, she'd been constantly chilly. She faced Cady. "I'm moving out."

The words produced an unexpected reaction in Cady. She stared and shook her head, her mouth in a silent "o". "No! You can't do that. Don't do that to me. Not because—" she broke off, looking over her shoulder "—not because of Will."

"No!" Cam shook her head and put her hand on her sister's arm. "No, it's not that. I swear. I just started thinking last night and I couldn't sleep, so I called Stan. He picked me up and we went to his place and talked. For hours. I just got back a couple of hours ago, actually, and I've been packing ever since. He's picking me up around lunchtime."

"You worked everything out?" Cady's expression was a mixture of envy and disbelief. "In one night?"

"Not everything, no. Enough, though. I don't want to live without him and I definitely don't want to have this baby without him. And he wants to be there for us, so I'm just going to have to learn to let him." Cam shrugged and looked at her coffee, then back up at her sister. "He makes me stronger, you know?"

Cady's expression softened and she nodded. "Yeah, I know."

Cam wondered who Cady felt made her stronger. Her husband or Will? She shook off the dread certainty of the answer and nodded. "Yeah. So I called Wade earlier."

"You did?" Cady looked startled.

"Yeah. I talked to him about Jeanne. He gave me her number. I want to see her." Cam looked at her sister appealingly.

"I know she probably hates me. Or worse, maybe she doesn't feel anything at all about me. I don't know. I don't know what kind of part in her life I can have now, but I'm going to try."

"Oh Cam." Cady's eyes filled with tears. "That's great."

"And Selena too. They moved a few years back and I lost the address. I have to track Frank down, but I've got some people I can call. I'll find them."

"I'll help you." Cady squeezed her sister's hand. "We'll find them."

Cam nodded gratefully. "Thanks." She hesitated, looking away. The last thing she had to say was the hardest, probably for both of them. "And Mom."

Cady froze. "What?" She pulled her hand slowly away, as if suddenly aware her sister's flesh had turned poisonous.

"We should call her. Maybe together. Maybe we should just go see her, I don't know."

"Go see her?"

"Sure." Cam tried to make it sound reasonable but from the look on Cady's face she might as well have proposed a trip to the North Pole. Cam sighed. "Look, I never felt right about the way you and Mom were after I left. I know how much it hurt you. I want to try to make it right."

Cady stood, but she gripped the bar with both hands as if trying to hold onto something. "Why?" Her voice came out as a whisper and she cleared her throat. "Why now?"

Cam bit her lip, trying to come up with an answer. "Because you need a mother. And so do I, to be honest."

Cady nodded. Then she came around the bar and threw her arms around her sister's neck with a muffled sob. Cam hugged her back and hoped she wasn't making one of her many mistakes where her mother was concerned.

EVERYTHING WAS SETTLED SHORTLY after Neil got up. He thought it was a good idea and he assured Cady he and Kelsea could manage alone for a few days. At least, that was what he told her, and she tried to believe he wasn't just happy to have her out of his hair for a while. As they discussed the trip over breakfast, Cady realized with a pang that it would mean taking time off from the restaurant and not seeing Will.

"I should tell Will." She spoke without thought and looked up to see every head had swiveled toward her. "To let him know I'll need to be away. He might need to get someone to fill in. I'll go in this afternoon to talk to him. After the lunch hour's over."

"Sure." Neil nodded. "Maybe Kelsea and I can come up and meet you for dinner after?"

"Not there." Cady barely concealed her horror at the thought of eating dinner with her family in Will's restaurant.

"I thought you liked Hubbard's?" Neil raised his eyebrows.

Cady shot her sister a look, but Cam seemed engrossed in her omelet. "I just have it so often. Something different would be good."

"I guess that's a drawback to working in the restaurant business." Neil glanced at Cam. "Would you and Stan like to join us?"

Cam looked uncertainly at Cady then shrugged. "I'll ask

him." She drew in a breath. "I guess I should call Mom, huh?" They'd decided it would be best if Cam called. If that didn't work, Cady would take over.

Silently, Cady handed her the phone and she and Neil sat frozen, eyes on Cam's face as she dialed the number and waited, perched on the edge of her chair, her head bowed, one hand holding the phone and half shielding her face at the same time.

"Hey, Mom. …. No, it's Cam, actually. … I'm, um, staying with Cady right now. …" Cady saw her sister take a deep breath as if preparing for the worst. "Listen, we were talking about coming up to see you. … Next week? Maybe Monday? We'd leave early and be there by early afternoon. We'll get a motel room nearby and spend the night. If that works for you… You are? Okay. Yeah. Bye." She hung up and looked at Cady. "She says she'll be home."

Cady nodded and took the phone from her sister. She wondered if Cam had even noticed the tears pouring down her face.

CADY WENT to the restaurant at three o'clock, hoping to provide herself a little time to see Will. The restaurant would be nearly empty, even on a Saturday at that hour, and the staff would be busy preparing for the early birds who would start arriving at four-thirty. Will wasn't in his office, so she poked her head into the kitchen to find him joking with the kitchen staff. He turned at her entrance, his grin broadening, and she knew with a rush of both triumph and panic that she was responsible for his good mood.

"Hey, beautiful. Didn't expect to see you today." He sobered at her expression. "Everything okay?"

"Sure, everything's fine. I just—can we talk for a minute?" How many times had he called her "beautiful" or some other pet name? Why did it sound so much more intimate now just because she knew he really meant it?

"Of course." Now he really looked concerned. He took her hand and led her into his office, shutting the door before turning back to her with the expression of a man who dreaded the answer to his question. "What's up?"

"I have to go out of town so I need some time off."

"Is that it?" He stared at her and when she nodded, he laughed and put his arm around her waist, pulling her against him and kissing her until her heart pounded and her breath came faster. "God, you scared me. I thought you were going to quit."

She bit her lip and laid her head against his chest. She knew she *should* quit, but the thought of intentionally never seeing Will again hurt too much. Hearing him voice his fear that she'd leave him didn't help her guilt, however. She clung to him, breathing in his scent as if she could somehow take enough of him with her to keep her satisfied while they were apart. It did nothing but make her aware of how much she wanted to continue kissing him. "Damn it, Will." She leaned back and looked at him, incapable of even attempting to disguise her hunger.

"I know." He touched her lips with his fingertips, then bent and kissed her again, hands on her hips pulling her more firmly against him.

After several minutes, she drew away, wondering how much time had passed since she'd arrived. "We've got to stop. Neil's going to pick me up in about an hour."

He moved away with a soft curse, sinking down behind his desk, picking up a coffee cup and making a face at its cold contents. He put the cup down and focused on her. "I'd say I'm sorry but I'm not."

The glint of humor in his eye made her smile, albeit weakly as she thought of Neil, possibly on his way there. And yet his kiss had summoned a wanton desire that threatened to break down any resistance she still could manage.

"Where are you going?"

The question reminded her why she had come to the restaurant. "To see my mother."

"Your mother?" Will frowned a little. "I thought you didn't get along with your mother."

"Cam suggested it. She's trying to mend fences or something. I don't know. But she called Mom and asked if we could come. And Mom said yes." Cady didn't try to hide her confusion. "I've seen her, what? Four times in the past five years, and once was at Dad's funeral. And Cam hasn't seen her *at all* since she was eighteen years old except for that one time at Dad's funeral. And they didn't speak then. So this morning Cam says, out of the blue, hey, let's go see Mom and she calls and Mom's all in favor of it." She realized she'd been pacing the little office, waving her arms wildly. She dropped them by her sides and turned. "So that's it. That's why I have to go."

He nodded. "Yeah, I can see that."

She sighed and dropped into the chair. "I don't even know what to expect. Mom and Cam might make up or they might have a huge fight as soon as we get there. Or we might go to lunch and realize we have nothing to say to each other. It's a toss up. And I don't even know what to hope for, either."

They sat for a while in the silence. Cady knew he had no idea what to say. What was there *to* say? She was afraid of going to visit the woman who'd given birth to her and finding out she meant nothing to her. And maybe she was even more frightened of finding that she'd broken her mother's heart all those years before.

A light knock on the door made her jump and she threw a terrified look at Will, as if they'd been caught doing more than sitting in thoughtful silence in Will's office. He made a calming motion with one hand, as if he were smoothing sand. "Come in."

Cady turned, expecting to see her husband. She'd already schooled her features into a welcoming smile when the door opened to reveal Cam. "Hey." Her gaze darted between Cady and Will. "Thought I'd give you guys a heads up that we're here."

Cady felt a rush of gratitude for her sister running interference. "Where's Neil?"

"At the bar. Talking to another lawyer of some sort. Stan's with him. And Kelsea."

"I should go." Cady turned to Will, who stood with her. "Thank you."

He came around the desk and took her hand. "It's okay." As Cam turned to the door, Will raised her fingers to his lips, kissing the backs of her knuckles with a tenderness that barely concealed his desire. "Call me when you get back. Or before." His voice was low, and he released her hand as Cam opened the door and turned.

"I will." Cady let Cam lead her into the restaurant where her husband, daughter and sister's fiancé waited.

14

*C*ady picked Cam up outside Stan's apartment building on Monday morning. She'd just hung up on a cell phone call with Will, and the warmth of his voice had almost made up for the distracted, absent good-bye from Neil that morning. However, as she watched the tenderness Stan used to help Cam into the little Volkswagen Beetle, she felt a lump form in her throat.

The sisters drove away in silence, but Cam soon broke it. "Everything okay at home?"

"Sure. They'll be fine without me. They're practically fine without me, even when I'm there, anyway." Cady tried to keep the bitterness out of her voice, but she knew from her sister's sharp look that she hadn't managed it completely.

"What about Kelsea? And the boy she's been dating?"

"They're not dating. And we're having him over for dinner on Friday. I talked to Kelsea about it and she says she understands our feelings that she's too young to date him."

"Are you sure she really does? She's a teenager, after all." Cam honestly sounded worried, but that just irritated Cady.

"For God's sake, Cam, she's not you, okay? My daughter isn't going to fool around and get pregnant before she even finishes high school."

Cam didn't reply and Cady felt immediate guilt. "I'm sorry, okay? It just sort of sucks that I'm leaving my family and the only person I feel like is really going to miss me is—"

"Will."

Cady shot her sister a look, surprised by her nonjudgmental tone. "Yeah." Tears threatened and she cleared her throat. "The only person who's going to miss me is the man I want to have an affair with. If I wanted to have an affair, which I don't but maybe I am, anyway." Her fingers tightened on the steering wheel.

Cam stayed silent for several minutes. Finally she said, "I'm sorry. I know I should just keep my mouth shut, but I can't because I'm scared for you. Are you sure you're in love with Will?"

Cady glanced at an old family cemetery plot situated beside the highway, surrounded by a cornfield. A large oak tree spread its limbs protectively over the gravestones, their family struggles forgotten in a final unity. She thought about Will's voice on the phone that morning, about how she could hardly wait to get to the car and call him, just to talk to him for the few minutes it took to drive to Cam's. She remembered the gentle timber of his voice as he'd told her to drive carefully and call him when she got a chance. Neil hadn't even said that much. Just a quick kiss on the cheek and a distracted, "Have a good trip."

"I don't know." Her heart thudded so loudly she wasn't sure if her sister could hear her or not. "I think so. I mean, I'm pretty sure."

Silence fell for a while. Finally Cam said, "How about Neil? Do you love him?"

Cady realized she'd never thought to ask herself this question. It was like asking someone if they needed oxygen to breathe. Her heart ached at the thought of losing Neil. He'd been her best friend and romantic partner for so long, she couldn't imagine not having him in her life. Even now while she struggled to figure out how their lives had diverged so much, she knew she didn't want to live without him.

And she didn't want to live without Will either.

"Cady?" Cam prodded her sister. "Do you love Neil?"

"I do." Cady heaved a long breath. "I always have and I'll never stop. And for the life of me, I can't figure out how I fell in love with Will, too." After another silence, she added, "Maybe it's just loneliness. I don't know."

"Maybe." Cam picked her lip nervously. "But Cady, you know you can't keep going this way, don't you? You're going to have to make a decision at some point. Or it may be made for you."

Cady made an impatient movement. "Can we not talk about this? I'm not having an affair."

"Okay." Cam nodded, her head bobbing up and down in Cady's peripheral vision. "It's not an affair. You're just in love with another man who is also in love with you. And don't tell me you weren't making out the other day before I walked into his office. You're just lucky it was me that came in there and not Neil."

Cady shrugged, turning on the radio and tuning her sister out.

CAM DROVE the last couple of hours and nudged Cady who was pretending to be asleep as they entered Brevard, the tiny North Carolina mountain town they'd grown up in. Cady sat up and looked around. "Oh my God."

"I know." Cam nodded. "I can't decide if it's way too familiar or way too different. Sort of both."

Cady surveyed the fancy new lampposts, the revamped storefronts and the rustic sculptures that hadn't been there the last time she'd been in town. She winced as she realized she hadn't been back to visit her own mother in five years. Had the rift between Cam and her mother been the real reason Cady had stayed away?

"Maybe it was just pride."

"What?"

Cady turned her head. "Pardon?"

"You said something about pride?" Cam arched an eyebrow.

"Oh." Cady hadn't realized she'd spoken out loud. "Just thinking out loud. I haven't been back here since Dad died. I was wondering if I was just too proud to come back here."

"You mean you had lawyer's wife syndrome?" Cam glanced sideways with a grin. "Maybe, but if you did, what's my excuse? I stopped being mad at Mom a long time ago, and I even knew it. I just couldn't bring myself to say it."

They pulled up in front of the assisted living facility their mother had moved into shortly after their father's death. Cady looked up at it. "It looks like an apartment building."

"It's not like she's an invalid. She's still pretty perky, right?"

The sisters looked at each other and began to giggle. Cam took Cady's hand and squeezed it. "Let's go see."

Susan opened the door to their knock and all three women stood dumb for several seconds. Susan broke the ice with a slightly acerbic "Long time, no see" and her daughters exchanged glances.

"C'mon, Mom, let us in. We wiped our feet." Cam held up one foot to demonstrate and Susan shook her head.

"Always the wit. Fine. You might as well come in."

"Might as well." Cady rolled her eyes to the ceiling. "We just drove seven hundred miles and it wasn't to check out the new yard décor at the courthouse."

"Those are horrible, aren't they? A statue of a moose? When was the last time we had moose around here?"

"They were probably plentiful in the seventeenth century." Cam sank onto the beige couch. "Glad you got rid of the plastic covers, Mom."

"Haven't had any teenage girls around spilling soda—or worse—on the cushions in a while." Susan raised her eyebrows and looked at Cady. "How is your family, Cady?"

Caught off guard, Cady stumbled. "Fine. I mean, Kelsea's good. Doing great in school."

"Um-hmm. And Neil?" Susan's gaze had sharpened.

"He's good. Working a lot." Cady didn't want to talk about Neil, so she glanced at Cam for help. Finding none, she blurted out, "Cam's pregnant."

Cam straightened, a startled and angry look on her face. "What the hell, Cady?"

"Like she's not going to notice." Cady gestured at Cam's swelling middle.

Cam glared. "Just because you don't want to talk about your husband when your lover is on your mind—"

"You—" Cady was so caught up in figuring out which expletive she wanted to call her sister she didn't notice her mother's amused look.

"Girls, please. You can both have my attention, I promise." Susan held out her hands to her daughters. "Just one at a time, please."

The sisters turned their heads at the same time, staring at their mother. Cady opened her mouth to say something and closed it again. Cam just stared as if dumbfounded.

Susan continued talking as if it were a perfectly normal conversation. "You've been like this since you were babies, you know. Always trying to one up the other one to get my attention first. I'd start feeding one of you and the other would need to be changed. And then I'd get one of you to sleep and the other one would start crying. Right there in bed with the first one, just wailing away until I'd pick you up and sing to you." Susan's voice trailed off and for a moment she looked like she had lost herself in the memory. When she recovered, her eyes sparkled with tears and she squeezed her daughters' hands. "I'm so sorry I forgot how to sing."

Cady sat frozen for a moment, then put her other hand over her mother's. She noticed Cam did the same, although she dropped it a few seconds later. Cam broke the silence, her voice foggy, as if she'd been underwater for a while. "Okay. But really. Who's hungry?"

Cady laughed, wiping her eyes, and Susan squeezed her hand and smiled at Cam. "I'm just so glad you called. But we've got plenty of time to eat and lots to do before then." She fixed Cady with a stern look. "What's this about a lover?"

Cam snorted and Susan raised her eyebrows. "Don't think you're off the hook. I'll get to the bottom of this pregnancy thing in a minute, but it looks like the damage has been done in your case." She turned back to Cady as Cam's expression changed from amusement to an almost comical despair. "Now, who is he?"

"He's not a lover. We're just friends." Cady thought about how many times she'd said that, especially in the past few days when she knew it wasn't true.

"Be serious, please." Susan frowned at her daughter, but Cady could tell it was more concern than judgment. "Why would your sister call him a lover if he's a friend?"

"And her boss." Cam raised her hands in a protective gesture at Cady's glare.

"Cady!" Susan looked shocked. "I expected better from you. And what about Neil? And Kelsea?"

"Geez!" Cady stood and walked across the room, turning only when she reached the bar that divided the living area from the kitchen. "What is this? Jump on Cady time? Why can't you guys just let it alone? It's my life."

Susan looked surprised and Cam started laughing. Cady glared at both of them. Cam continued giggling and even Susan smiled. "Honey, don't you know that's not what families do?"

Startled, Cady frowned at her still shaking sister who was now wiping tears of merriment from her eyes. "What's wrong with you?"

Cam grinned, facing her sister. "You. You've always wanted a big family. Didn't it ever occur to you that it just means more people to mess in your business?"

"Classic case of be careful what you wish for." Susan shrugged and turned to her other daughter. "Speaking of which, where'd the baby come from, anyway?"

By the time Cam had explained her pregnancy and ensuing engagement to her mother's satisfaction, Cady felt fairly safe again. She realized how wrong she was when her mother sat back and smiled at both of them. "I'm glad you came today, girls. I realize things haven't been exactly right between us in a while. I want to make that different, and from the sound of things, I might be just in time."

"Oh God." Cady covered her mouth just as the words escaped. She peered at her mother cautiously. "What do you mean?"

"Well, if Cam's moved in with her fiancé, it sounds like maybe you have an extra room. Then I can help you put your life back together, Cady."

Cam began to giggle again, but Cady decided it was time to put an end to such fantasies. "Uh-uh, no way. I just got *her* out." She jerked her thumb at Cam. "If my family needs anything it's a chance to get ourselves back into a groove we're comfortable with. And Mom, no offense, but really, we just did mend a few fences. Hadn't we better take it slower?"

Susan blinked. "Fences? What fences? I'm just glad you two finally came to see me."

"Don't do that, Mom." Cam's voice fell as flat as a well-ironed sheet over the conversation. Cady glanced at her and realized that although she'd been hurt by the rift between mother and daughters, it was nothing compared to what Cam had felt.

"Don't do what, dear?" Susan stood and moved swiftly to the counter. "Didn't you two say you'd like to go out for dinner? We should go now and beat the crowds."

"Don't pretend it never happened. Years are what we lost, Mom, and I'm not even saying it's your fault, but we can't just pretend it never happened. Not just because those years and what came before them don't fit into your perfect life." She crossed the room and stood in front of her mother, gesturing down at her pregnant form. "This is the way I left you, this is the way I'm coming back. I am who I am, and I need to know if you accept me for that." She glanced over her shoulder. "And I have a feeling Cady needs to know the same thing."

Susan looked stricken. "I'm sorry, I didn't realize—"

"Don't!" Cam's voice rose and Susan stopped, biting her lip. "Mom, you're saying you haven't noticed we haven't talked without fighting in twenty years? How is that supposed to make me feel?"

Cady put a hand on her sister's arm, but Cam shook her off, tears now evident on her cheeks. Susan's gaze fell. "I'm sorry. I thought—" She shook her head and looked at her daughter. "I didn't think. I just wanted to pretend it didn't happen. But you're right. It did. We can't get those years back, and I'm not even sure I'd do that if I could. Except to have your father back." Her voice broke and she covered her face with her hands. "I'm so sorry for the way it happened, Cam. I wasn't right, I just didn't know what to do anymore."

Cam watched her mother sob for several seconds and Cady had a horrible moment when she wondered if this was what Cam had come here for. Then she seemed to crumble inward, folding over her mother, her arms encircling her thin body, her head bowed over Susan's. A moment later, she reached over and held out her hand to her sister and Cady accepted it, letting herself be drawn into the family circle she'd longed for.

CADY THOUGHT LATER AS her mother bathed their faces with a damp washcloth—just as she'd done when they were children —that the tears of their shared grief and shame had bound them together in an irrevocable way. And when Susan brought out a bottle of wine, a glass of ginger ale, and a plate of cheese the three women gave up the idea of going out to eat in favor of an intimate session of catching up.

Susan told them about life in the "retirement home" (her name for the assisted living facility). They giggled about the bachelors and widowers Susan claimed vied for her hand at the dances and a seat next to her on bingo night. Susan wouldn't admit to any special man. When they pressed her on the subject she changed it to Cam's fiancé, wanting to know all about Stan. Cam obliged, talking enthusiastically about Stan and their plans for his education.

When Susan went into the kitchen and brought out a second bottle of wine, Cam began to laugh. "Geez, Mom, you keep a pretty good supply on hand, don't you?"

"Not much occasion to drink it." Susan carefully poured herself a half glass and filled Cady's. She returned to the kitchen and came back with a can of soda for Cam.

Already a little lightheaded, Cady nonetheless felt as if a great weight had been lifted from her. She wanted to celebrate, and she clinked glasses with her mother and Cam.

"So tell us about the extra man in your life, Cady." Susan sounded so casual, and the wine had lessened her resistance to the point where Cady didn't even mind the question.

"I like that way of putting it." Cam grinned. "She swears he's not her boyfriend—"

"He's not." Cady noted the slight slur in her words with surprise. How much had she drunk? She felt light and relaxed. How did her mother accomplish that, anyway?

"—but he's definitely one more than usual, right, Cady?"

Cady giggled. "I guess you'd be right about that. Mom, if you could meet him, you'd understand. I think even Cam understands."

Cam shrugged. "I'd like to say you're wrong, but you're not. Not really. I can see how it could happen at this point in your life, Cady."

Susan pursed her lips, tapping her wine glass absently with one finger. "I still think he's one more than you can afford."

The room had grown dark and Cady wondered absently how late it was. They'd made hotel reservations nearby but she couldn't imagine moving from this comfortable spot. And she wondered if her mother was right. Maintaining any relationship with Will was risky now that they'd admitted to their attraction.

"He says he won't push me into anything more than

friendship." Cady couldn't help but smile at the memory of their kiss before she left.

"I doubt he's pushing you into anything." Susan sipped her wine.

Cady turned her head to find Cam watching their mother with interest. She felt vaguely that she ought to take offense at her mother's words and even more vaguely that her mother and sister had coordinated this effort. Most important, however, was this relaxing moment to talk about Will.

"She and Neil have had problems for a while, Mom." Cam seemed determined to play the devil's advocate.

"Just one problem, actually," Cady said, laying her head back on the couch cushions. "He's never there."

"So Neil's never there, but this other man is?" Susan sat next to Cady and took her daughter's hand.

"Will." Cady smiled as she said his name, happy just to think about him. "Yeah. He says he's loved me for a while."

"But he's willing to just be friends?" Susan sounded doubtful.

Cady frowned. "That's what he says." She wondered if it sounded ridiculous to her mother and sister. And was it friendship anymore? Surely friends didn't kiss the way she and Will had done.

"Sweetheart, don't you think sooner or later he's going to want more?"

As she searched for an answer to her mother's question, Cady closed her heavy eyelids and because it was undeniably easier to keep her eyes closed than to answer her mother, she let herself drift off into a warm darkness.

CADY WOKE the next morning on the couch with an afghan over her shoulders but falling off her legs. Sitting up, she looked around and realized she was in her mother's apartment. She glanced at the closed bedroom door and wondered where Cam had slept. "Probably went to the hotel without me." Her voice sounded thick and she sat up, keeping her head as still as possible so her brain wouldn't rattle too much in her skull.

"Geez." She got up and stumbled to the bathroom where she splashed water on her face, found a paper cup and filled it. When she came out, her mother was in the kitchen and she could smell coffee. "God, that smells great."

Susan put a steaming cup in front of Cady as she sank into one of the old-fashioned wooden kitchen chairs at the little table. She wondered if this could be the kitchen set she remembered from her childhood home and realized it probably was.

Susan turned back to the cupboard and pulled a small white bottle from it, shaking two tablets into her hand. "You look like you could use these, too."

Cady examined the two offered pills. "Not sure I should trust anything you offer after last night. What's in these? Truth serum?"

"Just acetaminophen, I swear."

Cady swallowed the pills with a glass of orange juice her mother handed her. She coughed, wiped her mouth with her hand and said, "I guess that was the truth serum last night, huh? How'd you manage not to get drunk?"

"I only drank a little more than one glass the whole night. I paced myself and just poured a little more in my glass each time I filled yours. You wouldn't have noticed after the first refill."

"Pretty sneaky, Mom."

"What can I say? I'm not used to being a mother anymore, but I'm trying."

"Isn't it like riding a bike? Doesn't seem like a skill you'd lose from disuse."

"Did you know your sister is really worried about you?" When Cady looked at her mother, she shrugged. "She called me before you two came up. She laid it all out for me then, told me your happiness might be at stake and if I ever loved either of you, I'd help you now."

"She said that?" Cady stared at Susan.

Susan tapped Cady's coffee cup with one finger and Cady obediently picked it up and took a cautious sip. Susan folded her arms on the countertop and looked her daughter in the eye. "I honestly can't tell, even after last night. Is your life falling apart? Or are you handling it?"

"I'm handling it." Cady dropped her gaze, then looked back up at her mother. "I really am. I know what I want, and I know I love Neil. I just…I just can't stop seeing Will. He's been so wonderful to me. And I know he's not the type to try to seduce me."

After a moment's consideration with pursed lips, Susan nodded and straightened. "Okay."

"Okay?" Cady blinked. "Really?"

"Yeah. I believe you believe what you're saying." She hesitated, then nodded at the cell phone Cady had left on the counter the night before. "You might want to text him back, though. He's checked in at least twice since last night."

Cady's hand darted over to secure the phone and she realized as she did so that she hadn't heard from Neil since leaving the morning before. He'd never acknowledged her text that she'd made it all right. He hadn't called to say good night.

Susan touched her hand gently and when Cady looked at her, she saw understanding in her mother's eyes. "Just because I believe you doesn't mean I won't keep asking, though. Are you sure you know what you want, Cady?"

"Yeah." Cady looked at the phone in her hand and added in a low voice, "I hope so."

15

ady and Cam got home late that evening. They'd stayed for lunch with Susan and had left with a promise that she could stay with Cady when Cam had the baby. "I can't wait to see him," Susan said with tears in her eyes. "I've never been a proper grandmother, but I'll give it a try."

As Cam started to get out of the car in front of her apartment building, she hesitated and glanced over her shoulder. "You all right? I sort of apologize for last night."

"Sort of?" Cady raised an eyebrow and grinned.

"Yeah. Sort of." Cam gave her a sheepish smile. "I worry about you. I love you, you know?"

"Well I kind of accept your sort of apology. And I love you, too."

Cam hugged her and got out, and Cady waited until Stan came to the door and waved. Then she pulled out of the parking lot and onto Main Street. She didn't stop to let herself think about where she intended to go until she'd parked behind Hubbard's. Only one small light showed in the kitchen, and Will's car was the only one still there besides hers. Her restaurant key hung on a hook at home, so she pulled out her phone and texted Will.

"Still at the restaurant?"

A few seconds later, he texted back. "Yeah. You home yet?"

She smiled and got out of the car. "Not yet. Want to unlock the back door?"

He threw open the back door and pulled her inside in one motion. His arms encircled her and she leaned against his chest with a sigh of contentment, only slightly tinged with a sense that she shouldn't be there. After all, Neil and Kelsea were asleep a long time ago.

She limited her time at the restaurant to half an hour curled on her office couch in his arms. She told him about her visit with her mother and how she'd promised to come visit when Cam had the baby. She skipped over the fifth degree about him. And then she fell silent, her head on his chest as she listened to his heartbeat. He caressed her arm and kissed the top of her head, and when he spoke his voice was optimistic. "Sounds like it went well."

"I think it did." She sighed and sat up. "I should get home."

"Probably." He remained where he was, half reclining on the couch, one arm still stretched across its back. "Not that I mind, but why did you come here first, anyway?"

She blushed, looking away. "I wanted to see you. And Neil and Kelsea are already asleep."

"You think so?" His voice sounded noncommittal but a sudden doubt assailed her. She squelched it immediately, knowing there was no reason to hope Neil had stayed up waiting for her to get home.

She laughed and stood, picking up her purse. "Neil wouldn't wait up for me. Not that I blame him. It's been years since I waited up for him."

As she started to turn to the door, he stood, caught her hand and pulled her back to him. One hand raised to brush back her hair and he shook his head in wonder, then smiled and let go of her hand with a sudden sad certainty in his eyes. "He's awake. Trust me. If he isn't he never deserved you."

She turned again to the door but hesitated, looking over her shoulder. He remained where she'd left him and she could think of nothing to say, so she left without a goodbye.

WHEN SHE ENTERED THE QUIET, dark house, disappointment consumed her and only then was she aware how much she'd hoped Will had been right. But as she pushed her way wearily through the swinging door into the kitchen, it swung open in her direction instead, hitting her in the nose. "Shit!" She reeled back, holding her face.

"Fuck, are you okay?" Neil's arms surrounded her, his voice full of concern.

She stared at him, still clutching her nose, and began to laugh and cry at the same moment. She clung to him, shaking with a mix of emotions ranging from surprise and relief to sorrow and guilt.

"Baby, what's wrong?" He stroked her hair and held her. "Are you okay? Did I hurt you?"

So much, but not nearly as much as I could hurt you. She couldn't say it, so she shook her head, burying her face in his shirt, smelling his soap and wishing it didn't mix in her nostrils with Will's aftershave.

Neil took her upstairs and left her in the bathroom to clean up while he made her a snack and brought up her suitcase. She showered quickly and emerged to find him sitting on the side of the bed looking weary, a plate of cheese and crackers beside him. He beckoned her over and she went to him, wishing she couldn't still feel Will's hands on her.

"You look exhausted." She let him pull her onto the bed next to him. "You should have been in bed hours ago."

"Do you think I'd have been able to sleep?" He kissed her. "I've missed you. Tell me about it. How did it go?"

By the time they'd finished the cheese and crackers, Cady had told him the entire story, again leaving out her mother's trick with the wine. Feeling exquisitely sleepy, she let Neil draw her back into the blankets, realizing only as he lay on his side and turned her to face him that sleep wasn't the only thing on his mind. "I'm glad it went well," he kissed her lips and face. "I missed you."

She responded instinctively to him, and they made love slowly, tenderly, as if it wasn't nearly two o'clock in the morning and they both had alarms set for less than five hours away. Afterward, when she was sure he had fallen asleep, she moved to her side of the bed and muffled her tears in her pillow. She knew she'd already gone too far. It was too late.

She'd fallen in love with Will. Even though her heart still belonged to her husband.

THE NEXT MORNING, Cady went directly to her office, trying to bury herself in the stacks of invoices waiting for her after her long weekend off. A few minutes later, Will appeared in the door with two cups of coffee. "Good morning."

Her heart pounding in her throat, knowing she had to tell him how much she still loved Neil, she beckoned him in. He set the coffee on her desk before sitting across from her. "Neil was awake last night, wasn't he?"

"Yeah, he was." She wondered if he knew what it meant to her that her husband had waited up for her.

He sat with his elbows on his knees, looking into his coffee. "I figured he would be. He's a good guy. In another world..." He sighed and looked at her. "In another world I wouldn't be in love with his wife."

She met his gaze. "And I wouldn't be in love with you, either." She looked away at the glimmer of hope in his eyes. "But I love my husband, Will. And he is my husband. I owe him--"

"I know." He held up a hand, obviously unwilling to hear more. "Which leaves us where? Back where we were?"

She opened her mouth to say no, that they couldn't go back to kissing and cuddling and pretending to just be friends when they knew perfectly well that if anyone ever found out it would be the end of her marriage. But what came out of her mouth was totally different. "Is that enough for you?"

His silence drew out and she waited for him to tell her no, half hoping he would since she couldn't find the strength to tell him she couldn't continue to see him.

"It won't be one day. Every time I hold you I know I'm a step closer to that point. But if he makes you happy I can still let you go home. For now." He gave her a twisted smile and she wondered what her selfishness was costing them both. He stood, crossed the room and kissed her forehead. Then he wheeled around and left.

CADY AND WILL SETTLED back into a comfortable routine. A casual observer would never have noticed anything more than a close friendship and working relationship between them. In the morning she arrived early and he brought her coffee. They sat on the couch together and talked, sometimes holding hands. In the evenings when Kelsea had gone to bed and Neil had retired to his study to make phone calls and research his cases, she returned to help with the evening deposit. Only when she left did he kiss her, usually lightly, on the lips.

If anyone had asked Cady if she were having an affair, she would have said no immediately. And then she would have thought again.

On Friday she knew she wouldn't make it back in the evening, so when she was ready to leave, she knocked on Will's door. He waved her in, still talking on the phone. He looked happy and spoke animatedly into the receiver. "Yeah, thanks, thanks for calling. That's awesome. I really appreciate it."

He hung up and let out a whoop, bounding around the desk and seizing her around the waist to pull her into a deep kiss. She laughed breathlessly, trying not to worry about the open door. "Will! What's going on?"

He grinned down at her, playing with her hair and refusing to release her. "Just some good news. Want to know?"

She fought to keep her breath even. "Of course. What is it?"

He bent his head and kissed her neck just below her ear. When she sucked in a startled breath, he laughed softly. "We're going to be the featured restaurant in *Southern Dining* next month."

"Oh!" She gasped as his lips moved over her neck to her collarbone. She wanted to melt into his touch, but the open door at her back felt like a vacuum threatening to rip away all pretense and expose her to the world. "That's…that's great, Will." She tried to reach the door and failed.

"Is that worrying you?" She felt him grin as he pulled her closer, reaching around her to push the door shut at the same moment. "Better?" As she nodded, he spun her around and pressed her against the door, kissing her passionately, his hands moving freely over her body. "God, you're so beautiful."

They hadn't kissed so intimately since the day at his family's vineyard, and she couldn't deny how wonderful it felt. Her pulse beat so hard in her throat, he had no problem finding it with his lips. She trembled and when he nudged her legs apart with his knee, she didn't resist, molding her body even closer to him as his hands slipped beneath her blouse.

He stopped there, however, still holding her tightly against him, leaning his forehead against hers, his breath mingling with hers until she felt lightheaded. She could feel the warmth of his palms against her skin, aware she wanted him to keep holding her, keep touching her, to pull her to the couch or the floor and make love to her. And it horrified her that she could feel that way.

"I'm sorry." He stepped back, kissing her lips lightly as he did, moving his hands to hers, holding them tightly in both of his own. "I didn't mean to get so carried away, but once I had you in my arms, I couldn't seem to stop myself."

She closed her eyes, leaning her head weakly against the door. "Thank God you did." She bit her lip. "I don't think I would have."

He let go of her hands, turning away to lean on his desk for a moment, shoulders hunched. "Don't say things like that if you want me to be able to let you go." He moved behind the desk and sank into his chair. His voice sounded remote when he looked back at her. "Were you getting ready to leave?"

"Yeah." She swallowed hard. "The, um, payroll checks are done. I locked the safe."

"Tonight's the big night, then? You meet the boyfriend?" He smiled a little. "Take it easy on him."

"Yeah. I'll, um, do that." Her hand shook as she reached up to brush her hair back from her face. "Will, I—"

"It's okay." He nodded at the door. "You need to go, though."

"Yeah." She backed out the door and closed it behind her. She lingered for a second, her hand on the doorknob, knowing what her answer would have to be if someone asked her at that moment if she were having an affair.

CADY GOT ready for dinner before Neil got home. She knew she couldn't be naked in the same room with him so soon after being with Will. Surely Will's hands had left some mark on her, and even though she'd showered, she still felt as if she could smell his skin.

Sabrina and her mother dropped Kelsea off after cheer-leading practice and she bounced in, barely able to contain her excitement. "Rob called," she announced. "He's really looking forward to meeting you guys. I can't wait, I just know you're going to love him."

Cady tried to think of some way to answer. Rob would have to be pretty spectacular for them to agree to let a sixteen-year-old date their daughter. However, she didn't really think that was the thing to say to her daughter. "Well, we're looking forward to meeting him." She handed her daughter the potato masher. "Want to do the potatoes?"

"Sure!" Kelsea washed her hands and drained the potatoes. "You know how it is, right, Mom? He just looks at me and I feel all weak. And he's *so* protective. I just can't stop thinking about him."

Cady was saved from having to reply by the ringing of her cell phone. She snatched it up without looking at the caller i.d. "Hello?"

"I can't stop thinking about you."

Distracted by her daughter's confession, it took her a second to realize who was speaking. She glanced at Kelsea, rinsing the potatoes and humming. Keeping her voice low, Cady turned partly away. "Will?"

"Hey. I'm sorry. I know you're home and you can't talk to me. I just had to hear your voice one more time. And say good luck tonight."

She closed her eyes, savoring the timber of caring in his voice. "Thank you." She tried to put everything she felt into the only two words she trusted herself to say, and even though she knew she hadn't, she hung up anyway.

She stood for a long moment listening to Kelsea mash the potatoes and basking in the warmth of Will's voice and the memory of his touch. The sound of the front door opening startled her and she dropped her phone. "Damn." She stared at the smashed phone on the tile floor.

"Mom?" Kelsea sounded startled.

"It's okay, I just dropped my phone." Cady hurried to retrieve the handset and started when Neil placed a hand on her shoulder.

"Geez, you're jumpy." He frowned. "What happened?"

"Dropped it. Damn, what a mess." She sighed, running one finger over the cracked glass screen, then shrugged and tossed it into her purse. "It'll probably still work, though. Those things are designed to take a beating."

Kelsea stood with her hands over her mouth looking stricken. Cady looked at her daughter and laughed. "Honey, what's wrong? It's not like I ran over a puppy or something."

Her daughter shook her head. "That was just such a *nice* phone, though."

Cady glanced at Neil and they both snickered. Kelsea glared at them. "What? I was hoping you'd give it to me when you got a new one."

For answer, Cady plucked it from her purse and held it out.

"Here you go."

Kelsea frowned. "I don't want it *now!* It's got a big crack in it."

"Yeah, what are you thinking, anyway?" Neil smiled as he kissed Cady's cheek. "Our princess can't have anything less than perfect. But I think your old Motorola will have to do for a while yet, Your Highness." Still grinning, he thumbed through the mail. "So when does your prince get here, anyway?"

"Any minute." Kelsea's face lit up. "Thank you guys so much for doing this. I just know you're going to love him. I've got to go get ready." She sprinted up the stairs.

Neil looked after her with a sad expression. "Wow, she's growing up too fast."

"Yep." Cady tried to sound upbeat. "She's got a good head on her shoulders, though, even if it is a teenage girl head."

"Yeah." He sighed and glanced at her. "How was your day? Everything okay at the restaurant?"

"Yeah." She ducked her head, hoping her guilt didn't show. "Really good, actually."

"Really?" He uncapped a beer and raised his eyebrows at the same moment. "Don't keep me in suspense."

"Will just found out today. The restaurant's going to be featured in *Southern Dining.* It's a travel magazine that's got a national distribution."

He smiled absently. "That's great."

"Yeah." She wondered what he was thinking about as she pulled the pork roast from the oven and set it on the stove next to the mashed potatoes and green beans. "Well, dinner's ready. Where's our guest of honor?"

"I'm not looking forward to this." He frowned at the food. "This kid better be much more impressive than I'm giving him credit for."

"Yep." She glanced down the hall and lowered her voice. "I've got kind of a bad feeling about him, but when I talked to his mom, she just seemed clueless. Nothing wrong with her, but she doesn't seem to think her son can do any wrong. He puts on a good face in front of her, I guess, but there's something about him I don't like."

"You don't like the fact that he drives a motorcycle and wants to take our daughter out on it." He gave her a wry smile.

"Neither do you!"

"No. I don't." His smile faded as they heard the doorbell ring. A moment later, Kelsea's footsteps pattered down the stairs and they heard her answer the door and low voices in the hall. Then she appeared in the door with a tall teenage boy behind her.

"Mom, Dad, this is Rob." Kelsea stepped aside as if presenting a magic trick.

It might have been magic. Rob stepped forward with a very charming smile. "It's a pleasure to meet you, Mr. and Mrs. Summers. I've heard a great deal about you."

"Hello, Rob." Cady smiled and held out her hand. "We've heard quite a bit about you, too."

"Mom!" Kelsea widened her eyes impressively at her mother.

Rob, however, returned her smile with a grin. "Good to know."

Neil shook hands with Rob, and after pouring sodas for them all, they sat at the table. Cady reached for Kelsea's hand to say the blessing but hesitated when she saw Rob had already begun eating. Should she let it go this time? Before she could make up her mind, Neil said quietly, "Cady, would you say the blessing tonight?"

Rob immediately set aside his fork, actually looking a little embarrassed, and Cady decided he was only behaving as any awkward teenager would. She gave her daughter's hand a little reassuring squeeze and began the simple grace she'd offered every time her family had sat at the dinner table since Kelsea was born. She bit her lip as she remembered listening to Kelsea's childish voice lisp the words for the first time and sharing a smile with Neil over their daughter's bowed head.

Her own voice caught and she paused for a second, taking a breath. Looking up, she encountered Neil's concerned gaze and shrugged, glancing at Kelsea's bowed head with tears in her eyes, her throat still too constricted to go on. He nodded, understanding in his eyes, and said the last few words of the grace for her, winding up with a grin and "Let's eat!"

Cady recovered herself as she listened to Neil talking easily to Rob about his motorcycle. She wondered when he'd learned so much about motorcycles. Probably recently, for Kelsea's sake. The thought made her heart leap in her chest. Was there anything he wouldn't do for his daughter?

Dinner went smoothly. Rob answered questions about himself and school and his plans for the summer break. In fact, Cady found herself revising her opinion of him. Any young man who could speak so well and without reservation must not have anything to hide.

As she stood to serve dessert, she took their plates to put in the sink. A fork slid from the top of the stack to land between

Kelsea and Rob. It fell on the carpet unnoticed, and Cady bent to retrieve it. What she saw as she straightened took her breath. Rob had his right hand on Kelsea's left thigh, very high up. Cady felt her heartbeat quicken, now thundering in her chest. She stood quickly, walking to the sink and dropping the plates into it.

How could she handle this? In no way was it appropriate for a sixteen-year-old boy to be touching her still very young teenage daughter that way. Her maternal instinct reared up inside her and she took the dessert—chocolate cream pie—from the refrigerator, quickly cutting four slices and placing them on her best dessert plates.

Rob and Neil were discussing colleges while Kelsea sat very still. To Cady, her daughter almost looked terrified, and she made up her mind. She set Rob's pie in front of him with a clean fork and a napkin, but as she turned to set Kelsea's in front of her, she stole a glance downward and saw Rob's hand creeping further up her daughter's leg toward her crotch. Deliberately, Cady swept the second slice of pie off the plate and into her daughter's lap, catching Neil's startled glance as she did so.

Kelsea gave a shriek and stood abruptly. Rob also gave a start and jumped up, remembering too late that he shouldn't have been in the line of fire at all.

"Oh Kelsea, I'm so sorry, honey." Cady handed her a napkin. "What luck Rob's hand was in your lap to block most of the pie, otherwise I might have ruined your skirt." She glared at Rob whose face, now that he was caught, had hardened into insolence.

Kelsea burst into tears and ran from the room. Neil rose, looking at Rob. "You need to leave."

Rob shrugged and walked out, boot heels clipping smartly along the hallway. Cady glared after him. "Son of a bitch! Right under our noses, too. I knew that kid was trouble."

Neil sighed. "You couldn't think of a better way to handle it than to dump pie on your daughter?"

"It worked, didn't it? And if I hadn't, he'd've had his hand...oh God! And the expression on her face, Neil! She's not ready for this."

He held up a hand. "I'm not saying she is. God help me, if I'd caught him, I would have wanted to break his wrist. I wouldn't have done it, though."

"Well, neither did I. He'll recover."

"But will your relationship with your daughter?" He took the plate from Kelsea's place and dumping what was left into the garbage disposal. Then he began loading the dishwasher.

Cady glanced at the stairs. She knew what he meant. Kelsea no doubt saw her mother's stunt as a betrayal. She might not be ready for such sexual contact, but she was long past wanting her mother's protection. Cady blushed hot with anger at Neil's implied criticism. She was all the angrier because she was certain he was right.

Her anger didn't abate as she finished cleaning the kitchen with his help, then went upstairs and knocked quietly on Kelsea's door. Her daughter didn't answer, even when she called her name. Cady felt betrayed by Kelsea, her husband and, most especially, herself.

And she really, really wanted to talk to Will.

16

Cady arrived at the restaurant early the next morning in the hopes that Will would be there alone. He was. He'd made coffee for them and handed hers to her with a light kiss that nonetheless made her catch her breath. Just the thought that he could kiss her so nonchalantly made her heart skip, and she read the same surprised delight in his eyes when he stepped away.

His expression changed to concern, however, as he looked at her. "What's wrong? You look like you didn't sleep at all last night."

She told him the story. She still got angry at the thought of the boy's hand on her daughter's slender leg. She slammed her cup onto her desk, jolting hot coffee unheeded over her hand. "She's only *thirteen*! And I don't care what she says, she's not ready for something like that. I could tell she was terrified. A boy like that could ruin the way she thinks about sex, the way she feels she's supposed to be treated by men. And he won't stop if he doesn't get what he wants. He'll give her some sort of complex, tell her she's frigid or whatever boys tell good girls these days."

"Hey, calm down." He brushed her hair back from her face. "You're preaching to the choir. As far as I'm concerned, he's lucky you didn't do something worse. Did you tell Kelsea all this?"

Tears pricked her eyes. "She wouldn't let me." She remembered the scene in the kitchen that morning. Kelsea had refused to speak to her and Neil had remained silent over his coffee, leaving the house as quickly as possible. Anger returned, mixed with sadness. "And Neil! He was no help. He says I could have handled it better, that Kelsea will be angry until she gets over it, and I'll just have to wait it out."

"Maybe he's right." Will brushed a tear from her cheek with his thumb. "Kelsea's a smart girl. She'll come around and let you talk to her, and then you can explain to her how you feel and that even though she doesn't want you to protect her, she still needs you for the things she doesn't quite understand yet. Did Neil agree that she shouldn't see him anymore?"

"Yes, we told her together this morning. I'm not sure how much she listened to us, though. She just said 'whatever'."

"Well, that's good. And until she's ready to talk, it's all you can do."

Cady sighed and laid her head on his chest, feeling the comfort of his arms around her. She realized Will had taken Neil's side, and it didn't infuriate her the way her husband's lack of support and seeming criticism had. Why hadn't Neil just explained things this way? And why wouldn't Will just go ahead and take advantage of the friction in her marriage to drive a wedge between her and Neil?

She knew the answer to that question, even as she enjoyed the warmth of his embrace. Will loved her enough not to force anything from her. He wasn't trying to end her marriage, and he recognized that their relationship might have nothing in it for him. She drew away and looked at him. "Why are you so wonderful?"

He shrugged. "Sorry. Can't help it." His grin softened as he slid his hands from her shoulders to her waist and bent his head to kiss her. "It's not totally unselfish, though." His last words were just a breath on her lips, and then she surrendered to the delicious feel of his mouth on hers, the taste of his kiss.

Footsteps in the hall warned them of the approach of another person and they pulled apart quickly. Cady picked up her coffee cup and made it behind her desk as Will quickly sat on the couch. Cady wondered if she looked as guilty as she felt when Suzie poked her head in. "Hey, Cady, have you seen —" She paused as her glance took in Will on the couch. "Oh, hey. Sorry, you guys having a meeting?"

"Just coffee." Will's reply came easily. "Get yourself one and join us."

"No thanks, I'm just getting started in the kitchen, but I couldn't remember if you wanted to do the meatloaf sandwiches as the special today. If you do, I probably need to get them in the oven soon so they can be refrigerated before you grill them."

"That sounds good." He nodded. "Give me a minute and I'll be back to help you."

"No rush. Still plenty of time before lunch." Suzie waved cheerfully and retreated to the kitchen.

Cady gulped and laid her head on her desk. After a moment, she felt his hand on the back of her neck. "You okay?"

She raised her head. "Yeah. Yeah, I guess."

"I'm sorry." He took his hand away. "I forget how much you have to lose when I get close to you." His eyes were sad. "I guess I'm more selfish than I thought."

She sighed. In her heart she knew she wanted nothing more than to put her arms around him and assure him she wanted him as much as he wanted her. She managed a weak smile. "You're not. Selfish. I guess I forget sometimes, too, and then it comes back to me and frightens me all over again."

He nodded and squeezed her hand, but he had no words of comfort to give her. They both knew they'd come too far in their relationship to turn away from it. For better or worse, they were going to play it out.

As he left, she covered her face. She wanted his selfishness because it made it so much easier for her to cross the boundaries of her marriage. And she wondered how long she'd been cheating on Neil. She could measure it from the first time she'd kissed Will, or from that first intimate dinner they'd shared in the dark, deserted restaurant. But maybe it went back further. Maybe all the way back to their first dance at the benefit they'd worked on together. In memory, she was sure that on that occasion their hearts had beat in synchronicity when he'd held her.

And even as she wondered when their affair had begun, she also worried about where it would end.

CAM KNOCKED on the door of her sister's home early on Tuesday morning. She wanted to catch Cady before she left for work. Just as she reached for the bell, Kelsea opened the door. Happy to see her niece for the first time in several days, Cam started to greet her but froze when Kelsea glared at her. "If you're looking for my mother, she's in the kitchen." She stalked down the steps and out to the street. A moment later, a car stopped and she jumped into the back seat.

"Damn." Cam stared after her niece, feeling more than a little déjà vu. She shrugged and stepped through the open door. "Cady? What the hell's going on? Why's my niece stomping out of here like a prize fighter?"

Cady sat at the kitchen counter looking defeated and Cam realized she had neglected her sister in her own happiness. "What's going on?"

"What else?" Cady sighed. "I fucked up. I keep doing that for some reason. And Kelsea and Neil aren't likely to let me forget this one."

"What the hell did you do?" Cam sucked in her breath as a thought occurred to her. "Jesus, did they find out about Will?"

"No, but thank you very much for pointing out my other fuckup." Cady glared at her sister. "No, this has to do with Kelsea wanting to date a screwup sixteen-year-old whose only ambition is to deflower her and steal any girlhood she has left. And because I caught him at it and called him on it, I'm the bad guy."

Cam sat, more relieved than she cared to admit that Cady's

depression and Kelsea's anger had nothing to do with Will. "I think you ought to tell me about it."

Without further urging, Cady did. She got up and poured coffee for both of them, put the cups on the counter and spent the rest of her recital pacing the kitchen. "And Will agrees with Neil, too. He says Kelsea's a smart girl and she'll get over it when she realizes how much better off she is without him. But—"

Cam held up one hand, her heart sinking in her breast. "You've told Will all about this, then?"

"I did." Cady faced her sister with a tilted chin. "God-damnit, don't you dare judge me, Cam! I'm furious with both Kelsea and Neil; Will's the only one who's kept me even close to sane. God, Neil works until after dinner these days. Do you have any idea how difficult it is sitting across the table from a daughter who looks like she hates me? And she won't even talk to me. How can I fight that? I can barely wait for Neil to get home so I can go to the restaurant. And then I work late so I can be with someone who loves me."

After her sister fell silent, Cam took her hand. "I'm not judging you, sis. Seriously. I'm just worried about you. I guess I feel a little guilty, too. Maybe if I was here—"

Cady shook her head and sat, playing with her coffee cup. "It wouldn't make any difference. And it's not even fair of me to blame Neil for what's going on with me and Will. I just can't seem to stop myself, and I use every fight Neil and I have as an excuse to stay with Will." She sighed. "I usually love the summer, but now I'm dreading Kelsea getting out of school in a couple of weeks. She's got some camps lined up and I'm sure she'll want to hang out at the pool, but what am I going to do with a daughter that hates me?"

As surprised as she was by her sister's honesty, Cam realized she was also appalled by her behavior. She tried to dismiss the feeling, aware that it did little good to judge her sister. And why would she feel this way, anyway? It wasn't like Cady was doing anything Cam herself had never done. And there had never been any love lost between Cam and Neil. She'd always felt like he looked down on her. But still, it had always been nice to know her sister led a boring and commonplace life. Cady's life had provided a steady base for Cam's rocky one. Switching places with her sister disconcerted Cam, and she couldn't deny that her own love life was the steadier of the two at the moment.

Shaking it off, Cam picked up her own coffee. "That doesn't even matter now. What matters is Kelsea. Is she safe, do you think?"

"I have no reason to think she isn't. I've been there to pick her up from cheerleading practice. I've talked to Sabrina's mom and the cheer coach so they're aware she's not to be picked up by anyone else. I feel like a prison guard." She finally picked up the coffee and made a face at its lukewarm taste. "Ick."

"Are you going to work this morning?"

"Yeah. I should have already been there." Cady dumped her cold coffee in the sink and turned. Cam noticed that her sister looked better than she'd seen her look in a while. As if Will's attention and care had brought out a bloom in her that Neil's love had failed to elicit for some time.

"Listen," Cam took her sister's arm. "Get off work a little

early today. We'll go shopping and get something good to make for dinner. Call Neil and tell him to get home on time for a change. I'll call Stan and we'll make it a better evening than usual. And you can still go back in this evening, to help with the deposit or whatever."

"I can leave a little early." Cady sounded hesitant. "Maybe three? Kelsea has cheer practice until four."

"Make it two and it's a date." Cam squeezed her sister's arm and walked her to the door.

WILL APPEARED at Cady's door at a little after two o'clock with a rose in a bud vase. "Aren't you supposed to be gone by now?"

"Just finishing up a couple of things." Cady shut the ledger she'd been making notes in. She smiled at the rose in his hands, recognizing it as one from the dining room. "What's that?"

He came in, carefully shutting the door behind him, and placed it on her desk. "I can't give you much, but we had one extra today."

"Imagine that." Cady stood and he leaned over her desk to kiss her. The touch of his lips brought with it the normal mix of excitement, desire and guilt.

"Yeah, imagine that." He stepped back. "Are you coming back tonight?"

"Are you asking me to?" She gave him a coy smile as she gathered her keys, cell phone and bag.

"You know I want you to come back." He watched her walk around the desk.

"Do you need me?" This time she lowered her voice in a sexy way, deliberately teasing him with the double entendre.

For answer, he grabbed her hand and pulled her to him, lowering his mouth to hers and kissing her slowly and deeply enough to bring an inarticulate moan from the back of her throat. She realized her mistake as his desire threatened to overwhelm her defenses. He drew away, just far enough to meet her gaze when he spoke. "Yeah, I need you." He released her and cleared his throat. "Might be better for both of us if you didn't come back tonight though."

Her unuttered and inadequate apology died on her lips as he left.

CADY PICKED up Cam at her apartment building at a quarter to three. She ignored her sister's inquiries about being held up at work, in no mood for recriminations or accusing looks. "What did you have in mind for dinner?"

"Did you call Neil?" Cam raised her eyebrows instead of answering.

Cady tossed her sister her phone. "You call him. I asked him this morning if he'd be home for dinner and he said he wasn't sure."

Cam tossed the phone back. "That's your job. Stan will be there. And Kelsea. Let's make pizzas."

The suggestion surprised a smile from Cady. "Mom used

to do that. When we needed to make up after a fight. Remember?"

"That's probably what made me think of it. C'mon it'll be fun. We'll get pre-made crusts and lots of great toppings."

"Olives."

"Green peppers."

"Anchovies."

Cam laughed. "Ick. If you insist."

They had a great time shopping, teasing each other about their favorite toppings, and Cady almost forgot Will in the fun. It wasn't until they were leaving with four bags of groceries loaded in a cart that the mood was broken.

Cam stopped in the door and when Cady turned back curiously, she saw an odd look on her sister's face. "Cam?"

"Don't overreact." Cam took her sister's arm, her gaze on something behind Cady.

"What the hell?" Cady turned to look over her shoulder. She froze and then she jerked her arm free. "Ohmyfuckinggod." Kelsea stood across the parking lot with Rob. He had one arm looped over her shoulder, his hand lingering dangerously close to the girl's breast. His manner was so familiar, so blatantly possessive of her daughter, Cady felt her hackles rise. She turned calmly to Cam, handing her the keys. "Take the groceries to the car for me, please?"

"Don't overreact!" Cam's voice was frankly pleading. "Remember what happened the last time, and it obviously didn't do any good, did it?"

"Do you see me overreacting?" Cady shook the keys at her sister. "Just take the groceries to the car. I'll be there in a second."

Cam sighed, resigned, and took the keys. Cady marched across the parking lot. As she got closer, she noticed again how tense Kelsea looked, as if she were afraid to move. Her heart softened toward her recalcitrant daughter, but she knew she had to get her out of the situation she was in.

"Kelsea." She spoke her daughter's name as gently but firmly as possible.

Her daughter turned, startled, and might have even stepped away from Rob, but he tightened his grip on her, giving Cady an insolent look. "Hey, Mrs. S. How's it hanging?"

"Kelsea, go to the car, your aunt is waiting." Cady didn't look away from Rob.

"Go on, then, baby." Rob kissed Kelsea's forehead. "I'll see you later."

Kelsea didn't argue, either because she really was happy to get away from Rob or because she could tell her mother meant business. Only after she had gotten halfway across the parking lot did Cady say quietly, "Stay away from my daughter." She turned to leave.

"What's your fucking problem, anyway?" His voice cut across the parking lot, insolent to the point of rousing a primal fighting instinct in her.

She swung around, her lips curled to snarl out her next words, but stopped short when he spoke first.

"From what I hear, you know how to party. I figure your daughter oughta be at least as much fun for me as you are for guys your age." He gazed levelly at her. "Don't you think?"

Fear sliced through her, enhancing rather than extinguishing the anger. He knew. Somehow this little sonofabitch knew about her and Will. But it wasn't possible. She narrowed her eyes at him. "You keep your hands off my daughter. Don't even look at her and we won't have a problem."

He threw back his head and hooted with laughter, and the other kids gathered in the corner who had watched with silent interest joined in. Ignoring them, Cady walked back across the parking lot, teeth gritted against the anger and fear.

KELSEA STOOD in her room with her fists clenched, all fear forgotten or submerged in teenage angst and rebelliousness. "That's not fair!"

"What's not fair? You're grounded. Not only for being with Rob, which is bad enough, but for not being where you were supposed to be. Honestly, Kelsea, I don't know what's gotten into you." Cady's interaction with her daughter had reassured her somewhat that whatever Rob knew he hadn't yet shared with Kelsea.

But what could he know? As she closed the door to her daughter's room, she leaned against it, fear and relief equal waves washing over her. She pushed away from the door and went downstairs.

Cam waited for her in the kitchen. "I put the groceries away. I figured another night would be better?"

"Probably so." Cady picked up her phone and gazed at it. She needed to call Neil, but Rob's words stopped her every time she thought of it.

Cam said something about calling Stan and Cady should call her later, then she squeezed her sister's hand and left. Cady sat quietly in the empty room listening to nothing, her head too crowded with other people's words to think of anything herself.

From what I hear, you know how to party…

Might be better for both of us if you didn't come back tonight…

You couldn't think of a better way to handle it…?

She jumped when a hand touched her shoulder, whirling and holding her cracked phone out as if it were a weapon.

Neil laughed, but he looked uncertain. "Damn, I know I'm early, but I didn't really expect to be attacked." He grinned. "What's up?"

Instinctively, Cady put her arms around him, bowing her head into his chest. "I'm sorry. Oh God, Neil, I'm so sorry."

His arms surrounded her. "What's wrong, sweetheart?" His tone was very gentle. "Tell me."

She backed away, suddenly aware of how close she'd come to confessing everything to him. Taking a deep breath, she told him about seeing Kelsea and Rob together when Kelsea was supposed to be at cheer practice. "I feel so guilty. I should have made sure she was there. I don't even know how many practices she's skipped. I'm sure Sabrina's been covering for her." She groaned. "I had hoped to make up with her tonight. We were going to make pizzas and talk. Cam and Stan were coming over, and you're home early…" She covered her face and sat. "God, I feel like I screw everything up."

Neil stroked her hair. "I don't understand why you think you've screwed up, Cadence. I don't see that you could have done anything different." He sighed. "Listen, she's a teenage girl and we always knew these years would be difficult."

Cady leaned against him, enjoying the feel of his hand on her hair. As she relaxed, weariness consumed her, but she fought against it until he put a hand under her elbow and led her into the living room, directing her to the sofa. "Lie down. I'll make some sandwiches and take one up to Kelsea. You need to rest for a minute." He kissed her forehead. "You've been working too hard."

Too tired to protest, Cady lay on the couch, letting her mind drift away from the pain and fear of the previous hours, escaping from her own remorse. A while later, she sensed Neil in the room and sat up. He stood next to the couch, smiling down at her, two plates in his hands.

Her mind turned to Kelsea. "Hey, how'd it go?"

"She's eating." He sat, patting her leg reassuringly. "I think maybe she's starting to feel a little guilty. I told her you'd check in with her before you went back to work? Unless, maybe you don't have to go back?"

Might be better for both of us if you didn't come back tonight...

The memory of the desire choking Will's voice made her tremble a little, but she disguised it by shaking her head, knowing she needed to tell Will of Rob's veiled threat. "I wish I could skip it, but Will said he needed me tonight." Perversely, her words almost made her laugh. She bit it back firmly. "I think he's short-handed, probably won't have time to do the deposit. I'll try to be back early, though."

Neil nodded, putting an arm around her shoulders. "Tell Will I need you, too." He gave her a quick squeeze and she nodded, swallowing around a lump in her throat.

WILL WAS in his office when she arrived, and she went directly there, closing the door behind her. He frowned. "I thought I told you to stay home tonight."

"I'm sorry." She stood with her back to the door. "I really am. For everything, Will. It's just that something happened this afternoon. I needed to tell you." In a few sentences she told him about her conversation with Rob, watching his expression change to concern.

"Is Kelsea okay?"

Cady made an impatient sweeping motion. "She's pissed off at me, but there's nothing new about that. But I haven't told you the worst of it, Will."

"What do you mean?" His voice was very quiet.

"Don't you see? I think he knows about us, but how could he?" She spread her hands. "Maybe he's just blowing smoke. He knows I don't like him, maybe he's just pissed I've caught him twice."

"Maybe." Will didn't sound convinced.

"Don't, oh, please don't tell me you think he knows anything. How could he? The only place we're ever together is here and only when there's nobody else around." She knew she was trying to convince herself. Nobody else could know, especially not Rob, because then he could tell Kelsea and then Neil could find out and despite her feelings for Will, she still loved Neil and couldn't stand the thought of hurting him.

"Sweetheart, you know how I feel about you and I would never, ever do anything to hurt you, including tell Neil anything about us or allow him to find out before you're ready. But we have to be realistic. Yes, we're discreet and yes, we always think we're alone but we are not the only ones with keys to the restaurant." He raised his eyebrows at her.

"Oh my God." She sank into a chair and covered her face with her hands. "Then he could know. And he could tell Kelsea."

Cady knew they were both trying to accept the reality of the situation. What did it mean to Will? It could force her to tell Neil about her feelings for him. She had no doubt about Neil's reaction to such a betrayal, any more than Kelsea's. She would lose her family. The thought terrified her and she shivered.

She finally raised her head and found him looking at her helplessly. He held out his hands to her, palms out. "If I were a stronger, better man, I'd let you go voluntarily. I know what we're doing could ruin your life, Cadence. And if you ask me to, I will let you go."

Cady sat in silence, knowing what she needed to do but without the strength to do it, and the silence stretched between them.

17

*I*n mid-June Stan began taking night classes at the community college, but he worried about leaving Cam alone while he was gone. At eight and a half months, Cam had had contractions already, prompting her doctor to urge her to spend as much time off her feet as possible. Cady insisted on giving Cam a key to their house and Stan began leaving her there while he was at work or gone to class. Cam complained about being babysat, but between Stan and Cady they convinced her that she was far enough along in her pregnancy that she shouldn't be alone. At Cam's insistence, Cady put her in charge of making certain Kelsea got home from cheerleading practice and did her homework on time.

The presence of her sister made it even easier for Cady to spend more time at the restaurant, and she found her presence more and more required. Will was putting the finishing touches on the lasagna for the Great Lasagna Cook-off to benefit the

Neuse Riverkeepers Foundation. Although it wasn't a benefit Cady had helped organize, she found herself busier than ever helping Will prepare for it. And although they'd unintentionally cooled their relationship, she still enjoyed being around him, and his enthusiasm for the benefit was infectious. Cady worked harder than ever to make sure it went smoothly for him.

Nearly every independently-owned restaurant in the area was participating in the event, which was set for the last weekend in June. The restaurants paid for tents which they decorated in whatever style they wanted. Will had chosen to create an intimate Italian restaurant in his, complete with a rented parquet floor, small tables and chairs and a temporary bar. Cady found herself on the phone with the rental company quite a bit making sure the necessary supplies would arrive on time and working out the particulars of an ABC license so Will could serve champagne and wine with the lasagna samples.

HER LONGER HOURS at work did not go unnoticed by Neil, even though Cam was the one who realized he'd started coming home earlier and no longer spent so much time closeted in his study. He wandered into the living room one evening when Kelsea had already gone to bed. Stan wasn't out of class yet, and Cam had been trying to stay out of the way in the living room.

"Can I sit down?" He motioned at the couch.

She shrugged, looking down at her bloated body. "Your

couch. I realize I take up more of it than usual, but there's probably some room for you here."

He hesitated. "Is Stan in class?"

"He's taking Econ 10 tonight." She felt a little pride when she spoke. "It'll transfer to a bigger university when he's ready so he can get his degree in business administration."

"Good for him. Sounds like a solid plan." Neil sat, stretching his long legs out and propping them on the coffee table. "I wanted to apologize."

"How come?" Cam gave him a sharp look.

He sighed, and she noticed how tired he looked. "I haven't been much of a brother, have I?"

She shrugged again. "You're fine. You and I have never really seen eye to eye."

"Still." He took a sip of his beer. "I shouldn't have said some of the things I said. About you being a bad mother."

"Are you kidding?" She snorted. "I'm a shitty mother. Or at least I always have been. I can't ever make up for what I put my girls through, but maybe with this guy I can do better." She rubbed her belly and shot him a look. "I didn't need you to tell me I suck as a mother."

"Great." He looked glum. "I feel so much better."

"I wasn't really trying to make you feel better."

"I know." He groaned. "God, I've really screwed up, haven't I? With you, with Cady."

"Cady's problem is the same thing it's always been. She thinks the world revolves around her, so if things aren't going just right, somebody's being mean to her." She grinned at Neil's shocked expression. "C'mon, you know it's true. She's a sweet, loving, generous woman and I adore her, but she's a princess. And if you don't treat her like a princess…" She swallowed to keep from adding, "…she'll find somebody else who will" and shrugged.

"I guess I haven't really treated her like a princess recently." He looked thoughtful. "She works a lot."

She felt a wild desire to urge him to go find Cady. Out of loyalty to her sister, she bit it back. Whatever Cady and Will did alone in the restaurant every night, it couldn't possibly be beneficial for Neil to find out about it by accident.

"Well, yeah." She made her voice soothing. "It's a good outlet for her. She's always liked to feel useful."

He nodded, staring at the dark television screen for several moments. Finally, he looked at Cam. "Do you think I have anything to worry about?"

Cam turned away, uncomfortable. She couldn't lie to Neil. Though they'd never liked each other, she knew he was a very good man. "I know she loves you."

"Yeah." His shoulders slumped. "Yeah, I know that too."

NEIL WAS the farthest thing from Cady's mind that night. She worked steadily until well after the restaurant had closed, then she went to the kitchen to find Will wiping down the stainless steel counters. He looked up. "Hey."

"Hi." She glanced around. "Looks good. Are you about done?"

"Why, did you need something?" His gaze never wavered and she wondered if she'd imagined his slight emphasis on the word "need." Then he tossed the dishrag into a bucket underneath the counter and walked around to her. "Or was there just something you wanted?"

He stood very close, waiting for her reply, but she could find no answer for him. She longed to tell him she wanted him, needed his arms and his warmth, but her fear of where that might lead held her immobile.

"I um, wanted to let you know I confirmed all the arrangements for the tent and the ABC license for the weekend." She stared at the spot where he'd unbuttoned his chef's coat, exposing a bit of his smooth chest. She imagined putting her arms around his neck and kissing that spot, knowing what his reaction would be. She'd sensed it the last time he'd held her and every time since then when he kissed her good-bye at the back door. Soon, she would have to make a real decision about where to go with their relationship.

"Good. Thanks. I appreciate all your help getting ready for the Cook-off." His gaze caught hers and he smiled a little. "Like tasting the sauce."

She couldn't help smiling back. "Well, if you win, you can give me credit."

"I'd love to." He sighed. "Good-night, Cady."

"Good-night?" She couldn't deny she was startled by the obvious dismissal in his tone, but what else could she expect? She hesitated a moment longer at the threshold of the door, then nodded and turned away.

BY THE TIME Cady got home, Cam had left with Stan and Neil was in bed. Cady got ready for bed, intending to slip quietly between the sheets, but Neil rolled over as she came out of the bathroom. "Hey."

"Hey." She tried not to sound startled or to hesitate. When he held the covers up for her, she obediently lay down next to him and he put his arm around her, holding her close. She felt the warmth of his bare chest against her shoulders and took a deep breath, pushing away thoughts of Will and letting herself enjoy this rare moment of closeness with her husband. "Sorry I'm late. Will's putting the last touches to his lasagna for the contest this weekend. I stayed to help him."

"Hmm. Well, you have made some good lasagna in the past, so I can see how you'd be useful there."

"Well, you know. I'm more of an audience than a participant. I just taste and give him my opinion." Unbidden the taste of Will's lips on hers came to her and she had a sudden whirling sense of vertigo. Was she really in her husband's arms or back in the restaurant with Will, flirting with something so dangerous it would eventually destroy her life?

"Hey, you still there?" His arm tightened on her for a moment.

"Huh?" Cady blinked and came back to herself. "I'm sorry, I think I was drifting for a second. Just really tired."

"Yeah, well, I guess a split shift can do that, and you work a lot of those at the restaurant. I asked if I could take you to the Lasagna Cook-off this weekend."

"Of course. Are you sure you have time?"

"I have time." He kissed her cheek and released her. "Good-night, sweetheart."

She lay awake for a long time, thinking. Once upon a time she'd have been thrilled to have Neil with her at an event she'd worked hard on. Now she just wondered how it would make Will feel to see her with her husband.

SATURDAY DAWNED a beautiful day and Cady could almost believe everything would be all right with her family. Everyone slept in and when they got up, Cady made sausage biscuits and they sat on the balcony enjoying the drift of the water and the morning breeze. Cady reflected that part of the reason she loved Eastern North Carolina was the temperate climate. Although it could be hot in July and August and very cold in January and February, for the most part the temperatures were pretty moderate.

Kelsea and her father laughed and talked about plans for the summer. Kelsea wanted to learn to water ski and Neil offered to bring out the boat the next day and they could give it a try on the river. "And if it doesn't work, we'll throw the tube in."

"Great!" Kelsea's eyes sparkled as she turned to her mother. "You'll come, too, won't you, Mom?"

"Of course." Cady summoned a smile, glad her daughter had asked her, though she wondered if it would really happen. Most likely Neil would get a call and have to go somewhere. Although she had noticed he'd left his phone inside and seemed in no hurry to get rid of his newspaper to go get it.

She and Neil lingered in the warm sun. She wasn't in a hurry to get to the cook-off, and she sensed he wasn't either. Could he really just be interested in fixing things between them? Or had he ever realized how wrong things had gone?

"Cam seems happy." His voice as well as his words startled her.

"She's pretty much settled in with Stan, I guess. Probably best. She'll need the help when the baby gets here. And now that I'm working I can't really be there for her the way she'll need."

"Is Stan looking forward to the baby getting here?"

"I think so. He certainly seems to be an enthusiastic father-to-be." Cady smiled at the memory of the enormous teddy bear Stan had brought home and Cam had made him take back to the toy store. It had barely fit into the tiny second bedroom they had turned into a nursery. She opened her mouth to tell Neil the story, but stopped when she found him studying her thoughtfully. "What?"

"I just wondered if you had any regrets. About not adopting another baby back when we had the chance. We're not exactly young anymore, but if you wanted we could look into it…"

She shook her head. "No, you were right. I needed to find myself outside of my family. I need to be able to deal with the fact that you guys don't need me as much anymore."

"Have you found yourself, then? Is that what this job has done for you?" He reached across the table and took her hand, absently massaging her knuckles with his thumb.

She took a sip of coffee to quiet her yammering conscience. "Yes. Well, in a way. I mean, I've been able to find a purpose for myself. I'm not constantly needing to take care of somebody else, either."

"Good." He looked up and his smile was gentle. "Just

remember we still do need you, Cady. I need you, even if I don't always show it."

She nodded, biting her lip. "I'll remember."

THE LASAGNA COOK-OFF was held at Union Point Park, which had turned into a tent city of mini restaurants with chafing dishes of their offerings. Judges passed through, tasting each of the lasagnas, followed by crowds of eager tasters. By the time Cady located Will's stall, it was almost time for the prizes to be announced. Neil had been sidetracked by an acquaintance at another stall, and, eager to be with Will at the moment of truth, Cady excused herself to go ahead.

Will turned at her approach and smiled. "Hiya, beautiful." He put an arm around her shoulders and kissed her cheek, just as he might have done months before, when they knew each other only as friends. The small tent was crowded with well-wishers and employees waiting for the judging, but for a moment she felt as if they were alone. Then he released her. "Where's Neil?" His voice just missed the casual tone he was obviously aiming for.

At that moment a little girl flung herself through the crowd. "Uncle Will!" She threw her arms around his waist and hugged him fiercely.

"Well, I'll be jiggered." Will dropped to his knees and picked the child up. "Is it really my Pretty Polly?" He looked around. "Where's your mom?"

Brianne walked up, a shy but confident smile on her lovely face. "Hi, Will."

He gave her a hug and a warm kiss on the cheek. "Hey. It's great to see you two again."

Cady had an odd feeling of not belonging, as if she'd wandered into the reunion of a family she didn't belong to. She half-turned, looking for a way to back out just as Neil came up behind her. "Look who I found." He smiled and she noticed Cam and Stan behind him.

Will's grin wasn't quite as easy as usual when he shook hands with Cady's family. She noticed when he stepped back from the obligatory greetings that he stood even closer to Brianne. Knowing she needed to break the ice a little, she quickly introduced Brianne to the others in the group and asked her how school was going.

Brianne gave her an odd look, and Cady knew the other woman had picked up on some of the tension, probably through Will since she knew him best. However, she spoke enthusiastically about her courses at N.C. State University. "I thought I'd feel out of place there," she said. "But there are a lot of adults going back to school these days."

"That's good to know." Stan spoke in a deep voice unexpected enough to make them all turn to him.

Cam offered the explanation for his comment with a look of pride. "Stan's going back to school and he may end up taking some courses at N.C. State."

"That's well in the future." Stan smiled down at his partner. "Right now I'll be content with a business degree from Craven."

"I didn't know you had plans to attend N.C. State, Stan." Neil looked at the other man with more respect. "I can give you some numbers to call about transferring credits."

As the others spoke, Cady glanced at Will and found him watching her. The look of pain in his eyes was barely concealed, or maybe it was only obvious to the one who caused it. She couldn't be certain. She did know in that moment that what they had wouldn't last much longer. It was like trying to grow a rose bush in a jar. Sooner or later you had to transplant it or it withered and died.

Just as she realized both Cam and Brianne were aware of their silent interchange, someone yelled from the front of the tent, "Hey, Will, the judges are heading this way!"

On the heels of that remark, Sue Rumwalter, the president of the Chamber of Commerce, poked her head in and yelled, "Where's Will?" as she flourished a blue ribbon. A cheer went up and Will was half-pushed forward to accept the ribbon. Somehow Brianne was still beside him so that when he accepted the ribbon and turned, she flung her arms around his neck and kissed him.

Cady felt bizarrely displaced. As many times as she'd kissed Will, she'd never imagined what he'd look like in the act. His hands on Brianne's hips, he reacted without a hitch, obviously kissing her back, and Cady's heart shuddered with jealousy. She wanted to be the one in his arms sharing that moment with him. Another cheer went up in the tent, accompanied by laughter, and then he turned away, his gaze passing over Cady. "Anybody want lasagna? We've got plenty."

A party ensued. Will distributed champagne and beer and everyone had a plate of lasagna. Kelsea and Sabrina came by and Cady realized her daughter was supposed to be grounded but decided not to say anything. She spotted Lisa and Patrick at the bar together, but when her eye caught Lisa's and she smiled in greeting, Lisa turned away. A coldness swept through Cady's heart along with the certainty that Will's family knew about them and didn't approve. Of course. Had she ever expected they would? Brianne and Polly had disappeared and Cam wandered up with a plate of lasagna. She raised her eyebrows at Cady's empty hands. "No lasagna for you?"

"I've had it before." Cady tried hard not to look around for Brianne. Was she with Will? She shook off the lingering jealousy with difficulty. "Where's Stan?"

"With your husband." Cam jabbed her fork at one corner of the tent. "They're talking about education opportunities and small business loans and that sort of thing. Neil sure knows a lot about it."

"Yeah." Cady spotted Will coming back into the tent. He looked thoughtful, and his eyes scanned the tent, settling on her. She had a moment of disquiet, then he smiled gently and her heart warmed.

"You two have got to cut this out." Cam's voice was firm.

"What?" Cady turned to her sister, distracted. "What do you mean?"

Cam leaned closer, lowering her voice. "You and Will. Do you not have any idea how obvious it is you're in love with him? My God, your face when he kissed that woman. Well, it pretty much matches his when he looks at you and Neil together."

Cady felt a rush of anger. "Drop it, Cam."

"I'm just trying to warn you. You're going to destroy your whole life if you keep this up. Probably his, too."

Cady's anger faded in a flood of anxiety. She knew her

sister was right, and though Will didn't stand to lose as much as she did personally, his reputation was definitely at stake. And in a small town, a business owner's reputation was worth a great deal. She pushed the thought aside. "I'm going to get something to drink."

A tray with champagne glasses sat on the temporary bar and she ducked behind the bar to get a bottle of champagne. As she stood, she found Will next to her. "Hey." He took the bottle from her, filling a glass as he tilted it just right to minimize the foam. He handed the drink to her. "Having fun?"

She raised her eyes from the glass now in her hands to meet his gaze. "Sure. Congratulations."

"Thank you."

She dropped her gaze and took a sip of the champagne. "Good stuff. So what happened to Brianne and Polly?"

"They left. I just got back from walking them to their car, actually."

"Right." Cady couldn't look at him. "Well, I'm sorry I missed saying good-bye."

"Cady." Behind the bar, out of sight of the others in the tent, he reached for her hand. She could tell how much her coldness hurt him, how much he disliked the whole situation. She'd always known how difficult the cheating aspect of their relationship would be for him. He squeezed her hand. "I wanted it to be you."

And she knew he meant the kiss. He wanted to be able to kiss her in front of everyone. She looked around, seeing her sister, her daughter and her husband in the crowded tent, and knew what he wanted would probably never happen.

"Cadence?" Cady jumped and turned to see Neil approaching. His brow was wrinkled with worry. Behind the bar, Will dropped her hand. "I'm sorry, honey, I just got a call—"

"—and you have to go to work." She smiled. "Actually, so do I."

Neil hesitated, blinking. He shot Will a glance. "Really?"

Will shook his head. "Not really. Your wife has an overdeveloped sense of duty."

"You know you'll need help getting things straight at the restaurant when you get there. And Jeannette's not there, so things are probably a mess anyway. I'll at least total the receipts for you while you get the truck unloaded." She took a sip of the champagne and met Will's gaze directly.

"I didn't intend to make you feel obligated." His eyes looked very dark in the shadow of the tent.

"I don't. You know that."

"Well, you may have to give her a raise if she remains so dependable." Neil sounded bemused and they both turned to him, distracted from each other. He shrugged. "I just know how difficult it is to find good help." He leaned across the bar to kiss Cady and paused before drawing away. "I'm really sorry, sweetheart. I can stop by the restaurant after and give you a ride home?"

Cady nodded. "Sure, but don't worry about me if you run late. I can make it home."

Will paused in the act of putting champagne glasses into a bin to be transported back to the restaurant. "I'll be sure she makes it home safely."

Neil glanced at the other man and Cady noticed a slight twitch in his eyebrows, as if he was briefly curious about Will's motives. Then his cell phone buzzed and he turned his attention to it, muttering something. He glanced back at Will. "Thanks. Yeah, I appreciate that." He kissed Cady again, but as he turned away, she noted he'd already pushed the button to answer the phone as he put it to his ear.

WITH NEIL AND BRIANNE GONE, no one seemed to find it odd that Cady assumed the spot at Will's side. He accepted congratulations from friends and even a few rival restaurant owners who stopped by with good-natured compliments. By five thirty, almost everyone had cleared out and those remaining were employees busily packing away dishes, food and furnishings. Everyone looked tired but cheerful.

Cady threw herself wholeheartedly into the cleanup process, and eventually found herself alone with Will in the tent. Even the bar and floor were gone, but the tent itself wouldn't be removed until the next day. It felt odd being in the tent with the green grass under her feet—as if a curtain of illusion had been drawn back.

"I guess everyone is gone, then." Will stuck his head out the tent flap, undid the catch that held it open and let it fall closed behind him. He turned, crossed the small space to her and put his arms around her waist, pulling her against him.

She relaxed, happy to be in his arms and suddenly feeling playful. "I just realized something."

"What's that?" He rubbed her back with one hand, stroking her hair tenderly. He seemed in no hurry to release her and she reveled in the feeling of timelessness in the displaced tent.

"Except for that one day in the vineyard, you've never kissed me any place except the restaurant before."

"Hmm." He kissed her hair. "Actually, you're mistaken. I've kissed you in a lot of places."

She pulled back and frowned at him. "Have you got me confused with someone else?"

He laughed. "Nope." He kissed her gently on the lips. "I've kissed you here." He moved his lips to her neck. "And here." He moved lower. "And here." He knelt in front of her, holding her hands and looking up at her. "Or wasn't that what you meant?"

Her heart pounding wildly, even as she was aware of the chance they were taking, she let him pull her down to him, his lips covering hers as he lay beside her in the grass. They kissed for several long luxurious minutes, the grass itching the back of her shoulders, until he rolled over onto his back, pulling her with him so she straddled him. He moved his hand from the back of her neck to her ponytail, releasing the elastic with deft fingers so that her hair fell over her shoulders.

When she finally pulled away a little, he let her go, lying back on the grass and looking up at her with a little smile. "God help me, loving you hurts so much."

She brushed a hand across the light stubble on his face. "I know what you mean."

"I doubt it." He put both hands on her hips and moved against her so she could feel the hardness of him through his jeans. She gasped and he laughed. "It's not just this." He released her and rolled them over so he propped himself on his elbows above her. "It's knowing you're going home to him. Knowing he can have what I can't, just for asking for it.

Knowing you belong to him, and I'm not even sure anymore that he deserves you."

Tears suddenly threatened to strangle her. "Oh God, let me up." She tried to push him away, and he levered himself off of her. She sat up, hugging her knees and burying her head in her arms. She fought against the sobs, feeling his arm around her shoulders, knowing he felt contrite and half-hating him for it. "You're so wrong." She whispered the confession in a trembling voice. "I don't deserve either of you."

"Cadence—"

"Don't!" She stood, moving quickly away from him. "Oh please, don't. Do you honestly think I don't want to make love to you? Every time I'm with you I think, maybe this time I should just push it a little further. Just take us a little too far to turn back. But Neil—he's never done anything wrong. He works too hard, but he's always had to, he's just like that. And you're so wonderful and he's so fantastic. How can I betray either one of you, but I do every time I'm with you. You should be free to find someone you can spend the rest of your life with. I interfere with that every time we're together. And Neil should have my loyalty and I've betrayed that every time I'm with you, every time I think about making love to you, every time—"

He took her by the shoulders then and pulled her against him. "Shh." He kissed her hair and held her. "I think I got the gist of that." She laughed, but without any real amusement. He kissed her again and sighed. "So you're as torn as I am. I guess I knew that."

He tightened his arms around her. "You know of course

that there's only one place this conversation can take us? You love your husband."

"I love you, too." She kept her head bowed when she said it, ashamed to feel the way she did.

"I know." He stroked her hair back, tilted her face up to his and kissed her very gently. "I love you, too." He stepped away, pulling her with him to the tent flap. "Let me take you home."

18

On Monday Cady filled in for the hostess again. This time she was surprised by how easy the work was. It felt good to be in a visible role at the restaurant and she considered asking Will if she could do it more often. Will worked the bar during the lunch rush, chatting with the customers, and she caught him looking at her a few times. Once while Patrick stood at the bar talking to him, Will's gaze was so distracted by her, his brother snapped his fingers in front of his face to get his attention back. Patrick looked annoyed and maybe even a little worried when he glanced over at Cady.

At three, Cady went back to her office and a few minutes later, Will followed her. Instead of coming in, however, he paused at the threshold. "You should go home for a little while."

"I don't need to." She tried not to let his curt tone hurt her. "I'm fine. And Cam's going to bring Kelsea home today. She's planned on it for a while. She's staying with us while Stan's gone back to Georgia to handle something with his old boss. He didn't want to leave her alone, and she's too pregnant to travel." She knew she was talking too much, but she couldn't seem to stop herself.

He shrugged. "That's great, but you've already been here since nine o'clock."

"I didn't realize you knew." She didn't look at him, knowing he'd stayed away from the office that morning on purpose. He didn't want to be alone with her.

"Cady, I'm trying—" He stopped as Suzie came down the hall and handed him the moneybag.

"There's the afternoon's haul, boss." She gave them an odd look. "Did I interrupt something?"

"Nothing." Will looked at the bag in his hand. Then he stepped over and dropped it on Cady's desk. "Go home after you finish the deposit, Cadence."

Suzie had already disappeared back into the restaurant. Cady stood as Will turned to follow her. "Will."

He paused, gripping the doorframe with one hand. Slowly he turned back. "Yeah?"

"Tonight. We need to talk."

He nodded, looking sad. "Yeah. We do." He looked as if he knew what they'd say to each other already.

Cady wished she did.

FOR THE FIRST TIME, Cady dreaded Will's arrival at the door of her office. She'd finished the deposit and locked it in the safe, gone over the receipts a second and third time in an effort to keep her mind off what she knew they needed to say to each other. By the time he entered her office, she'd given up trying to work on the books and simply sat at the desk, her face in her hands.

When she heard his step, she raised her head. "Hi. Everybody gone?"

"Yeah." He closed the door and stood for a moment with his back to her before swinging around. "Let's talk."

She froze and nodded. "Yeah." All this time she'd known it was coming, and she wasn't ready for it yet. She knew she was taking far more from him than she was giving. Was she ready to give him more? The choice was hers, but she wasn't totally certain she was ready to make it.

"I can't keep doing this." His voice was very soft. "Part of me wants to, part of me hates myself for betraying you this way—"

"Betraying *me*?" She blinked, startled.

He laughed. "I know you think you're the only one betraying anything, but I'm stealing you away from your family. These hours we spend together—you could use them to help mend your marriage, to be better friends with your daughter. You're not the only one with guilt issues. I could've fired you months ago or never hired you or whatever."

She nodded, accepting his words. "Okay, but—"

He touched her lips to silence her, brushing his hand through her hair. "Forget all that, though. I can't stop thinking about how much I want you. And not just for a couple of hours at a time. I want you forever. And I can't have you. I can't even have you for an evening, and it's killing me."

The pain in his voice tore at her heart. She wanted so much to take that pain from him. She reached out to him, but he stepped back. "You have to go."

"I can't." She knew if she left half of her heart would stay behind with him.

"Go home to your family and be happy." He turned resolutely to the door, his hand on the knob.

"I don't know if I can be happy without you." The words came unbidden to her lips even as she thought that she couldn't love him when she still loved Neil. Fifteen years of love with her husband couldn't just disintegrate. But even in her confusion she knew what she said was true. "Please don't leave."

He froze in the doorway, then turned slowly. His eyes on hers, he took two steps back to her, surrounding her with his embrace. He held her still for several seconds, eyes searching for some uncertainty, but when her gaze didn't waver, he bent his head and kissed her, a hungry, probing kiss, and she opened her mouth to his tongue with a soft moan of release. His hands slid under her blouse, warm against the skin of her back, belly and then breasts. She gasped as he moved his lips to her neck and began to edge her toward the couch.

He sat and pulled her with him, still kissing her neck as she straddled him. She trembled at the touch of his hands on her bare skin, at the thought of what this could do to her marriage, but she had gone so far now and she did love him, she did want him. She drew away, her eyes on his, and reached for his belt.

His breath came faster as she undid his belt and pants. She could feel how hard he was through the thin material of his boxers, but as she reached for him, he stopped her, drawing her to him again, holding her close for a long moment and breathing deeply. "Not now."

"I want you." Her lips trembled on the words. "I don't care where we are."

"God." His hands on her hips, he pulled her down to him, and she obliged, moving her hips against his until he gasped. "Not here. Not like this." He kissed her again, brushing her hair back from her face and looking at her. "I want you, too, but not here, not sneaking around on a couch in your office. You mean too much to me for that."

"When? How?" She pulled back and shook her head. "I can't—" God, did she have to tell Neil she was leaving him? How could she do that? She covered her face, her entire body shuddering at the thought of hurting him in such a horrible way.

"Shh." He took her hands away from her face, peering into her eyes. "I don't expect you to. Can you get away for a few hours tomorrow night? More than just the hour after closing."

"I don't know. Maybe." She could lie. She could come up with something. She would. Inventory or working on the menu. Neil was usually asleep or close to it when she got home. Her breath came faster. He was still so hard against her. She longed to tell him to forget making things perfect for them. She wanted to move against him until being outside her was too much agony for him and he had to take her. Her heart beat wildly in her chest, but he stood, refastening his pants and belt.

He touched her face gently. "I can't do it this way. It's not just sex for me and I don't think it is for you, either."

She dropped her gaze, ashamed at her own wantonness. "It would be so easy."

"Too easy." He bent and kissed her again, taking her hand and holding it against his chest. "If we're going to do this, I want it to be about more than just sexual satisfaction, even if you can't let go of Neil yet."

Yet. She managed a smile even as the word chilled her, and she realized her mistake. Calling him back to her, telling him she needed him, had made it possible for Will to believe she would leave Neil. Now she could see her desire for the one man seemed likely to destroy the love she shared with both.

IN SPITE OF HER MISGIVINGS, Cady had every intention of keeping her date with Will. As she looked at her reflection in the mirror the next morning she was torn between excitement and self-loathing at what she saw. How had she become the type to cheat on her husband? She had always looked at women who had affairs with disdain. Why make a vow if you had no intention of keeping it?

...in good times and in bad...

If she looked at it that way, she could find the strength to stay away from Will. She even tried to do it. But then she'd remember how Will had been there for her over the months when Neil hadn't. And her mind would drift to how her spirit lifted when he smiled at her and called her "beautiful".

"Tonight." She said the word to her reflection so she could grasp it. Tonight she would make love to Will. She would give herself to a man other than her husband. She wondered how it could be true. She didn't look any different from the woman she'd seen in the mirror yesterday. She fluffed her hair, feeling the sensuous way it fell around her shoulders and imagining what it would feel like when Will brushed it back to kiss her neck…

The water stopped in the shower and she hurriedly grabbed her hair clip, binding her hair back in a loose ponytail as if it might give her away if Neil saw her with her hair around her shoulders. He came out of the shower wrapping a towel around his waist. He seemed even more absent and withdrawn than usual, and she squelched her irritation as he brushed past her to reach for her toothpaste. It never failed. They had an enormous bathroom with two sinks, a whirlpool tub and a separate shower enclosure. And he was always using her toothpaste.

He brushed his teeth and dressed in silence and she had pretty much given up on even a greeting from him when he slid his arms around her waist from behind, kissing her neck. Startled, she looked at his reflection in the mirror and he smiled. "Sorry, you just look so beautiful I couldn't resist."

She bit her lip. "Thanks. No different from any other morning, though."

He studied her reflection and shook his head. "I don't know what it is. You're always gorgeous, but today…" He shrugged and kissed her neck again. "I hate that it's going to be late tonight, but maybe there'll be something to celebrate when I get home, if you're up."

"I'll be up." She thought of her plans with Will. "It'll be a late night for me, too. Will is still working on the menu and he wants my opinion."

"Is that really in your job description?" He raised his eyebrows at her in the mirror.

Deciding that the lie, once begun, should be done right, she shrugged. "If you look at it from an economic view, I guess. I know how much the ingredients cost, so we can figure out what's the most cost-effective."

"Hmm. I may have to talk to Will about keeping you so late." He gave her one more squeeze around the waist and moved back to his sink. "Stan's getting back tomorrow?"

"Yeah. Cam said she'd be going home with him then, but she'll be here tonight so Kelsea wouldn't be alone. So no problem with both of us being gone."

"That's good." He nodded. "I'll try to be home by nine."

She leaned against the sink after he left and hated herself because even her love for Neil couldn't squelch her desire for the passion Will's touch produced in her.

WILL KEPT his distance from her most of the day, although he managed to brush her hair from her shoulders once as he stood next to her at the bar and he smiled at her often enough so she knew he was looking forward to their evening. As she was preparing to go home for a few hours at four o'clock, he came to her office, closed the door and put an arm around her waist, burying his face in her neck. "God, you smell good. I'm not sure I can wait for tonight."

The way he held her reminded her of Neil's embrace that morning. She felt a twinge of guilt, but when he turned her to face him, the pleasure of Will's hands on her body, his lips on her neck and his knee edging between her legs helped her push it away and enjoy the moment in his arms. She tilted her head back, welcoming his kisses in a very wanton way, losing herself in his caresses. She forgot everything except her desire to be in his arms. Abruptly he froze. Puzzled, she opened her eyes and turned to follow the direction of his gaze.

"Shit!" She jerked back from Will, her attention caught by her daughter's startled face. Her head whirled as she realized in an abstracted way that Kelsea had opened the door without knocking. Had she suspected she'd catch her mother in Will's embrace?

Will released her and she took a step toward Kelsea, trying not to let her knees buckle beneath her. "Honey, what are you doing here?"

Kelsea shook her head, her features marred by disgust, and backed away. Then she turned and ran.

Cady started after her daughter, then turned back to Will. He had a stricken expression on his face. "Go. Catch her." He bowed his head. "I'm so sorry."

She wasn't sure if he was talking to her or Kelsea, but she didn't stop to ask.

SHE DIDN'T SEE Kelsea in town. Either she'd ducked into a store or the library or someone had given her a ride to the restaurant and taken her away as well. Cady dreaded who that might have been. "Please let her be at home."

Her tires squealed a little as she swung into the driveway

and slammed out of the car. Cam stood in the door. "Kelsea just came in. She's upset about something…"

"She saw." She still couldn't get over the horror of seeing her daughter's shocked face catching her kissing Will.

"What?" Cam seemed not to understand.

Cady pushed past her and bounded up the stairs, calling over her shoulder, "She saw me kissing Will."

Her daughter's door was locked. Cady could hear music thumping through the door and she knocked. "Kelsea, let me in."

"Go away."

Cady banged on the door. "You don't understand, Kelsea! We have to talk about this."

"Talk!" Kelsea slammed the door open. "What's there to talk *about*, Mom? You're cheating on Dad."

"I'm not—"

"I *saw* you! I didn't believe it at first, but when I went there and fucking *saw* you kissing that other guy and looking like a total slut, there wasn't much doubt. What the hell would you call that if it wasn't cheating?"

Cady decided it wasn't the time to mention her daughter's language. "Honey, you don't understand. Sometimes adults have problems. And sometimes we don't handle them quite right, either. I know I didn't. I'm sorry. I never intended for anyone to know…"

Kelsea swung around and for the first time, Cady saw the young woman her daughter would soon be. She caught her breath at the beauty of her daughter and tears started to her eyes as she wondered how much she'd messed things up for her.

"I knew! A lot of people know! That's what I'm trying to tell you! How could you do it, Mom? How could you cheat on Dad?" The pain in Kelsea's voice slashed at Cady and she recoiled.

"Kelsea, you don't understand…" She let her protest die in the face of her daughter's anger and distress. She bit her lip and felt her cheeks burn in shame. She'd never meant for this to happen. She'd never meant to hurt Kelsea. She couldn't tell her daughter that it wasn't too late, she hadn't really cheated on Neil. She and Will had never made love, but how could that matter? To Kelsea or Neil? In every way that was really important, she'd cheated every time she looked at Will with longing, every time she kissed him, and definitely when she promised to make love to him.

Kelsea looked at her mother with thinly veiled disgust under her anger. "Yeah, I probably don't understand. And I hope I never do!" She flung the bedroom door open and stumbled past Cam who had her hand half-raised, either to stop her or to knock on the door.

Cady covered her face with her hands, but when she heard the sound of the motorcycle engine, her head shot up and she raced past Cam to the front door. "Kelsea!"

"Shit!" Cam stood at the front door next to her, clinging to the frame as if for support. "Damn, I'm sorry, Cady. I didn't know he was out there. I would have stopped her."

"It's okay." Cady whirled, grabbing her purse and searching for her cell phone. She was done blaming everyone else for her own mistakes. It didn't matter. All that mattered was making sure her daughter was safe. She started sprinting down the stairs, Cam stumbling behind her. "I have to go find her. I'll call Neil from the car. I'm sorry, Cam, I'll be back as soon as I can."

"Go!" Cam waved her out the door. "Go, don't worry about me." For a moment she looked like she would cry, but she took a deep breath. "Just make sure she's okay."

Cady gave her sister a quick hug, then rushed out the door, dialing Neil's cell as she went. It went straight to voice mail. "Shit." She glanced at her watch as she waited for the beep. It was after five. "Shit. Oh shit." She backed as carefully as possible into the street. "Neil, it's me. I'm going to keep trying to call you, but this is an emergency." Her voice broke. She took a deep breath. "God, I've screwed up so bad. I'm so sorry. I-I had a fight with Kelsea and she took off. I don't know where, but she's with that boy. Rob. Please, please call me back. I'm so scared, and we've got to find her."

She hung up and dialed his office number. To her surprise, he answered. The sound of his voice made her weak. "Oh thank God, Neil." She was so relieved, she pulled over to the side of the road and stopped, trembling.

"Cadence?" His voice was concerned and she closed her eyes at the sound of her name on his lips. "What's wrong?"

"Kelsea. Oh God, everything. I just left you a voice mail. Please, Neil, you've got to help me find her."

"Find her?" The timber of his voice changed from concern to alarm. "What do you mean? What happened? Take it slow, baby. Tell me the whole story."

"She's gone. We had a big fight. God, I screwed everything up. It's all my fault and she'll never forgive me even if you do, but she took off with Rob on his motorcycle." She choked on a sob and clutched the phone like a lifeline.

"Hush, baby, it'll be okay." He was silent for a minute. "Where would they go?"

She took courage from his calm. "There's a concert at some bar. At the beach. I found the flier in her room earlier this week. I thought it was over with her and Rob, so I didn't think much about it."

"I'm leaving now. I'll call you when I get there."

"I'll pick you up." She looked over her shoulder and pulled back onto the road.

"No, you need to go home. Check out some places in town first. The arcade, the skate park, anywhere you can think the son-of-a-bitch might have taken her. Call her friends. Call his parents. I'm leaving right now, sweetheart. We'll find her. I promise."

She hung up as she approached a stop sign. She hesitated at the four-way stop, wondering which way to go. She thought of the park and turned that way. She knew teenagers hung out there, smoking, drinking, making out. She cringed at the thought of her beautiful daughter there, but she knew she had to try it.

The phone rang and she seized it, hoping it was Neil saying he'd found her already, or Cam saying she'd come home or Kelsea herself saying she'd come to her senses. "Kelsea?"

"Cady? Is everything all right?"

Will. Caught off guard by his voice, Cady fought for the right words. "Will. I'm not going to make it tonight." She choked back a laugh at the inadequacy of the statement.

He was silent for a second, then he spoke gently. "What happened with Kelsea? Why was she here?"

"She found out about us. I don't know how."

"Oh God." His voice sounded like ideals crumbling and she cursed herself for what she'd taken from him. Why had he wasted his love on her?

"She took off. With that boy I told you about. Rob. Now my daughter thinks I've cheated on her father and she's off riding around on a motorcycle with a scumbag kid who thinks he's going to live forever and it's all my fucking fault!" She slammed her hand on the steering wheel and hot tears of self-hate poured down her face. "I'm sorry, Will, I've got to go find her."

"I'll help you."

She shook her head, wiping her hand across her face. "No. She doesn't want to see you. Hell, she doesn't want to see me. And God only knows what she'll tell Neil when she sees him. But all that matters is getting her back safely and if she sees you she'll take off."

"I won't let her see me. If I find her, I'll call you, but I'll keep my distance. And I'll call Patrick. He won't do anything official yet if I ask him not to, but he'll look for her. I've got some guilt to deal with here, too, Cady. You've got to let me help."

"Okay." She didn't feel like arguing. Her energy had to be devoted to Kelsea. "Just for the love of God don't let her see you."

She hung up and began dialing numbers from memory, getting wrong numbers at least half the time and no answers half of the rest. The friends of Kelsea's that she could reach hadn't heard from her. Rob's parents didn't answer. She drove slowly past the arcade, the park and the library. She stopped and went into the library although she didn't think she'd find Kelsea there with Rob. She did find Sabrina at a table with several other giggling girls and a couple of boys. Sabrina stood when she saw Cady.

"Hi." She didn't look Cady in the eye and she wasn't as friendly as usual. Cady realized in a distracted part of her mind that Sabrina knew about her and Will. Perhaps she'd been the one to tell Kelsea or maybe Kelsea had confided in her. It didn't matter.

"Sabrina, I need to find Kelsea. Do you know where she is?"

Sabrina shrugged carelessly. "I thought she was grounded."

"We had a fight and she took off." Cady waited, her breath held.

The other girl gave her a look of barely concealed disgust. "I'm not really surprised. You know Rob told her, right? He found out from his cousin who works there and saw you guys. She didn't believe him, but I told her I'd heard it, too, so she went. She called me when she left. I've never heard her so upset." She met Cady's horrified gaze. "I bet half the town knows by now."

"None of that matters!" Cady refused to be sidetracked by the horror of being found out. She seized the girl's arms, resisting the impulse to shake her and lowering her voice when one of the girls at the table stood. "I've got to find Kelsea. She's with Rob and I'm afraid she'll get hurt. Please, for the love of God, tell me where they went, honey. You know Rob is trouble."

The girl still hesitated and Cady realized everyone at the

table was staring at her. She didn't care. Reckless in her worry, she nonetheless forced herself to calm down and took Sabrina's hands in hers. "Sweetheart, it doesn't matter what you think of me. I love Kelsea and I'm trying to keep her safe. Please, please help me do that."

Sabrina looked up and their gazes met. She sighed and nodded. "Okay. She said they were going to the concert. She was so upset when she found out about—" She lowered her voice, "you know. She said she didn't care what you thought about Rob, and she really kind of scared me the way she talked. I've been pretty worried about her…"

Cady pulled the girl into a tight hug. "Thank you, sweetie." She raced from the building, dialing Neil's number.

"I'm almost there." He sounded tired and worried when she told him what Sabrina had said. "I'll call you as soon as I find her."

"Oh God, Neil, please bring her home." Cady stood outside the library, her eyes still scanning the nearly abandoned street for some sign of her daughter. "Please. I have to make it right with her." And with you.

"I will. Go home and I'll call you. I love you."

She closed her eyes and wondered if he would change his mind before the night was over. "I love you, too."

19

She found Cam waiting in the living room. She struggled to her feet as Cady entered. "Cady? Did you find her?"

Cady shook her head. "I found Sabrina. She says Kelsea's at a concert. Neil's on his way there now."

Cam nodded and sank back onto the couch. She looked pale and Cady frowned. "Are you okay?"

"I'm fine." Cam waved off her concern. "I've been tense and worried about Kelsea. And you. You said Kelsea saw you with Will?"

Cady sat next to her sister. "Yes. God help me, she did. I have fucked everything up, Cam. I can't believe how stupid I've been." How could she have thought she couldn't live without Will? In the face of losing everything that really mattered, she realized that she could give up Will to save her family, no matter how much it hurt.

Her phone rang and Cady jumped for her purse, looking

quickly at the display. Neil's cell number. "Neil?" The background noise on the other end was overpowering. She raised her voice. "Neil? Have you found her?"

When she could finally hear him, he sounded shaken. "I can't find her. I found some kids that know Rob, but they claim Rob and Kelsea didn't come."

Real fear sliced through Cady's anxiety, and she realized what terror tasted like. Her daughter was gone. She'd disappeared. She wasn't where she'd told her best friend—the only person she was likely to confide in—she was going.

The doorbell rang and Cady looked at the door dumbly. "Hold on a second, Neil." She opened it with a dreadful certainty that whoever was there had some news about Kelsea.

Will's brother Patrick stood just outside. "Cady?"

"Just a minute." She lifted the phone back to her ear. "Neil, come home. She's not there." She hung up and looked at Patrick. "Where is she?"

"At the hospital. I'll take you there."

Cady looked back at Cam. Cam waved at her. "Go. I'll tell Neil where you are."

Patrick explained as they walked to their cars. "I got a call from one of the patrolmen. A couple of kids had broken into the Palace gardens. A security guard heard a girl yelling for help and found her running. He couldn't catch the boy, but he got a plate off the motorcycle. He called me because I'd put out a call for a girl with Kelsea's description."

Cady nodded, feeling numb. "Thank you, Patrick. Have you told Will?"

"I, um, figured I'd let you do that." Patrick looked uncomfortable enough for Cady to realize he knew all about the two of them. But then, why should she expect Will to keep his secrets from his brother? She'd told Cam everything.

She reached for her phone, but before she could dial, it rang. It was Will. "Hi Will." She noticed Patrick's sharp glance. "I'm with Patrick now. He's found Kelsea."

"Thank God. Is she okay?"

"She's at the hospital. I don't know."

He cursed. "God, I'm sorry. I'm coming, but it will be at least an hour. I'm on the other side of Jacksonville. There was a biker hangout I wanted to check out."

"Okay." She hung up and held the phone to her chest. "I should have told him not to come."

"Probably." The sound of Patrick's voice startled her. She'd almost forgotten he was standing there, waiting for her to get into her car. When she looked his way, he shrugged. "Look, it's none of my business what's been going on between you two, but I do know this is a family matter and if Will gets mixed up in it, he's going to get hurt." He hesitated, then added in a resigned tone, "Not that he's not going to get hurt, anyway."

She thought of Neil and nodded. "If it makes you feel any better, he won't be the only one."

He shot her a look and a half smile that reminded her of his brother. "Not really."

She slumped, feeling weak. "Me neither." She reached for the car door and hesitated. "How long have you known?"

"About you and Will? I don't know much really. I've never paid attention to gossip. I just know my brother and we've all been a little suspicious of the way he talks about

you. Will's not a very good liar. Maybe you've noticed that."
He reached around her to open the door for her.

"Not like me." Cady dropped into the driver's seat,
remembering the way she'd lied to Neil, to Kelsea, even to
herself. She didn't want to end her marriage, even if she did
love Will.

She followed the patrol car to the hospital, and Patrick
escorted her to the Emergency Room. A very old nurse told
them where to wait. Cady paced while Patrick sat in a corner,
apparently trying to be as unobtrusive as possible. When the
door opened and Neil appeared, Cady thought she'd never
been happier to see anyone in her life. She rushed into his
arms and he held her tightly. "Have you heard anything?" He
sounded anxious.

She shook her head, clinging to him. "The nurse wouldn't
tell us anything except to wait for the doctor here."

As she spoke, Patrick stood and Neil noticed him. He
pulled Cady over to his side, keeping one arm around her.
"Officer? Did you find her?"

"No. Not really." Patrick looked awkward. "I'm not really
here in an official capacity. More of a friend."

"I don't understand." Neil frowned, confused.

"I found out about Kelsea and brought Cady to the hospital." Patrick held out his hand. "Patrick Hubbard. Will's
brother."

"Oh." Neil nodded, still appearing a little confused. "That
was great. Very kind of you."

"I should go. Now that you're here." Patrick took a backward step toward the door.

"Thank you, Patrick." Cady found it difficult to speak

above a whisper. Her fear and shock combined with her guilt had nearly paralyzed her.

Patrick nodded and backed away another step as Neil pulled Cady back into his arms. "It's going to be okay." He stroked her hair. "She'll be fine."

Over his shoulder, Cady saw Patrick turn just as Will came around the corner. Will froze at the sight of her in Neil's arms and their gazes locked for a moment. She saw the pain and desire to be with her in that moment, followed by a sad resignation as his brother grasped his arm and pulled him away. Cady closed her eyes and leaned her head against her husband's chest, cursing herself again for all she'd done wrong over the past months.

The door opened to admit a very young doctor. Cady thought confusedly that he looked more like a friend of Kelsea's than the doctor who had attended her in the Emergency Room after she was attacked by her boyfriend.

"Oh God, am I really here?" She closed her eyes for a second, but when she opened them again the young doctor still stood there.

Neil looked at her quizzically. "Are you okay?"

"Yeah." She nodded. "I'm going to sit down now."

The next thing she knew, she was lying on the couch in the waiting room and a nurse was handing a cup to Neil, who sat next to her. She accepted it dreamily, taking a sip, then sitting up as a shock of realization went through her. A wave of nausea threatened to overwhelm her, but she fought it off, searching for the young doctor. Not finding him, and no longer certain he had ever been there, she turned to Neil. "What happened? Did I faint? Where's Kelsea? Is she okay?"

"Shh." He stroked her hair. "She's fine. They're bandaging up a sprained wrist and a couple of scrapes and then we can take her home. I've been to see her. She asked about you."

"I have to see her." Cady sat up, pushing away his restraining arms.

"Sweetheart, just rest. She's fine. The doctor said she got a good scare, but she's fine. They're not even keeping her for observation. We can take her home. You need to rest." His brow furrowed in concern, and her already broken heart ached a little more. "I'm actually a little worried about you."

"Don't. Don't worry about me. I don't deserve it." She shook her head to clear a peculiar buzzing in her ears and staggered a little. When he reached for her, though, she propelled herself out the door and straight into a nurse. Catching herself, she asked where she could find Kelsea and was directed to an alcove.

Kelsea looked up when her mother entered. Cady saw a tired, lonely, hurt little girl and crossed the room, putting her arms around her daughter. Kelsea leaned against her. "I'm sorry, Mom. I should've listened to you."

"God, no, baby." Cady's arms tightened around her daughter. "It's not your fault. None of this is your fault. It's that damn boy's fault. And mine. I messed everything up and I'm so sorry, but if you'll let me I'll do my best to make it all right."

Kelsea sniffled. "You think you can do that? With Dad, I mean?"

Not for the first time, Cady honestly wondered if she could. "I don't know, but I'm sure as hell going to try."

"I'm scared, Mom." When Cady opened her mouth to

reassure her daughter, Kelsea shook her head. "Not of Rob. He's a wuss. I kicked him in the balls and he doubled over like I'd stabbed him or something."

"What then, sweetie?" Cady felt her old protectiveness rising up in her.

Kelsea lowered her voice as if she were ashamed of her fear. "I'm scared of you and Dad splitting up."

Cady bit her lip. She wanted to chase her daughter's demons away, but how was that possible when her daughter's demons were her own? She sighed and sat next to Kelsea on the exam table. "I wish I could tell you it won't happen, baby."

"You don't want to leave him? For Mr. Hubbard?"

Her daughter's words hurt more than Cady had expected. She realized her actions had made Kelsea doubt the power of their family. "No. I love your dad. I never stopped. I wish I hadn't— But I did. And I can't swear I can make it right."

"Because you've never lied to me." Kelsea swung her legs, cradling her hurt arm in her lap.

"I've always tried not to. And your father is a wonderful man. Maybe he'll be able to find it in his heart to forgive me. I hope so." She wrapped her arms around herself, suddenly cold.

"Do you have to tell him?" Kelsea turned appealing eyes to her mother. "I mean, you're not going to see Mr. Hubbard anymore are you?"

"Not...not like that, no." Cady shook her head decisively. "That's over. But yes, I have to tell your father. He...deserves to know. Whatever happens, you have to remember you are *not* responsible. I hate that you were dragged into this at all, but you finding out has nothing to do with anything that happens between your father and me."

Even as she spoke and her daughter leaned her head on her shoulder, Cady wondered if what she said was true. In truth, Kelsea's discovery of her secret had a great deal to do with what would happen between her and Neil. If Kelsea hadn't found out, Cady and Will would have made love and that was something she could never take back. But maybe even now Neil could forgive her.

Maybe, because of Kelsea, it wasn't too late.

CADY STAYED with Kelsea while Neil handled the discharge papers. Then Neil walked the two of them to Cady's car and Kelsea got in the front passenger seat. She sat and immediately closed her eyes. Neil knelt beside the car and took her hand. "I'll be right behind you guys."

Kelsea opened her eyes and nodded. She looked exhausted and Cady realized it was after two o'clock in the morning. Kelsea reached out to give her father an impulsive hug. "Thanks, Dad."

Neil checked her seatbelt as if she were a little girl again and stood, closing the door. Standing, he pulled Cady a little away. "Are you sure you're okay? I can drive us and we can come back tomorrow for my car."

"I'm fine."

"You fainted."

"The nurse said it was just stress. My blood pressure was

through the roof. I feel okay now." She looked away from him, knowing she didn't deserve his worry.

He took her hands. "You've been through a lot."

He looked so handsome in his rumpled shirt and tie, so strong and exactly what she needed. She felt a rush of shame accompanied by dread. She'd stolen so much from him, and even more from herself by becoming involved with another man. The emotions of the night surged up inside her again and she shuddered. He pulled her against him. "It's okay. She's fine. She'll be fine."

"I know." She clung to him, wondering how much longer she'd be able to. "Oh God, what if she hadn't been? It was so close, Neil."

He stroked her hair. "Hush, baby. It's okay. She's safe. Let's take her home."

She nodded and dragged what felt like her last bit of strength together, getting into the car. She glanced over at Kelsea and realized with a rush of tenderness and affection that her daughter had fallen asleep.

Neil followed her home. She was intensely aware of his headlights hovering in her rearview mirror. Even as she worried about confessing everything to Neil, she was haunted by her glimpse of Will. She'd hurt him so badly and now she had to do the same thing to another man she loved.

She pulled into the garage with Neil right behind her. She got out and motioned to him. "She's asleep."

"I'll carry her upstairs. You get the door."

She did as he instructed, then followed her husband and daughter up the stairs to Kelsea's room. The guest bedroom door was shut and Cady thought vaguely that her sister had given up waiting for them and gone to bed. Cady opened her daughter's door, turned down the bed and smiled a little as Neil came forward. Kelsea's arms were looped around her father's neck, her face pillowed on his shoulder. How many times had he carried their sleeping daughter to bed? She realized with an ache in her heart that this might be the last. Parenthood was full of those bittersweet "lasts," most of which passed unnoticed. The last time a child rode in a stroller, the last time a baby was breastfed, the last time she sat on a parent's lap.

Taking a deep breath, Cady committed that moment to memory just before Neil laid his daughter gently between the sheets and kissed her forehead. As he reached for the blankets, she whispered, "Let me." He glanced at her quizzically and she blinked the tears back, struggling past the lump in her throat. "Please."

He smiled and put a hand on her waist, keeping his arm around her as she pulled the blankets over her daughter and bent to kiss her. Then they crossed the hall to their bedroom together.

20

He shut the door behind them and she stood for a moment a few steps inside the room, wondering how to start. She turned slowly. He took his wallet and keys from his pants pockets, putting them in the tray on his dresser. He glanced over. "Don't you want to go to bed?"

"I don't think I'll be able to sleep."

He nodded. "I know what you mean. It's been quite a night." He crossed to her, putting his arms around her and she let herself relax against him.

How could she tell him? If she told him how she'd betrayed their marriage, how could he forgive her? And if their daughter hadn't found out and been brutally attacked, Cady would have slept with Will. Only her search for Kelsea had kept her out of another man's bed.

"I have to tell you something." She took a deep breath but it caught in her throat with a sound like a sob. "I've really screwed up. I-I don't know if you'll forgive me."

He turned her to face him. His brow furrowed, but his gaze was steady. His voice had a kind of forced lightness. "We won't know if you don't tell me, will we?"

She took courage from his gentle tone, but when she began to speak, she dropped her gaze from his, her cheeks burning with shame. "It's about tonight. About why Kelsea and I were fighting. She found out something. About me. And Will."

She stole a look at him and saw his puzzled expression begin to break apart. What it left behind was hard for her to look at. "You and Will?"

"Yeah." She looked away again, then forced herself to face him. She was about to break his heart and if she had to do it, she should have to watch it. "Tonight I was supposed to meet him. We've been sort of seeing each other."

"Seeing each other?" He released her and his expression, though it didn't change to anger, hardened in a way she'd never seen before. "You were having an affair?"

"No, I mean we never…not really." It sounded weak and she sighed, defeated. Whether they'd had sex or not, she'd betrayed her husband and the vows she'd made to him. "Yes. We were having an affair. We never had sex, but we kissed and—other things—and we talked like I've never talked to anyone but you."

He took a step away from her and dropped into the chair at his desk. "What did you talk about?"

"Does it matter?" Her lips felt numb. She wanted to fall on her knees and beg him to forgive her, but she was too frightened of his answer.

"It matters." He sat with his shoulders hunched, his expression stony. She remembered how she'd thought he didn't care, that maybe he knew about Will, that maybe he was having an affair of his own.

How could she have been so wrong?

She sat on the bed, summoning her conversations with Will, trying to remember what had seemed important to her over the past few months. "We talked about you and our marriage. We talked about Kelsea and Cam and the baby. I told him how much I wanted another baby and how it wasn't fair that Cam could have so many she didn't even take care of."

"And about how I'm never home."

"Yes." Silence fell. Cady felt strangely empty, as if her confession had taken a part of her soul. Or maybe she felt the absence of his love for the first time in her married life. The thought filled her with horror and she looked up in time to meet his gaze.

"And tonight?" His voice was filled with the expectation of pain.

She looked away and nodded.

"You were going to have sex with him." His words fell into her silence, lingering like something unpleasant released from the darkness.

"Oh God." The words were torn from her. It sounded so cold and calculated. It hadn't been, though she'd been an idiot. In her quest to avoid the pain of what she'd seen as Neil's desertion of her, she'd acted selfishly and possibly destroyed the best thing in her life. She lowered her head and whispered, "Neil, I love you. I always have. I've just been…God, I don't even know what. I've been lonely and selfish and not worthy of you…or Kelsea." She covered her face with her hands, tears hot on her cheeks and fingers. Her shoulders heaved with her sobs and she heard him get up. She thought he'd left, probably forever, but a moment later, she felt him sit on the bed next to her. She felt his hand on her back and raised her head, eyes still blurred by tears, to stare at him in astonishment.

He held out a tissue, not quite looking at her. "Here."

She took it, her gaze not leaving his face, almost afraid if she looked away he'd vanish. His expression was sad and angry, but he sat stoically beside her. After several moments, he spoke. "If you had told me this yesterday, I probably would have left you."

The words were like tiny knives of fear slicing through her heart. She nodded, unable to deny their veracity. She tried desperately to read his mood. Anger? Sadness? She couldn't tell. She took a deep breath. "And now?"

He shook his head, still not meeting her eyes. "Everything we've been through tonight. Searching for Kelsea…going to the hospital…now this." He shrugged, and his mouth quirked. "I won't lie to you, Cadence. I've been trying to find my way the past few months, myself. I had sort of lost myself. Work took a lot out of me. But I figured out what's important tonight. You and Kelsea. That's it. I can live without the house and the cars and the boat and my job. If something happened tomorrow to take all that away, but I could still have the two of you in my life, I'd figure everything else out."

She lowered her eyes. "I know. I feel the same way."

"Do you?" He sighed. "I won't deny my part in this, Cady." He held up a hand when she would have protested. "I know. You're willing to be the villain, but I think we've both always known there were two people in this partnership. Right or wrong, if you felt lonely, it's because I left you alone." He drew a deep breath, letting it out slowly and she saw some of the anger fade. "I never wanted my job to interfere with us, so I didn't talk about it. I didn't want it to touch you. I didn't want you to know about the evil things two people can do to each other. Two people who once swore they'd love each other until death. So I didn't talk about work, but it consumed me most of the time. I guess when I was here, I wasn't really even here."

His hand still rested on the small of her back and she gathered a little courage from that. She reached for his free hand. Almost instinctively, his fingers closed over hers. He turned his head and looked at her.

"I'm sorry." His voice broke and he took a deep breath, shaking his head a little. "I was trying to protect you...you and Kelsea. I shouldn't have. I should have talked to you about work and--"

"Stop!" Her hand squeezed convulsively on his and she struggled to keep another storm of sobs from ripping through her. After several deep breaths, she felt strong enough to continue, her voice hoarse. "None of what I did is your fault. I don't know what I was thinking, but I know how wrong I was. And now I've hurt you and Will and, oh God, Kelsea." She caught her breath on the hard rock of another sob.

He nodded. "Will." A silence fell between them and she wondered uncomfortably what he was thinking about Will.

"It wasn't Will's fault. He tried so many times to stop what was going on. He told me to work things out with you. Even yesterday—" Eager to keep Neil from blaming Will, Cady ignored the growing pain in her husband's expression until he stood, yanking his hand from hers, and paced to his dresser before turning. She started to speak, but he held up a hand to stop her, shaking his head.

Silence fell between them. When he finally spoke, the question wasn't unexpected. "Do you love him?"

"I love you, Neil. I never stopped." She didn't want to think about Will or the way he'd looked when Patrick dragged him from the hospital. "Everything that happened with Will, it was because I wasn't secure enough, I didn't believe enough in your love, but not because I ever stopped loving you."

He shook his head again. "I know. But that's not what I asked. Do you love Will?"

She dropped her gaze, unable to find a way to answer him without hurting him. Much as she wanted to, she couldn't deny her feelings for Will. He had been too good to her to be written off as a simple mistake. Yes, she loved him, even though the heart she loved him with belonged to Neil.

"God." The pain in her husband's voice was almost worse than anything else she'd borne that night. He turned away, one hand covering his mouth as he leaned against the bureau.

She bowed her head and a tear ran down her cheek and fell onto her blue-jean clad leg. "I'm sorry. I didn't mean to. I didn't even know I could. He was so good to me when I was so lonely and confused and he never meant to…"

"Jesus! Stop telling me how wonderful he is!" His tone startled her, and she stole a look up at him to find him staring at her in disbelief. "You think that matters to me? You've just told me you love another man and you think I care how it started? What I want to know is how it's going to end." He crossed the room back to her in two strides. His voice was clipped and angry. "I love you. You are the only woman I've ever loved. You are my life and my life is with you, but only if you are mine." He knelt in front of her, his gaze holding hers, his voice determined but softer. "Are you still mine, Cadence?"

She bit her lip and nodded. Without dropping his gaze, he ran his hands up her thighs, pushing them apart and feeling her tremble as he did so. Still on his knees, he moved closer to her, sliding his hands further up her thighs, to her waist, beneath her blouse to her skin. She gasped. "Neil."

He held her in place when she would have moved closer to him. "Say it. Say you're mine." His hands edged higher, finding her breasts, caressing her nipples through the fabric of her bra.

The unexpected intimacy on the heels of thinking her marriage was over made her head whirl and she found it difficult to think straight, but she gasped the words he wanted to hear. "Yes. I'm yours."

He nodded, satisfied. "Yes." He pulled her blouse over her head and discarded it in the corner, following it with his shirt and tie. He rose, putting one arm around her waist and half lifting her onto the bed, pushing her back onto the pillows. Straddling her, he looked at her thoughtfully. "Yes. You're mine." He bent to kiss her, his lips caressing hers, his tongue coaxing her mouth to open. His touch was very gentle, but Cady sensed a strength and determination in him that she'd never felt in his lovemaking before. It both excited and conquered her, and she surrendered every part of herself to him. As he bent to kiss her neck, his lips hovered by her ear just long enough to whisper, "And I'm yours."

She trembled with the intensity of every emotion she'd felt through the day, but mostly with wonder that he could offer her this opportunity. Releasing the shame and despair, she wound her arms around his neck, giving in to her body's response to his caresses, wanting only to affirm to him again that she was his alone.

They helped each other get rid of their remaining clothing, kicking them away. Just as her jeans and his pants joined their shirts in a pile, someone's cell phone buzzed. Her heart sinking, Cady looked at the pile of clothing. A call so late at night (or early in the morning) could only be an emergency that would take him away from her. He took her face in his hands and turned her back to him. "Everything we have that's truly important is safe in this house right now."

Kissing her, he gently unwound her arms from his neck, lacing his fingers through hers. She felt the cool pressure of his wedding band against her right hand, but everything else about him was warm. He kissed her neck and breasts, then moved between her legs. Before entering her, he rolled them over, hands still linked, so she straddled him. Then, supporting her hands with his, he arched up, sliding into her. She gasped at the familiar pleasure of having him inside her, and he released her hands, pulling her back down to him, kissing her and winding his legs through hers. He rolled her over onto the bed, stroking her hair back from her face, his touch both tender and powerful.

He drew away and looked at her. "I love you." He spoke the words in a way that made her realize how much they meant to him.

Tears slid down her face as she reached up to him,

caressing the lines of his forehead, touching his lips and really appreciating the gentle strength of the man she'd loved for so long. Feeling the solemnity of renewing something between them, she whispered her reply. "I love you, too."

This time when he returned his lips to hers, they both let go of their emotions. She tasted the saltiness of her own tears, knew he tasted them too, but they were no longer tears of regret. As he began to move and then to thrust into her, bringing her to climax, the tears came from joy, and when he cried out, at last releasing himself into her, she wound her arms around him, holding him and feeling his own tears hot on her shoulder.

THEY LAY TOGETHER for a long time after. Cady looked out the window at the lightening sky. "It'll be dawn soon."

He tightened his arm around her, nuzzling her neck. "I've never felt less sleepy."

She smiled. "Me either. I hope Kelsea will be able to sleep late."

"She was out cold when I checked on her." He kissed the top of her head. "Did she find out about you and Will? Is that why she was so angry?"

She nodded, swallowing hard. His forgiveness had alleviated her guilt, but she still felt panic rise up in her when she thought of what could have happened to Kelsea. "God, if anything had happened…"

"It didn't." He caressed her arm gently. "She's all right. Or she will be."

They were silent for a while, then Cady said softly, "There's still something I have to talk to you about."

"Will." His voice betrayed nothing.

She pushed herself up on one arm, rolling over so she could look him in the eye. "I know you don't want to talk about him. I understand that. I just have to know you won't--"

He grinned without humor as her voice broke off. "Hurt him? Beat him up? Does that seem like me, Cady?" His expression turned gentler and he put both arms around her. "We have forgiven each other. That's enough for starters. But you have to know I don't want you to see him again."

"I know." She laid her head on his chest. It felt good not to fight him. "I'll quit tomorrow."

He kissed the top of her head. "Which means you have to see him."

Her muscles tensed. "One last time. I may have hurt him more than anyone else, Neil, even you. And I have to live with that."

He caressed the back of her arm with the palm of his hand for several seconds before he answered. "I think you're wrong. You didn't hurt Will the most. He'll recover. I hope you will, too."

She shrugged, saved from answering when his cell phone buzzed angrily. Cady laughed when he cursed. "It's okay. Answer it."

"I don't want to." He kissed her, pulling her closer and she realized he wanted her again. She smiled. How long had it been since they made love twice in one night? She looped her arms around his neck and responded whole-heartedly to his kiss. His phone stopped buzzing, but a moment later hers began. She was on the verge of ignoring it, when it suddenly struck her that if someone from work had called Neil, they wouldn't immediately call her when they failed to get him. It was a personal call and it was in the very early morning hours.

The same thought seemed to have occurred to Neil. He leapt from the bed, grabbing her jeans and his pants and searching them. He found her phone and tossed it to her. The number was unfamiliar, but Cady punched the answer button. "Hello?"

"Where the hell have you been?" Cam sounded tired and irritated.

"Cam?" Cady was confused. Her sister was asleep in the guest room. Why was she calling?

"I've been calling and texting you all night. Well, ever since the baby was born. Is Kelsea all right? How could you not call me as soon as you found out?"

Cady sat upright. "The baby was born?" Neil handed her his phone with a picture text of a tiny bundle of blue. "Oh Cam, he's gorgeous."

"Thank you and about time. Now, how the hell is my niece?"

"She's fine. Well, okay, anyway. She came out of the whole thing with a pretty bad scare and a sprained wrist, so we're counting it as a win."

"That little twerp of a boyfriend attacked her? God, give me a couple of days to recover and I'll turn his whole rear end red."

"Yeah, I'll hold him, you hit him. But when did you go into labor? And how did you get to the hospital?"

"I guess I was in labor most of yesterday. You know I

didn't feel good. Stan got home early and came to pick me up after you left for the hospital last night, but I didn't want to leave until I heard from you. We were, um, watching television and all of a sudden I started getting these horrible, ripping contractions."

Cady noticed the "um" and wondered if it represented what she figured it did, but decided not to ask. "So he took you to the hospital?" She wondered at what point Cam had come through the emergency room. It had to have been right after she and Neil left with Kelsea.

"Yeah, and a good thing, too. I had little Eddie half an hour later."

"Eddie." Cady's eyes misted. "You named him after Dad."

"Yeah, it's pretty terrible, isn't it? Edgar. What a horrible name for a kid. But then his parents are Cam and Stan. We sound like a couple from the burbs."

"I like Cam and Stan. And I like Eddie. You make a nice family."

"Thanks. But you didn't answer my question. Hold on a sec." Cady heard a rustling and the soft murmur of voices. After a moment, she came back. "Sorry, they brought the baby in a little while ago and woke us up. I'm sending Stan home to get some rest."

"I'm really happy for you, Cam." It felt good to say the words and know there was something in her sister's life to really be happy about. "Will you stay in town, though?"

"I think so. Stan really likes his job. Hey, maybe we'll come live out in the burbs with you."

"There are no 'burbs' here. There's nothing to be a 'burb' of." Cady smiled and leaned back against the pillows. Neil had put on sweat pants and a t-shirt. He paused on his way out the door, came back and kissed her so deeply she nearly forgot she was on the phone. As he drew away, she offered him his cell phone, but he grinned and shook his head.

"Hello? You still there?" Cam's voice was acerbic.

"Yeah. I mean, sorry. I got a little distracted." Cady watched her husband leave. She knew he was going to check on Kelsea and probably make coffee. But he'd be back. She felt certain he wouldn't leave her that day.

"I was asking if everything was okay, by which I meant, are you and Neil okay? But I get the feeling from your voice everything is fine."

"You have no idea." Cady hugged herself in a wave of almost perfect happiness. "I don't know how, but somehow I managed to find the most wonderful man on earth to marry." She sobered. "And I'm going to work really hard not to forget that from here on out."

"Good." Cam yawned. "Well, baby's fed and happy and I'm tired. If you and Mr. Wonderful would care to come visit later, I'd let you in."

"Can't I come right now?" Cady teased. "C'mon, sis, you've got to let me hold my baby nephew. It's past time to start spoiling him."

"No. You missed your chance. Now you have to wait." Cam paused. "But, Cady?"

"Yeah, babe?"

"Thank you. For everything."

"Yeah, you too." Cady hit the button to hang up and set the cell phones together on her bedside table as Neil came back in with two steaming cups of coffee.

"She okay?" Neil handed her one of the cups.

"She's fine. A little upset with me. Now that I'm thinking straight it *was* pretty dumb of me to assume she had gone to bed. She adores Kelsea and she never would have rested until we got home. Fortunately, Stan was here." She smiled a little remembering her sister's hesitation when she said they were "watching television." She sighed, blowing on the hot coffee. "I don't think we'll have to worry about having a newborn living here, though."

"I'm sorry." He didn't sound apologetic. "Are you worried you're going to miss too much?"

She grinned. "Not really. They're staying in town, at least for now. And I don't think Cam will ever be as far away from me as she was before this visit." She looked at him suspiciously. "So what are you still doing here, anyway? How come you haven't called work or answered your phone or checked your messages?"

"Because I quit." He grinned at her shocked look. "It's okay. One of the other partners and I are going out on our own. There's no non-competition clause in our contracts, so we can stay in town. But I can make my own caseload and more decisions about how things will be done. I'm not going to say it'll solve everything, but I do believe it will help some."

"That's—wow. A surprise?" She shook her head. "This is what you were talking about when you said you were working on it. How long have you been unhappy?"

He sat Indian-style on the bed, propping his elbows on his knees and holding his coffee in both hands. "I don't honestly know. It sort of crept up on me. Everything at the firm was so competitive. The more cases you had, the better your standing and the bigger your salary. And I could handle a lot of cases so I got ahead. But I sort of lost sight of why I was doing it. I started out wanting to help people who couldn't think of another way to be happy. I hated seeing marriages end, but I thought maybe if I could help them make a clean break, maybe I was doing something worthwhile. I still think that, by the way, but at the firm I felt like a vulture, preying on the dead marriages. I didn't make the divorces, but the more that happened, the better off my career was."

Cady cringed, remembering how often she'd resented him leaving her to help a client. She set her coffee cup aside and stood on her knees behind him, putting her arms around his waist and laying her head on his shoulder. "I'm sorry. I never realized how painful your job was for you."

He nodded. "It sucked. You know what's worse, though?"

"What?" She lifted her head curiously.

"Feeling you behind me like that, knowing you're naked and imagining what you look like, and completely unable to do anything about any of it because I'm holding a cup of hot coffee."

She smiled at the yearning in his voice and slipped her hands under his t-shirt to feel his skin, pausing at the waistband of his sweatpants, then slipping beneath the material to the revealing hardness of his erection. He gasped as her hands closed on him, caressing the length of him, applying pressure and, from the quickening of his breath, doing all the right things.

"God, take this damn cup of coffee already." He held it out at arm's length and she obliged. The second it was safely on the bedside table, he turned, caught her by the waist and flipped her over onto the pillows. "That was *not* fair."

She laughed, touching his lips with one finger. "I think you might want to look up the terms of our contract, Mr. Lawyer. According to my memory, all's fair in love, and especially in making love."

"Huh. Maybe I need to rewrite it then." He lowered his lips to hers, kissing her deeply enough to leave her breathless, then drawing back with a wicked grin. "And I'll pay particular attention to the clause on equitable use of your beautiful body."

21

———

When Kelsea woke around two o'clock, the family went to meet little Eddie. Stan held his son while Cam sat in the chair next to the bed. Both of them looked exhausted but very, very happy. Cady couldn't stop smiling as Stan handed the blue bundle to her to cuddle and she passed it on to Kelsea, who stared with wonder at the tiny face pillowed on her injured elbow. Cady looked around her and thought that when her mother arrived, they'd have a very big family indeed.

"I talked to Jeanne earlier." Cam's voice broke into her thoughts.

"Really?" Cady returned her attention to her sister.

"I thought she should know about her brother. She sounded really happy about it. And she's been in touch with Selena, so she told me she'd call her. They might even come up to visit this summer."

Cady smiled, taking Eddie from Kelsea, kissing him

tenderly and returning him to his mother. "That's great, sis. I'm really happy for you."

"Yeah, me too." Cam ducked her head to kiss her son's tiny fist. "I hope it'll happen." She looked at Kelsea and smiled. "Cousins would be nice, huh?"

"They'd be awesome." Kelsea gave her aunt a hug. She still looked tired, bruised circles under her eyes.

"Yeah, that would be nice." Cady put her arm around her daughter, thinking that if Selena and Jeanne came at the same time as Susan, the dinner table would be very crowded and hopefully very lively, and she would love a chance to adore and spoil her nieces. But in her heart she knew the only people she had to have in her life were the ones easily within reach at that moment.

NEIL AND KELSEA dropped Cady off in front of Hubbard's. They drove on down the street to the little coffee shop Cady liked. Cady would join them when she had done what she had to do.

Will was not in the dining room. Very few people were. Suzie stood at the bar talking to the bartender and she turned when Cady approached. "Hey."

"Hey." Cady managed a little smile. "Is Will around?" She was conscious of a few curious looks and knew the rumor mill had reached the restaurant.

Suzie's hesitance confirmed her theory. "He's in his office," she said after an awkward pause.

Holding her gaze level, Cady marched into the back

offices, passing by her own without a glance. She reached Will's and hesitated. He sat behind his desk, looking at her without smiling. "Hey."

"Hey." She summoned another smile, this one more painful than the last. "Can I come in?"

He nodded toward the chair. "You want something?"

She hesitated, shifting uncomfortably. Maybe it wasn't the right time. Then again, when was the right time? She took a deep breath and faced him. She knew this would be the second hardest conversation she'd had in the past twenty-four hours. "I quit."

"Great. I was going to fire you if you didn't." He leaned back in his chair and studied her. "If you quit, we'll get fewer questions. Anything else?"

She sighed. "God, don't make this easy for me, please. I hate myself for what I did to you, to Neil…to everybody. I shouldn't be allowed to have the love of one wonderful man and somehow I managed to rate *two*."

"Yeah, you suck pretty bad." His voice was bland. "I can't really figure out what I ever saw in you." When she looked at him sharply, he shrugged. "You said not to make it easy for you."

She laughed. "Yeah. I guess I did." She bit her lip and wondered how to approach what she needed to say. Everything sounded too trite. Finally, she spoke, her voice very low. "Thank you." He sat forward as if to hear her. "For being there. For giving me everything I thought I needed. I'm so sorry for how it turned out." She stopped herself there. She could have kept going, telling him what a wonderful person he was and how it hurt her to know she'd hurt him, how she still remembered his arms around her, his lips on hers, his hands on her skin…but when she met his eyes, she knew he knew. And nothing would ever change it, any more than anything would ever change her love for Neil.

After a moment, he nodded, and his face relaxed a little. "We both knew what we were getting into, Cady. I always knew what my chances were, but I don't regret it. Even a second of it. I had you in my life, more than a friend, even if it wasn't as much as I wanted."

She nodded. "Please tell me you'll find someone. You deserve to have someone to love you."

He shrugged. "I'll find someone." He spoke with enough confidence to reassure her. She hadn't ruined anything for him.

Cady cleared her throat and looked around. "Um, what about the books? Do you need me to work until you find somebody to take my place?" Even as she said it, she hoped he wouldn't say yes.

"No." The word fell between them and she winced a little even as she was relieved. He didn't try to soften it, either. "I'll do the books myself until I find someone else. I don't anticipate needing much time for anything else for a while."

"Maybe Brianne will come back when she's done with her degree?" Cady thought of the way Brianne had kissed Will. She looked up and found him smiling at her in a bemused way.

"You know it won't be that easy, don't you?" When he spoke, she realized his practiced nonchalant attitude was cracking, and she spotted a little of the pain behind it. "I can't just replace you, even with Brianne."

"Will…God, I'm so sorry."

He shook his head. "Don't. It'd be best for me if I didn't see you very often, though. As soon as things settle here, I'm going to turn over the day-to-day management of the restaurant to Suzie for a while. I talked to her about it this morning." He hesitated. "You did tell Neil everything, didn't you?"

"Yeah." She remembered the terror of the previous evening and shivered. "It was really the only way."

"Good." He nodded. "Because Suzie already knew. She figures one of the waitresses found out somehow. Maybe just guessed."

"What about your family? Do they know?"

"Patrick, yeah. Maybe Lisa. I don't know. Depends on who she's talked to. I don't think Patrick would say anything. Guess I'll find out when I go home." He played with a pencil, studying the planes and angles of it as if they were the most important things in his world. Then he looked up at her. "I figure I'll be a full-time grape grower for a while."

She imagined him working in the vineyard every day and knew it would be good for him. He'd get back to the basics and when he came back to town the scandal would have blown over. At least half of her envied him the opportunity to get away. But she knew if she stayed to take the brunt of the gossip and blame, Will's reputation would come closer to escaping unscathed. She owed him that much. She could be New Bern's Lolita who ran a decent man out of town with her bad behavior.

None of that mattered if she had her family beside her. She stood. "I have to go."

"Your last paycheck is on your desk." He returned to his pencil study.

Cady left his office and stepped into hers. A small box with her personal belongings was already packed. On top lay an envelope and she opened it to find the check he had mentioned. In the memo line were two words: No regrets. Tears pricked her eyes and she took a deep breath, picking up the box. As she stepped into the hall, she glanced back at Will's office. He stood at the sight of her and smiled. "Good-bye, Cadence."

Not trusting her voice, Cady nodded and fled. The first of the evening crowd had arrived and she had to fight her way through them, but when she got to the door, she took a long, deep breath, collecting herself. Then she turned to the little coffee shop where her family waited, knowing at last where her place was in life.

ABOUT THE AUTHOR

Michelle Garren Flye is a hard-working romance author. Reviewers have described her work as: "an engaging novel with charming and likable characters", a story that "will make you believe in love and second chances", and a "well-written and thought-provoking novel."

In addition to romance, Michelle writes short stories, poetry and a children's mystery book series. She has served on the editorial staffs of Horror Library Butcher Shop Quartet and Tattered Souls. Her popular *Jessica* children's series can be found on Amazon and most other online book retailers under the pen name Shelley Gee.

Michelle has a Bachelor's degree in Journalism and Mass Communication from the University of North Carolina at Chapel Hill and a Master's degree in Library and Information Science from the University of North Carolina at Greensboro. She lives in eastern North Carolina and runs a beautiful bookstore when she's not writing. (And sometimes when she is.)

A NOTE FROM THE AUTHOR

If you enjoyed this book, please consider posting a review on Amazon. I read all reviews and very much appreciate your comments.

Connect with Michelle Garren Flye online:
Website: http://michellegflye.com

ALSO BY MICHELLE GARREN FLYE

Want more?

Sleight of Hand Series:
Close Up Magic
Escape Magic
Island Magic
Movie Magic
Becoming Magic
Dickens Magic
Magic at Sea
Pirate Magic (Coming Soon)

Carolina Wine Country:
Ducks in a Row
Saturday Love

Published by Carina Press:

Where the Heart Lies

Published by Lyrical Press:

Secrets of the Lotus

Winter Solstice

Set in the North Carolina Mountains:

Weeds and Flowers

Tracks in the Sand

Synchronicity Series

Strange Path: A Synchronicity Story

Out of Time

Time Being

Timeless

The Jessica Series by Shelley Gee

Jessica Entirely

Jessica Naturally

Jessica Gravely (Coming October 2020)

Praise for Michelle Garren Flye's other novels...

WHERE THE HEART LIES

"A romance with heart, heat, and a big ambitious story covering miles of emotional terrain. You'll be swept away."
   -- Ellen Meister, author of The Other Life

"An ambitious and engrossing tale, full of complexities of both character and plot. Read this one on the beach, by the fire, in your bed… wherever. Just read it!"
   -- Stephanie Stiles, author of Take It Like a Mom

"...a brilliant stroke of amazing and entertaining story telling."
   -- Smitten with Reading

WINTER SOLSTICE

"…outstanding characters, wonderful storyline, great dialog, and delicious humor that just adds flavor to the story."
   -- Booked Up Reviews

"The love scenes were exquisite and beautifully done."
   -- The Romance Studio

"Well-written, with just enough sexual tension, plus believable conflicts that are finally solved satisfactorily."
   -- Manic Readers

SECRETS OF THE LOTUS

"A glorious, sweeping love story packed with surprises. Brava to Michelle Garren Flye on her splendid debut."
-- Ellen Meister, author of THE SMART ONE

"…a delightful story with a confident heroine who is not afraid to be herself … I found it difficult to tear myself away from this enchanting story."
-- Single Titles

"I would read this story, and any story by Michelle Garren Flye again in a heart beat."
-- Happily Ever After Reviews

"Sweet love story featuring a playboy billionaire who falls in love with a reporter. … Very nicely written contemporary romance."

-- Romance Book Scene

"Michelle Garren Flye has successfully woven a modern day fairytale in her novel, Secrets of the Lotus."

-- Book Martini Reviews